The
New Young
Oxford Book
— of —
Ghost Stories

Other Anthologies edited by
Dennis Pepper

For Older Readers
The Oxford Book of Christmas Stories
The Oxford Book of Animal Stories
A Book of Tall Stories
The Young Oxford Book of Ghost Stories
The Young Oxford Book of Supernatural Stories
The Young Oxford Book of Nasty Endings
The Young Oxford Book of Aliens

For Younger Readers
The Oxford Book of Scarytales
The Oxford Christmas Storybook
The *Happy Birthday* Book
(with David Jackson)
The Oxford Funny Story Book

The
New Young Oxford Book
of
Ghost Stories

DENNIS PEPPER

OXFORD
UNIVERSITY PRESS

OXFORD

UNIVERSITY PRESS

Great Clarendon Street, Oxford OX2 6DP

Oxford University Press is a department of the University of Oxford.
It furthers the University's objective of excellence in research, scholarship,
and education by publishing worldwide in

Oxford New York

Athens Auckland Bangkok Bogotá Buenos Aires Calcutta
Cape Town Chennai Dar es Salaam Delhi Florence Hong Kong Istanbul
Karachi Kuala Lumpur Madrid Melbourne Mexico City Mumbai
Nairobi Paris São Paulo Shanghai Singapore Taipei Tokyo Toronto Warsaw

with associated companies in Berlin Ibadan

Oxford is a registered trade mark of Oxford University Press
in the UK and in certain other countries

British Library Cataloguing in Publication Data
Data available

ISBN 0 19 278154 5 (hardback)
ISBN 0 19 278178 2 (paperback)

Cover image reproduced by kind permission of Millennium Images Ltd.
Photograph by Herborg Pedersen

Typeset by
Mike Brain Graphic Design Limited, Oxford

Printed in Great Britain by
Biddles Ltd, Guildford and King's Lynn

Contents

Introduction   vii

Marian Abbey *Watching Over You*   1

Francis Beckett *A Separate Peace*   11

Ruskin Bond *Topaz*   20

Tanya David *Dogends*   25

Louise Francke *Alicia*   37

Shamus Frazer *Florinda*   47

Adèle Geras *Rowena Ballantyne*   57

John Gordon *If She Bends, She Breaks*   65

Catherine Graham *Snookered*   79

Dennis Hamley *Incident on the Atlantic Coast Express*   89

Kenneth Ireland *Who is Emma?*   102

Shirley Jackson *Home*   111

Gerald Kersh *The Extraordinarily Horrible Dummy*   121

Rita Morris *Hallowe'en*   126

T. V. Olsen *The Strange Valley*   134

Susan Price *The Haunted Inn*   143

Alison Prince *The Fire Escape*   147

Robert Scott *With Vacant Possession*   163

Contents

Laurence Staig *Love Letters*   166

Rosemary Timperley *The Sinister Schoolmaster*   179

Barbara Ker Wilson *The Honeysuckle Trap*   190

Mary Frances Zambreno
   The Ghost in the Summer Kitchen   201

Acknowledgements   214

Robert Scott *The Opening Match*   216

Introduction

I once knew someone who claimed she had seen a ghost. She was at school and was walking by the wall outside the school chapel one afternoon when she noticed someone sitting on the seat at the end of the path. As she approached, the figure—a woman—stood up, took a few steps forward, and disappeared. No trick of light, my friend said, no one playing a joke, no mistake of any kind. And nothing sinister or threatening, but she was very shaken all the same.

I can understand that, but for someone who wasn't there it really is a very unsatisfactory encounter. I mean, if you are a ghost why appear at all if you're not going to *do* something? Now I can think of good reasons for such inaction but then I was, I recall, simply annoyed by the whole episode. What was the *point* of it? The truth is I was expecting a real-life encounter to be more like a story.

Even when they are not scaring you out of your wits, fictional ghosts behave very differently. Adèle Geras's story is set in a school not too dissimilar, I imagine, from the one my friend went to. Her ghost is not especially scary (though she does give the visiting speaker a nasty shock), but there is a reason why she appears when she does and she has a purpose which she achieves. For the reader it is a very satisfying story.

The ghost of Sergeant Major Smith, who haunts the First World War military cemetery in Francis Beckett's story, is much more frightening. He had knowingly ordered one of his men to a gruesome death and now takes possession of the dead man's great grandson in order to expiate the crime that has not let him rest for eighty years. There is more to Smith and Rowena, and to the ghosts in all the other stories here, than simply appearing and disappearing.

There are ghosts of all kinds in this book, from a three-year-old child protecting her twin sister to a drunken old nanny determined to punish the innocent occupant of the room where she alternately neglected and abused her charge; from a dog in search of a new owner to a tyrannical ventriloquist insisting still on training his son; from a disappointed lover to a bullying headmaster. There are ghosts who insist on helping, ghosts who are out to destroy, ghosts who have become lost in time and, even, ghosts who do not know they are ghosts. But there are no ghosts who simply get up and walk away, leaving you to wonder why they bothered to appear in the first place.

As with the earlier *Young Oxford Book of Ghost Stories*, I have brought together stories originally intended for adults and those written with readers like you in mind. In this collection, however, I have concentrated on more recent stories: most of those you will read here have been written in the last ten years; indeed, a third of them appear in print here for the first time, having been written specially for this book.

Dennis Pepper
May 1999

Watching Over You

MARIAN ABBEY

We only moved here last year. I still remember when I first saw the garden, saw it properly from 'my' window. Mum and Dad had let me choose first, because I was the oldest. I chose the back bedroom and the boys had to make do with sharing the middle room. They moaned like anything of course, they always do. But they should be used to it by now, being so close in age. Only a year apart. They're lucky, actually. They get to do everything together.

Anyway, I remember looking out. It was late summer, and some kind of vine was growing up the back wall and covering over the glass. Dad wanted to cut it back, but I wouldn't let him. It was good, like looking out through a curtain. The leaves were green and red and pink as they turned. They were dying actually, but you don't call it that, do you? 'Turning' is so much safer.

Our garden isn't very big, but it's OK. In the middle there's a great high tree, with grass all the way round it, and flower beds and things at the edges. There's a red brick wall which borders the garden, and a gate in it at the far end that leads to the canal. That was what we all liked about the new house, that it backed on to a canal. From my window you can see over the wall and watch the water. It's not a great canal—a bit oily, a bit smelly sometimes—but we like it.

Looking out, I saw her for the first time. The only moving thing apart from the ducks paddling on the sluggish water. A little girl, playing in the next-door garden. The neighbours had one little girl, we knew that already, although I hadn't yet seen her. And here she was.

The sunlight was poured into the garden like into a bowl. It turned the bricks orange, warm, as if they were on fire, and it made her hair gleam. Beautiful light hair, glowing gold. *I dream of Jeannie with the light brown hair*. But her name wasn't Jeannie, though I didn't know her name at all at first. Later on I found out she was called Tamsin. But it wasn't until the end that I really knew her name.

I watched. It was an odd game she was playing. I remember I noticed that. Noticed that she moved strangely, slowly, as if accommodating something. She was playing tea parties or something—some little-girl game anyway. There were some toy cups and plates that she'd arranged on the grass, and she was busy collecting things from the garden to add to them. I watched her walk along the side of the flower beds like a little bee, looking and choosing. After a while she'd stop, and put her head on one side as though she were listening, or asking a question. You know how little children do it, when they're trying to get your attention, or wanting to ask you something. And then she'd pick a stalk from the grass, or pull a leaf from one of the shrubs, and come back to the tea party again. But she always walked in that odd manner, head on one side, questioning. Listening.

My window was open, but I couldn't hear anything. She didn't speak. Her game obviously didn't need words.

I must have watched her for ages, organizing her tea, dancing attendance on someone or something. *Polly put the kettle on*. I remember smiling as I worked it out suddenly: she must be playing with an imaginary friend. I knew children had them. Someone totally real to the child. The sort of friend you could take anywhere. I never pretended I had an imaginary friend, and my brothers have always had each other, of course, so they never had to make anyone up.

I watched her playing, learned the way our garden fitted alongside everyone else's, got used to the sounds of the canal and the pattern of the red brick walls, and eventually someone from next door's house called her in. The little girl got up off the grass, held out her hand, and waited until her friend had had time to get up and join her. Then, carefully holding hands, she went inside. ,

I didn't see her parents for ages. I went to my new school (which was OK-ish, but the other girls were all in pairs before I got there and it was difficult to join in). Mum and Dad 'got the house sorted out' and Mum started her new job. My brothers went off to the Infants together, coat by coat, lunch box by lunch box.

I used to go to my room every day after school and usually I'd just watch the garden and the little girl and think.

She was always alone. She was three—I know that now—and I'm sure that when I was three Mum got other little three year olds round to play with me and their mums to drink coffee with her. But the girl's mother never seemed to have visitors. During the week there was never anyone in the garden except for the girl. *Mary, Mary, quite contrary, how does your garden grow?* At weekends the father used to appear, gardening or kicking a ball around with her, but that was all. And sometimes, when we saw the mother at the front door, going out or carrying shopping in, she'd say hello with a dip of the head which begged you not to ask any questions or say any more than a basic remark about the weather. I asked Mum about it a couple of times, but she just shrugged it off. Perhaps she's shy, she said. Perhaps she's busy. The little girl seems OK, doesn't she? She seems happy enough, playing on her own.

And she did seem happy enough. But then, she wasn't playing on her own, was she? She always had a friend. And the friend was just the same as her. You could tell that. When she spoke to the friend, she just looked across at her own shoulder, where the friend always was. When she held hands, she reached out her hand just at the same level as her own. The friend was exactly the same.

It got colder and mistier, as autumn came and winter got nearer. The leaves died off, leaving the booms and masts of trees. The little girl didn't go out into the garden so often, and when she did, she got called in earlier and earlier. A few times I saw her mother come walking down into the garden to fetch her. Sometimes she didn't hear herself being called in, being so engrossed in her conversation, and she would startle when her mother touched her on the shoulder. She'd look up, surprised, as though she were expecting to see someone quite different standing there. And then they'd shuffle back up the garden together, Tamsin holding her mother's hand, her other arm outstretched to bring back the third to make up the party. As if they were incomplete, Tamsin and her mother. As if it wasn't enough, just the two of them.

By then we knew Tamsin's mother wasn't well. It was always put like that. Lower your voice and say it. *Not well*. But that was all. We didn't see her much, never really heard anything from next door, so it didn't affect us. My school got a bit better. I was allowed into one of the gangs—only on the fringes, but tolerated, so that was OK. The boys were fine, as usual, living together in their exclusive childish world.

So we all carried on, our family and Tamsin's family, side by side, through autumn and Christmas and the New Year.

It was winter when it happened. And, of course, when it happened it wasn't in the way you thought it would. Perhaps danger, real danger, always works that way. You think you know what to worry about. Dad's always there ready and waiting outside the gates when it's time to pick the boys up from school. I always have to be home by half-past four unless I've phoned first. The canal was the source of Mum's constant warnings about playing by the water: how we had to be careful of the depth of the water, and the weeds, and the rats. How the little ones weren't allowed to open the gate unless there was an adult with them, or me, their big sister. How we had to look after the little ones. Keep them safe. Keep them alive.

It was the dead bit of the year, January to February, when the garden gave itself over to mist and cold and bitter frosts. The houses had all been built at the same time, a hundred years ago, and through the skeleton trees and bushes you could see clearly down the row of terraces, each house with its red brick façade and its gable windows and its old red brick garden walls.

The little girl was playing, as usual, in the garden, and I was watching, as usual, from my room, still with my coat on because the house hadn't warmed up yet. She was wrapped up heavily against the chill, and I remember the red scarf, scarlet as berries against bare twigs.

This time she wasn't playing tea parties, or anything like that. She was walking up and down, slowly, with one gloved hand outstretched, of course, to meet the invisible matching hand that she was holding. Walking and talking, and earnestly nodding her head from time to time. I suppose it crossed my mind just then that she might be mad, just a flickering, fleeting thought that was over as soon as it formed. No, I said. She's only three. She's just being a kid.

I don't think I can explain why I used to watch her so much. I suppose that she was intriguing, so contained, so complete in her own world. And it was quite relaxing. After all, I wasn't responsible for her, not like I was, sort of, for my brothers. She had her own parents to look after her. Even so, I suppose with a bit of my brain I'd always looked out for the accident. Always been prepared, in the back of my consciousness, for her to head for the gate and pull it open and walk out to the canal (although surely their gate would be firmly locked, just like ours always was). The grass would be slippery, the edge unsafe. The oily water would soon saturate her clothes, pull her down. I'd see it and yell for help, and at the same time I'd tear down the length of the garden, and dive in and rescue her from the sucking water. I'd be a hero.

In the event I don't think I uttered a sound.

She had stopped walking by now and was sitting down, resting against the opposite wall to us, so I could see her quite clearly. The sun was nearly gone, and the last lines of pale light were lying along the bricks. It was very cold. You could see her breath on the still air. The sky was clear. There would be another frost tonight.

She sat still, on the cold earth, in companionable silence. It crossed my mind that she might get cold sitting there, but that was nothing to do with me, and I was about to leave the window and fish out my homework when suddenly she moved. Only she didn't so much move as jerk upright, like a puppet with someone invisible pulling the strings. Her face changed, shocked. One arm was pulled out in front of her. At first I thought she must be having a fit. She staggered to her feet, slipped and was pulled upright again. She had been sitting about halfway down the garden, and now she half fell, half lurched across the end towards the canal gate. And I saw that the gate was open.

I don't remember racing downstairs or getting through the kitchen door to the garden. I only have a half memory of forcing myself over the wall that divided her from me and hearing my coat as it ripped. But I remember the rushing blood in my head and my heart banging in my ears and the screams and screams and screams as someone flung herself past me as I landed, ran and dived almost on top of the little girl before she reached the gate, wrapping her in a grip that choked the air from her body.

There was a grinding sound behind us. A crack, then the sort of noise that an earthquake might make. The wall bowed and swayed, and then crumbled, collapsing in on itself where the frost had cracked away all the cement and mortar which held it up.

London Bridge is falling down.

Bricks and mortar fell, in slow motion, burying the flower bed, burying the place where Tamsin had been. There was a great heavy pile of jagged bricks, far higher than a three year old sitting on the ground. It covered the side of the garden. The canal gate was the nearest safe place to be.

Tamsin's mother stared at me over her daughter's head. Petrified, like a cornered rabbit. None of us moved. Tamsin's red scarf had been left behind, and was lying on the soil, running out from under the bricks like a trickle of blood.

That was when people came running and shouting, stumbling over the broken bits of wall and reaching out for us. Dad, torn between checking Tamsin and wanting to make sure that I was all right. The man from the other side of Tamsin's garden, picking his way along the canal bank. What happened? they said. So lucky. So *very lucky*!

Tamsin sat calm and huddled in her mother's lap. Her mother and I looked at each other. We knew it wasn't luck.

'It was her.'

She said it to me, over Tamsin's head. Then she held her daughter at arms' length, away from her on her lap. 'It was her, wasn't it?' she said over and over. 'Wasn't it?'

The little girl gazed back evenly and nodded.

'Sarah?' Dad was confused. He looked from me, to the mother and daughter tableau, and back again. 'Sarah? What did you . . .'

'No.' Tamsin's mother broke in. 'Not Sarah. *Her*.'

Dad glanced round, hopelessly, but there was no one there. Of course there was no one there.

'Don't you see?' Her voice rose, shriller. 'She was there all the time. She's always there. Isn't she?'

Again, Tamsin nodded.

Her mother held Tamsin tighter, until you could see the little girl stiffen against the grip.

'Come on,' Dad said.

But Tamsin's mother paid no notice. 'Leave her alone.' She was speaking to someone in front of her. 'Leave us alone,' she said. 'Please . . .' And then suddenly, 'No! No, please don't leave . . .' And she reached out her hand at three-year-old height into the freezing empty air.

It wasn't the chill that made me shiver. I didn't want to look round. But I made myself. I turned, slowly, as though by doing so I wouldn't frighten whoever it was, might catch a glimpse out of the corner of my eye. But there was nothing to see, careful as I was. Only a strange stillness in the air. And, of course, the way Tamsin gazed fixedly, focused, in front of her.

'Come on.' Dad shook himself, like a dog, flicking off awkwardness and uncertainty. 'Let's get you inside. It's too cold to hang around out here.'

The other neighbour surveyed the wall. 'It must be happening all over the place,' he said, as an excuse. I guessed it was his wall. 'It's the frosts. They've finally had it, these old walls. But you can't tell, can you? Not before . . .' He drained to a halt, spreading his hands.

It did, actually, happen all over the place. That winter was famous for it. All those hundred-year-old walls and the sharp frosts working together to change the face of the gardens. People put up fences, rebuilt brick, called in surveyors to pronounce on the walls they still had standing.

We walked back up the garden. The men went on ahead, purposefully, to put on kettles and make phone calls, whatever they thought was needed. But they didn't see.

Tamsin's mother put her hand on my arm to stop me. 'You understand, don't you,' she said, fiercely. 'You saw.'

'I didn't . . .' I began, and then stopped. Thought of how Tamsin had been dragged to her feet and away from the wall. Thought of how she played all the time. Thought of how she was never alone. 'I don't know,' I replied. 'I don't know what I saw.'

'She looks after her.'

'Sorry?'

'The baby.' The words came hissing out. 'She looks after Tamsin.'

I glanced up, hoping that Dad would be there to rescue me from this, but he was already at the house.

'Haven't you seen them together?'

Ahead of us, Tamsin was walking along. Calmly and companionably.

Of course. That was what Tamsin was. Together, just like my brothers. But with someone only she could see.

Her mother went on. It was like the wall falling, as though she couldn't stop the words tumbling out of her mouth. 'The baby died, at birth. We never told Tamsin. Perhaps we should have. We always meant to, when it was right. We will one day . . .'

I shook my head. The little girl walking ahead of us didn't need telling.

'We will,' she said urgently. 'We will. But she's still so little. How do you tell a kiddie about . . .'

I took a deep breath. 'About her sister?'

'No.' She shook her head. 'No. Her twin. Identical. A little girl.'

Down will come baby, cradle, and all.

I felt sick.

'You see, it's different with twins.' Her hand gripped tight on my arm, not letting go. 'Babies take what they need. So one grows, and the other . . .' She sighed. 'One baby's always bigger. Stronger. That's the one that survives, you see. How do I tell her that?'

Tamsin had disappeared now, inside the house. I wasn't going in. I stopped at the back door, like a horse refusing to go any further. I couldn't look at Tamsin's mother. Couldn't listen to her voice any more, telling me things I didn't want to hear.

'You know, don't you?' she said, earnestly. 'You understand.'

I backed away. The path was slippery with frost. I shook my head.

'You've seen her, haven't you? I know you watch, from your window. You've seen her.'

I wanted to run, but didn't. I tried to walk away calmly, heading back to my own wall, my own garden, my normal mother and my normal brothers.

The words cut through the air behind me as I walked. Stabbing.

'But she will know,' she called out to me. 'I'll tell her one day. She carries it with her, don't you see. Tamsin. Her name. It means "twin". Didn't you know that? Tamsin means "twin".'

I didn't watch from my window after that. Sometimes I would glance out, notice the canal gate in next door's garden firmly shut and the new fence where the wall had been, see a little girl playing alone and not alone, and quickly turn away. And the following summer, when the vine grew down again over the glass, I begged Dad not to cut it. It didn't matter if I couldn't see out, I told him. I didn't want to. I liked it like that. And so the leaves shut out the world. My room swam in a sea-green light. And the new growth nearly, but not quite, cut out the sounds of laughter from the garden next door, the sound of childish laughter and of returned laughter.

A Separate Peace

FRANCIS BECKETT

If you want the sergeant major, we know where he is
We know where he is
We know where he is
If you want the sergeant major, we know where he is
He's hanging on the old barbed wire.

The voices singing the old First World War song were hollow and mocking, and seemed to come from all sides. But Smith could not see anyone: only endless rows of identical white gravestones, a regulation eighteen inches from each other, cold and dignified and sad in the cold, damp early evening.

So many graves. So many young men, only just out of school, who should have been drinking beer and picking up girls, brought here to die in a stinking trench.

Smith had walked the weary length of the huge graveyard just outside Chauny, fifty miles north-east of Paris, more often than he could count. Each time he thought: this time, this time they'll come for me. But only the trees whistled their mocking song at him.

People don't congregate in graveyards much. So when he heard a voice behind him, it startled him for a moment. He turned and saw a young man—a very young man, probably about eighteen: the same age as some of the men in these graves. He was, Smith thought, the sort of young man who, in 1918, would have been in a trench a few miles away from here, frozen, tormented by lice, terrified, and probably about to die.

The young man called out. 'Here, Dad, this is it.' Smith turned to see an older man walking across the graveyard, looking doubtfully at the darkening sky as he came. 'Hope you're right,' he grunted as he walked. 'We haven't got long. The storm's on its way. I can feel it in the air.'

The two of them, both tall, the father running to fat but fighting it, stood peering in the half light at the fading inscription carved on one of the gravestones, as Smith himself had done a thousand times. 'You're right, Gary,' said the father. 'It's him all right. It's my grandfather. Rifleman James Cutmore, died of wounds, March 1918.'

Smith stared at the two men. So these were Jim Cutmore's descendants. Who'd have thought it? Jim Cutmore.

'Cutmore. Take this message to Captain Michaels in B trench. At the double. At the double.' Smith remembered, with sickening fear in his heart, the order he'd given, and he remembered what Jim had said.

'But Sergeant Major Smith, they're potting everything that moves out there.'

'Get out there right now, Cutmore, if you don't want to be shot for disobeying an order.'

Jim didn't need to be at the Front at all. Forty years old, he was, with a wife and three little girls. Little tiny girls. The oldest was seven. Jim wouldn't have been conscripted, he was too old. He volunteered, the silly bugger. Smith never saw the three little girls, of course, but he knew that they loved Jim and sent him their chattering letters, and Jim wrote back. Jim's letters were long, in his fine, careful handwriting, and he only commented on what the children were doing, never a word about himself because he didn't want them to be sad or frightened.

He'd shown Smith some of the children's letters once. That was when Cutmore and Smith were both riflemen. They were friends in those days, before Smith got promoted.

Smith moved right up beside the two, the father and the son, to get a closer look. He felt it was a little rude, crowding them like that, though he knew they couldn't see him. He was just a cold nothingness, like the rapidly closing night itself.

The father was speaking.

'Ruined my mother's life, losing her father when she was seven. I think she spent the rest of her life looking for him.' His voice, Smith noticed, had just that gentle, almost musical quality that Jim's voice had had.

'That was a pretty stupid thing to do, looking for someone who was dead,' said Gary, who, like most young people, took everything rather literally.

'I don't mean looking for him in that way.'

'You said looking for him.'

'I know what I said.' Gary's father's voice had that grim, strained I-am-firmly-in-control-of-myself sort of tone. 'What I meant was . . .' Then he stopped, took a deep breath, and said, as though he was starting on a completely new subject: 'You remember I told you about my father, how he was much older than your grandma? Well, I think your grandma wasn't really looking for a husband when she married him. She was looking for a father. A father figure, I mean.'

'Oh,' said Gary. It was the sort of 'oh' that meant: if I tell him I haven't the faintest idea what he means, he'll start to explain, and we'll be here for ever. His father had the sense not to pursue the point.

Hearing them squabble amiably, Smith felt angry with Jim all over again, just as he'd felt that terrible day eighty years ago. Why did the stupid bastard have to come to the Front? Why didn't he stay at home where he belonged, and look after his daughters? It's not even as though he was much use as a soldier. He was so short-sighted he couldn't shoot straight. He was only good for stopping a bullet.

Why did he join the army? Smith had asked him once. 'It's not like you was in my place, Jim,' he said. 'I was conscripted. It was out 'ere or the bloody prison. But it wasn't like that for you. Why did you come?'

So Jim told him. He'd been feeling guilty, he said, about not 'doing his bit'. There were younger men out there dying for their country, and he was safe at home. At first he comforted himself with the thought that he was putting his wife and three little daughters first. Then one night, walking home from the office, a woman stopped him and gave him a white feather.

'Other men are out there doing your work,' she said crossly. 'They're not cowards like you.' And with withering contempt, she turned her back and walked off. Jim enlisted the next day.

'You stupid bastard, Jim.' Smith stared at the grave and wished tears could still roll down his cheeks. 'What did you want to get mixed up for, and make me send you out?' And he saw Jim's frightened, contemptuous face as he heard the order. He saw Jim pick up his rifle, poke his head over the top of the trench, look back once more in mute appeal, then run as fast as he could go.

Jim was too short-sighted to see much in the gathering darkness, and at first he wasn't running in quite the right direction. Smith shouted at him and he swung round, but it was too late. A younger man might just have made it before the sniper got him. Then again, quite likely no one would have made it.

'I 'ad to send someone, Jim. They'd a shot me else. I 'ad to. Wish you'd understand that. Didn't 'ave to be you, a course. You was a bit like a father to me, Jim. Fifteen years between us. I'm sorry, Jim.'

He watched Gary and his father take careful notes from the gravestone. 'You knew why I picked you, Jim. You knew. You gave me that look. How you looked when I was shouting out orders, shouting my head off, you used to look at me kind of sideways. Like you was saying, you knew who I was, I could fool the others but I couldn't fool you. I could 'ave 'ad you up for bloody insubordination for that look, Jim. I din' do it though.' He looked miserably at Gary and his father and thought: I killed you instead.

'When they shot him,' said Gary's father, 'he was carrying a message from one trench to the next. That's how they did things. If they had an errand to run, they'd send them, one after another, until finally one of them made it. They sent him running a hundred yards across part of no man's land. It was as good as killing him. And the stupid war was practically over anyway. You know, the same day my grandfather was killed they executed some poor sod of a sergeant in the same platoon. Sergeant Smith. It says on his army record: Shot for Desertion.'

'How do you know all this?'

'You can look at the army records. The captain kept a day-to-day record of what was going on. There's a place in London where you can go and look at them. It's called the Public Record Office. I do a lot of my research there. Most historians know it.'

'Oh, yes. Historians.' Sometimes Gary wished his father could have found another way of earning a living that didn't involve giving lectures. What he said was: 'Right, let's go, Dad. Storm's on its way. You said so yourself.'

'Just a minute,' said his father gently. 'It's a grandfather I never knew, and I've only just found him.'

'He's not very talkative,' said Gary, 'and that café in Chauny is calling to me. Chips, it's saying.'

Smith was now so close to the boy that, if he could touch anything, they would have been touching. He knew that once Gary and his father were through the cemetery gate, they were gone forever, and he could not bear to let them go, not yet. He and Gary looked at the gently rising hill just beyond the cemetery gate, the bare horizon at the top, and he sensed a change come over the boy.

'All right,' said Gary's father. 'You win. Chips and a beer for you and a *croque monsieur* and a pastis for me.' He looked at the sky, and a sudden flash of lightning lit up the hillside. He said, 'You're right. The storm's coming.' They heard the angry rumble of thunder, and he started to walk briskly towards the gate. Then he turned to look at his son, who had not moved. 'I thought you wanted to go.'

'I do,' said Gary quietly. 'I do.' But he didn't move.

'Fine.' His father thought he knew all Gary's moods, but this was new to him. He came slowly back to the grave. 'Fine.' He stood, silent, watchful, waiting for something that would tell him what was going on in his son's strange and irritating mind, and he said cheerfully: 'You haven't got long. I'm not getting soaked to the skin.' Another brilliant flash of lightning lit up the hillside, closer this time, and the thunder came sooner. Gary said nothing, but stared at it.

For Smith, locked in the memory of that awful day, a fresh bombardment was beginning.

When Gary did speak, he said the last thing his father expected to hear.

'It was Sergeant Smith sent your grandpa on that errand, and got him killed.'

'And how do you make that out?' His father was still puzzled, but pleased that he seemed to have captured his son's interest at last. Another flash of lightning, and thunder immediately afterwards, made him add: 'Tell me in the car.' But Gary stood restless, apprehensive. The bombardment moved closer.

'Smith sent Jim out,' he said quietly. 'He chose Jim because Jim was brighter than he was. He'd got a sort of—a sort of feeling against him. He—get down!' The last two words came out in a great scream and Gary took his father's shoulders. The two crouched behind Jim Cutmore's gravestone as another flash of lightning lit up the skyline.

'Gary, can we get up?' said his father. 'Crouching like this plays hell with my sciatica.'

But Smith's nightmare had taken hold of Gary. 'Stay down,' he shouted, as though he had to strain to make himself heard above a great noise. 'Down!' And this time he pulled his father right to the ground, and they lay there on their stomachs while the lightning flashed over them, and the cold wind chilled his father's bones.

'They got Jim, you see,' Gary shouted. 'I knew they would. I knew when I sent him out. That he'd never come back. And I still have to get that message to Captain Michaels in B trench.'

'To whom?'

'To . . .' Gary stopped speaking. For a moment he looked utterly bewildered, then he spoke very quietly. 'I must have made that name up. Let's say the message was for someone called Captain Michaels in B trench. OK?'

'OK, Gary. OK. Just—tell me what's on your mind.'

'Smith's captain, he was called Captain Osborne, a real public school type, cold as ice. "Right, Sarn't Major Smith," he said quietly, so the men couldn't hear, "you'll have to send another of your men."'

There was a pause. Gary's father thought of saying something, and decided to wait. Suddenly his son bellowed, in a strange and strained voice: 'No, sir. I'm not sending another man. I've sent dozens of men out there to 'ave their brains blown out. I'm not doing it no more. I'm not. Down!' Gary looked over his shoulder as the lightning flashed and the thunder bellowed insistently in their ears, and the first few drops of rain fell on them.

'Gary . . .' His father tentatively put an arm over Gary's shoulders, but Gary shook it off, but spoke quietly, in his own voice. 'Captain Osborne whispered in Smith's ear. He said: "If it's not done in five seconds, you will be disobeying the orders

of a superior officer on the field of battle, and you know what that means." Oh, yes. He'd do it.' Gary shook his head, as if to try to get rid of a memory.

'Then, very quietly, so no one else could hear, Captain Osborne counted down: five, four, three, two, one. And as he got to one, Smith rushed over the top of the trench and ran towards the German lines. I had . . . he had some vague idea that if he could get into the German trenches, they'd arrest him and he'd be a prisoner of war. That way he might live.'

Now the thunder and lightning was all round them, and the rain was starting to get heavier. In a few moments it would be a downpour, but Gary turned suddenly to lie on his back and stare upwards into the darkness, and he shrieked in sudden terror. 'I forgot the barbed wire. Wouldn't have run like that if I'd remembered. Hangin' on the bloody barbed wire, full of bullet holes. Christ. It hurts. Come and get me, boys. Come and get me off. You can shoot me after, I don't mind, just make it quick.'

'Gary!' Now his father was on his feet, taking Gary's arms and pulling. But the arms were limp in his hands, and the eyes stared at the dark, electric sky and seemed not to notice the rain. His father was alarmed now. 'Gary . . .'

'It's OK.' Gary sat up, his eyes focused, he talked in his own voice. 'It's OK, Dad. You know, Captain Osborne never told anyone what had really happened. He just reported to his superior officer that he'd shot Smith for desertion, though of course it was really the Germans who shot him. No one even knew what happened to old Smith. And that's it.'

Gary stood up as the heavens opened, and the cold rain came suddenly down in a great sheet. Gary noticed a sudden extra chill in the semi-darkness, like frozen tears. By the time they got to the car they were as wet as if they had jumped in a river.

Rain didn't bother Smith. He was remembering the cruel barbed wire. Both sides put up tangled barbed wire between the trenches. Smith was a good runner, and he got to the wire before the bullets hit him, but he didn't get over it. He was like hundreds of men he'd seen, stuck to the barbed wire like a fly in a spider's web. It took him two hours to die, and he prayed for death every minute of it.

Sometimes, when a man got trapped on the barbed wire and he was still alive, they'd send a patrol out to try to get him back, as they did, eventually, for Cutmore. But no one came for Smith. Captain Osborne saw no point in risking lives just to bring a man back to face a firing squad. And the men had grown to dislike Smith as soon as he was promoted. They thought his new rank made him bullying and self-important. A sergeant major was someone who barked orders at them and denied them comfort and dignity, and forced them out to die. That was why they sang their cruel song at the tops of their voices as he died, and their voices floated to Smith across no man's land:

> *If you want the sergeant major, we know where he is*
> *We know where he is*
> *We know where he is*
> *If you want the sergeant major, we know where he is*
> *He's hanging on the old barbed wire.*

There were a dozen men in this graveyard whom Smith had sent to their deaths on patrols, and hundreds whom he had forced over the top when the order came to attack. Smith heard them singing the song yet again. But this time, as the words died away, he knew there was someone else with him. Slowly he lifted his gaze from the ground to the sky and said: 'You've come for me. I told someone, Jim. I said what I done, all of it. Someone knows now. That's why you're here. I bin waiting. I bin waiting a long time.'

Jim's voice was quiet and careful, just as he remembered it. 'I wanted to see him, that's all. My grandson. I'd been wondering, you know, what he might be like.'

'If it weren't for me,' said Smith miserably, 'you'd a known. You'd a bin around when he were born.'

'If it weren't for the war. You didn't start the war.' He moved away and Smith felt himself abandoned again. Then Jim turned, and said:

'Come and join us, sarn't major. I think the lads would be happy to see you.'

If you ever go to the English graveyard at Chauny, you'll find that it isn't haunted any more.

Topaz

RUSKIN BOND

I t seemed strange to be listening to the strains of 'The Blue Danube' while gazing out at the pine-clad slopes of the Himalayas, worlds apart. And yet the music of the waltz seemed singularly appropriate. A light breeze hummed through the pines, and the branches seemed to move in time to the music. The record-player was new, but the records were old, picked up in a junk-shop behind the Mall.

Below the pines there were oaks, and one oak tree in particular caught my eye. It was the biggest of the lot and stood by itself on a little knoll below the cottage. The breeze was not strong enough to lift its heavy old branches, but *something* was moving, swinging gently from the tree, keeping time to the music of the waltz, dancing...

It was someone hanging from the tree.

A rope oscillated in the breeze, the body turned slowly, turned this way and that, and I saw the face of a girl, her hair hanging loose, her eyes sightless, hands and feet limp; just turning, turning, while the waltz played on.

I turned off the player and ran downstairs.

Down the path through the trees, and onto the grassy knoll where the big oak stood.

A long-tailed magpie took fright and flew out from the branches, swooping low across the ravine. In the tree there was no one, nothing. A great branch extended halfway across the knoll, and it was possible for me to reach up and touch it. A girl could not have reached it without climbing the tree.

As I stood there, gazing up into the branches, someone spoke behind me.

'What are you looking at?'

I swung round. A girl stood in the clearing, facing me. A girl of seventeen or eighteen; alive, healthy, with bright eyes and a tantalizing smile. She was lovely to look at. I hadn't seen such a pretty girl in years.

'You startled me,' I said. 'You came up so unexpectedly.'

'Did you see anything—in the tree?' she asked.

'I thought I saw someone from my window. That's why I came down. Did *you* see anything?'

'No.' She shook her head, the smile leaving her face for a moment. 'I don't see anything. But other people do—sometimes.'

'What do they see?'

'My sister.'

'Your *sister*?'

'Yes. She hanged herself from this tree. It was many years ago. But sometimes you can see her hanging there.'

She spoke matter-of-factly: whatever had happened seemed very remote to her.

We both moved some distance away from the tree. Above the knoll, on a disused private tennis-court (a relic from the hill-station's colonial past) was a small stone bench. She sat down on it: and, after a moment's hesitation, I sat down beside her.

'Do you live close by?' I asked.

'Further up the hill. My father has a small bakery.'

She told me her name—Hameeda. She had two younger brothers.

'You must have been quite small when your sister died.'

'Yes. But I remember her. She was pretty.'

'Like you.'

She laughed in disbelief. 'Oh, I am nothing to her. You should have seen my sister.'

'Why did she kill herself?'

'Because she did not want to live. That's the only reason, no? She was to have been married but she loved someone else, some-one who was not of her own community. It's an old story and the end is always sad, isn't it?'

'Not always. But what happened to the boy—the one she loved? Did he kill himself too?'

'No, he took a job in some other place. Jobs are not easy to get, are they?'

'I don't know. I've never tried for one.'

'Then what do you do?'

'I write stories.'

'Do people *buy* stories?'

'Why not? If your father can sell bread, I can sell stories.'

'People must have bread. They can live without stories.'

'No, Hameeda, you're wrong. People can't live without stories.'

Hameeda! I couldn't help loving her. Just loving her. No fierce desire or passion had taken hold of me. It wasn't like that. I was happy just to look at her, watch her while she sat on the grass outside my cottage, her lips stained with the juice of wild bilberries. She chatted away—about her friends, her clothes, her favourite things.

'Won't your parents mind if you come here every day?' I asked.

'I have told them you are teaching me.'

'Teaching you what?'

'They did not ask. You can tell me stories.'

So I told her stories.

It was midsummer.

The sun glinted on the ring she wore on her third finger: a translucent golden topaz, set in silver.

'That's a pretty ring,' I remarked.

'You wear it,' she said, impulsively removing it from her hand. 'It will give you good thoughts. It will help you to write better stories.'

She slipped it onto my little finger.

'I'll wear it for a few days,' I said. 'Then you must let me give it back to you.'

On a day that promised rain I took the path down to the stream at the bottom of the hill. There I found Hameeda gathering ferns from the shady places along the rocky ledges above the water.

'What will you do with them?' I asked.

'This is a special kind of fern. You can cook it as a vegetable.'

'It is tasty?'

'No, but it is good for rheumatism.'

'Do you suffer from rheumatism?'

'Of course not. They are for my grandmother, she is very old.'

'There are more ferns further upstream,' I said. 'But we'll have to get into the water.'

We removed our shoes and began paddling upstream. The ravine became shadier and narrower, until the sun was almost completely shut out. The ferns grew right down to the water's edge. We bent to pick them but instead found ourselves in each other's arms; and sank slowly, as in a dream, into the soft bed of ferns, while overhead a whistling thrush burst out in dark sweet song.

'It isn't time that's passing by,' it seemed to say. 'It is you and I. It is you and I . . .'

I waited for her the following day, but she did not come.

Several days passed without my seeing her.

Was she sick? Had she been kept at home? Had she been sent away? I did not even know where she lived, so I could not ask. And if I had been able to ask, what would I have said?

Then one day I saw a boy delivering bread and pastries at the little tea-shop about a mile down the road. From the upward slant of his eyes, I caught a slight resemblance to Hameeda. As he left the shop, I followed him up the hill. When I came abreast of him, I asked: 'Do you have your own bakery?'

He nodded cheerfully, 'Yes. Do you want anything—bread, biscuits, cakes? I can bring them to your house.'

'Of course. But don't you have a sister? A girl called Hameeda?'

His expression changed. He was no longer friendly. He looked puzzled and slightly apprehensive.

'Why do you want to know?'

'I haven't seen her for some time.'

'We have not seen her either.'

'Do you mean she has gone away?'

'Didn't you know? You must have been away a long time. It is many years since she died. She killed herself. You did not hear about it?'

'But wasn't that her sister—your other sister?'

'I had only one sister—Hameeda—and she died, when I was very young. It's an old story, ask someone else about it.'

He turned away and quickened his pace, and I was left standing in the middle of the road, my head full of questions that couldn't be answered.

That night there was a thunderstorm. My bedroom window kept banging in the wind. I got up to close it and, as I looked out, there was a flash of lightning and I saw that frail body again, swinging from the oak tree.

I tried to make out the features, but the head hung down and the hair was blowing in the wind.

Was it all a dream?

It was impossible to say. But the topaz on my hand glowed softly in the darkness. And a whisper from the forest seemed to say, 'It isn't time that's passing by, my friend. It is you and I . . .'

Dogends

TANYA DAVID

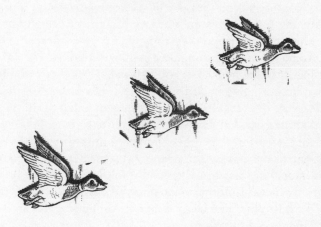

For as long as Robbie Buckley could remember he had wanted a dog. It didn't really matter what kind of dog, as long as it wasn't one of those daft looking ones like a poodle or one that was so small that you had to carry it around in your pocket, just an ordinary dog that he could take for a walk and teach a few tricks, that was all he wanted. But his mum didn't want a dog. Dogs were too much trouble, they ate too much and they made too much mess, and when you wanted to go away on holiday you couldn't just ask Mrs O'Donell from next door to come in and feed it. No, dogs needed too much looking after.

'I'll look after it,' Robbie had said, but he knew that his mum would just think of another excuse.

'This house is too small for a dog, Robbie. It wouldn't be fair to keep it cooped up all day when there's nobody at home.'

Robbie thought about all his friends who had dogs and lived in houses the same size as his, some even smaller, but he didn't mention them to Mum. He had learnt that it was no good trying to change her mind about anything. So after a while he gave up on the subject of getting a dog and promised himself that as soon as he was grown-up and old enough to leave home he would have as many dogs as he wanted.

It was the Tuesday that Robbie cleaned Mr Spatchley's office that changed everything. When he woke up on this particular day Robbie had no idea that it was going to be any different from any other but later, when he had time to think about it, he knew exactly when everything had begun. Tuesday, the 3rd of August, halfway through the summer holidays. He had been sitting at the kitchen table eating a bowl of cereal and wondering what he was going to do for the rest of the day. All his friends, at least the ones that lived nearby, were on holiday. This year his parents had decided they were too poor to go anywhere, even to Butlins, so Robbie had been left to amuse himself. Even his sister had gone away to Ireland with her best friend. Robbie was munching his cornflakes and thinking about how unlucky he was when his mother came into the kitchen.

'Well, Robbie,' she said, 'what are you up to today?'

'Dunno,' said Robbie.

His mother began to clear the table. Robbie sat and watched her.

'What about Jeremy?'

'He's gone to his aunt's.'

Robbie's mum took some dishes to the sink and began to wash up.

'Well, what about Matthew and Simon?'

Robbie told her they were on holiday too.

'Mum, why can't we go anywhere? We could go to Scotland again and see Trina.' (Trina was his mum's sister.)

'Don't start all that again,' his mother sighed. Robbie watched her dry up the things on the draining board and put them away in the cupboard.

'But I'm bored. There's nothing to do here. Everybody goes away on holiday except me. It's not fair!'

As soon as he had said this, Robbie knew he shouldn't have. His mother slammed the door of the cupboard and turned around. Her face was hard and angry.

'OK,' she said. 'If you're so bored you can come along to the offices with me and do a bit of work for a change. Then you'll really have something to moan about! Put your shoes on and brush your hair. And you'd better hurry!'

Robbie tried to tell his mum that he wasn't that bored, but she wasn't about to let him off so easily. Why, oh why, had he opened his big mouth? As they walked down the road Robbie glanced at his mum striding beside him and his heart sank when he saw the determined, stubborn look on her face. When she looked like that it was no good saying anything.

Robbie's mum was a cleaner. She cleaned offices and people's houses and a school in the afternoon. The offices they were going to were not far away. When they got there Robbie's mum showed him where the cupboard with all the cleaning things was then put him to work in the first office, Mr Spatchley's.

'Mind you dust everything. Mr Spatchley's away on his holiday and I promised him I'd give his room a thorough going-over,' she said, putting a yellow duster firmly in his hand. 'And be careful. If anything gets broken it's coming out of your pocket money.' Robbie scowled at his mother's back as she disappeared into the office next door. This wasn't funny. He wished for the hundredth time he had never opened his mouth about being bored. He would give anything to be sitting back at home being bored now.

Mr Spatchley had a thing about ducks. They were everywhere you looked in his office. Not live ones, of course, but all sorts of wooden and plaster and painted ones. Three very large blue and green ones sailed across the wall at one end of the room. A stuffed duck in a glass case watched Robbie with beady eyes from above the fireplace, and several smaller ones marched in rows across the mantelpiece. Robbie had never seen so many ducks all together, in fact he had never seen so much anything all together. Mr Spatchley had duck bookends and duck pictures and duck paperweights on his desk. He even had a duck pencil sharpener. He was duck crazy. Which was all right if you liked that sort of thing, thought Robbie, wandering around the room looking at them, and then he remembered he was the one who had to dust them all, which was not all right at all. 'Mind you dust everything,' his mum had said. Everything. He glared at the duck in the glass case. It seemed to be laughing at him.

It took Robbie a long time to dust all those ducks and he was in a very bad mood when he'd finished. His mother poked her head round the door. She was carrying the hoover.

'Still bored?' she said in a teasing voice. Robbie didn't bother to answer. She put the hoover down in front of him and nodded at it.

'That's next,' she said. 'And mind you hoover everywhere. You'll have to move things around.' She disappeared again and Robbie heard her begin to whistle from somewhere down the corridor. He kicked the hoover four or five times, but this only made his toes hurt. The duck in the glass case watched him gleefully.

Robbie plugged in the hoover and started vacuuming the floor. He was so angry now that he was not bothering to be careful, and he was certainly not going to bother to stop and move anything out of the way. He pushed the chairs back so hard with the end of the hoover nozzle that one fell over but he didn't bother to pick it up again. He didn't care. He dragged the hoover behind him, zigzagging it around the room getting its lead tangled around Mr Spatchley's desk legs and several large potted plants that stood under the window, then around a large standard lamp that had a duck sitting on it, and then several more ducks that just seemed to be sitting on the carpet getting in the way.

At the other side of the room between an armchair and a bookcase was a little antique table that had a funny-looking pot standing on it. Robbie was so busy concentrating on the carpet that he didn't see the pot until it was too late, at least until it was too late to do anything about what happened next. The hoover lead had somehow got around the legs of the little table and when Robbie yanked it the table wobbled so much that the funny-looking pot rolled off and fell on to the carpet. Robbie heard it and turned around. There seemed to be dust everywhere; a cloud rose up around the pot whose lid had come off and rolled somewhere else. Robbie hoovered up the dust without thinking. When all the dust had gone (and there seemed to be an awful lot of it) he picked up the pot and looked inside. There was still a bit of dust inside so he took the end off the hoover and stuck the nozzle inside until it was all gone.

It was a funny thing to use as an ashtray, thought Robbie, and nobody seemed to have bothered to empty it for a long time. Well, it was empty now. He put the pot back on the table and then noticed it had some pictures stuck on it. They were photographs of a dog. Robbie liked the look of the dog; it was one of those scruffy little dogs with long wiry hair and a stumpy tail that was always wagging, a friendly, happy sort of dog. Then he noticed something else. Behind the little antique table was a dog's collar and lead hanging on the wall. Robbie took it down and read the silver name tag. 'Jasper,' it said on one side, and then the address of the Spatchleys on the other. And then Robbie noticed something else. On the side of the urn was a small silver plaque with three words engraved on it. 'Our Beloved Jasper,' read Robbie, and underneath, two dates '1980–1995'.

Robbie stood, holding the hoover nozzle, for a long time. So it had not been cigarette ash he had spilt all over the carpet. It had not been cigarette ash he had so carefully vacuumed up, and it had not been cigarette ash he had cleaned out of the urn. He felt vaguely sick. No wonder there hadn't been any cigarette ends. What was he going to do now? He had hoovered up the ashes of Our Beloved Jasper and now those ashes were in the hoover bag with all the dust and dead leaves and carpet fluff and dirt that hoover bags got filled up with. What would he say to his mother? Worse still, what would they tell Mr Spatchley? For a few moments Robbie saw himself emptying the hoover bag and rescuing what remained of Jasper and putting it safely back in the urn without telling anyone. Surely no one would be able to tell the difference between what was Jasper (at least, what used to be Jasper) and ordinary household or office dust? But supposing they could? Supposing someone . . .

'Robbie?' shouted his mum from the corridor. 'Have you finished yet?'

There was no time to do anything now. He heard his mother coming closer. The next minute she was coming through the door.

'Well, that's not a bad job,' she said, looking round approvingly. 'Get everything straightened out and then we'll go home. Not bad at all. You'll have to come and help me another day . . .' She laughed at the expression on Robbie's face. 'Only joking.

Come on, we've been here long enough. I'll put the hoover away.'

Robbie watched her carry the hoover and Jasper out of the door. When she had gone he went over to the urn and very carefully lifted up the lid. He peered inside, just to make sure. Not a speck of Jasper remained.

'You're very quiet,' his mother said as they walked home. 'You did a really good job in Mr Spatchley's office. I don't think you left a speck of dust in the whole place. So how about an ice cream? I think you deserve one.'

They crossed the road to where the ice cream van was. His mother smilingly bought him an enormous vanilla cone with chocolate and strawberry syrup. It didn't cheer him up very much though. All Robbie could think about was poor Jasper's ashes, locked away in the hoover somewhere and lost forever. He hoped it would be a long time before anyone thought to look in that urn again.

That night Robbie was woken by a howling noise. He opened his eyes . . . it was coming from outside his window somewhere down in the garden. He looked at his clock and the luminous hands glowed in the dark. It was 3.45 a.m. The howling turned into whimpering. Robbie knelt up in bed and looked out of the window. The garden was bathed in ghostly moonlight, the trees seemed to glow strangely, everything was still. Down at the bottom of the garden, just outside the gate, he could see a crouching, doglike shape. It didn't move but the whimpering continued. And then, as Robbie watched, the dog seemed to see him too and sat bolt upright and started barking. Robbie got out of bed and went downstairs. The barking stopped when he got to the back door. He saw the dog sitting at the gate as if it was waiting for him so he ran down the path in his bare feet, but as he got close he saw the dog stand up and begin to walk away.

'Hey,' said Robbie, but the dog didn't stop. By the time Robbie had reached the gate it was gone. There was no sign of it at all.

A few nights later the same thing happened. This time Robbie was dreaming about Mr Spatchley's ducks. They had all come alive and were flying around the office whilst Robbie desperately tried to hoover the floor. There were ducks everywhere, on the desk and mantelpiece and padding around on the floor, knocking things over and quacking indignantly. All of a sudden there was a loud barking and Robbie turned round to see Jasper standing in the doorway. That was when he woke to hear real

barking coming from the end of the garden again. Robbie peered through the curtains and sure enough there was the dog standing at the gate as if it was waiting for him. Robbie sprinted downstairs and outside. This time the dog waited until he was very close. Then it turned and ran off down the street. Robbie saw its stumpy little tail disappearing into the shadows and that was that.

After that, strange things began to happen. There was the feeling Robbie got whenever he left the house. He would sense it as soon as he went out of the front gate. It started off as a feeling that he was being followed. He kept thinking there was someone behind him. Sometimes he could almost hear their soft footsteps, but when he turned round there was never anybody there. After a while he felt that they weren't behind him any more but walking beside him, near to the ground, and it wasn't two feet he could hear, but four. This went on for some days but after a week Robbie found he was getting used to it. It was hard to explain, but he stopped feeling frightened and instead felt as if whatever it was was keeping him safe. He didn't mention this to anyone. There was no one to tell in any case: if he told his mum she would just get worried, and if he told any of his friends they would probably laugh out loud at him, so he kept quiet.

One day Robbie decided to go to the park. The soft pad-pad sound stayed beside him all the way down Richmond Street and round into Turner Avenue. When Robbie started to run, the sounds got quicker too as if there was something running beside him. He reached the gates of Turner Park and stopped. The noises stopped too, as if whatever it was was waiting for him. It was just like having an invisible dog beside him—a ghost dog! That's what it was, thought Robbie, a flipping ghost dog! He ran along the path and all the way to the lake. The thought of a ghost dog made him run very fast. But when he reached the lake he was so out of breath that he had to stop. He sat down on a bench feeling slightly dizzy. The padding sound seemed to go on towards some ducks that were resting by the water. There was a great deal of quacking and fussing and they all flew away. A ghost dog! A ghost dog that liked chasing ducks! Why would a ghost dog be following him around? And then he thought of poor Jasper and the hoover. His mum had probably emptied it by now and Jasper's ashes were in a dustbin somewhere lying on top of all kinds of rubbish, soggy tea bags and egg shells and toilet rolls. It made Robbie wince to think of it.

After a minute or two he suddenly realized that he was alone. The strange sounds had gone and he no longer had a feeling that there was something beside him. Had he imagined them all along? No, of course he hadn't, but . . . A mother with a baby buggy was walking down the path towards him. Her little boy was tagging behind. He was playing with something shiny, throwing it up into the air and catching it. Then he dropped it. It rolled down the hill a bit and stopped very close to Robbie's feet. Robbie bent down and picked it up.

'Come on!' the little boy's mother said crossly. But the little boy ignored her. He was looking around on the ground, frowning. Robbie looked at the small round silver disc in his hand. It was rather battered, like a 10p piece that had been run over by a ten ton truck. He turned it over and read the word on the back. It made him nearly jump off the bench in shock.

'Jasper!'

The woman and the boy both stared at him.

'Is that your dog?' asked the boy's mother. 'Kenny found that in the grass just over there. It must have dropped off its collar. Kenny saw the dog, didn't you?' Kenny nodded.

'You saw it?' asked Robbie. 'What did it look like?'

'Dunno,' said Kenny, who was looking very intently at the disc in Robbie's hand.

'Come on, Kenny love,' his mother said wearily. The baby in the buggy started to cry. She started to walk away from the pond. 'We've got to go home and have our tea.' But Kenny wasn't listening. He walked over to Robbie and held out his hand.

'Can I have my money back?' he asked petulantly. 'I found it. It's mine.'

'OK, if you tell me about the dog. What colour was it?'

'Brown,' said Kenny.

'With curly hair and long ears?'

'Yes.'

'Big or small?'

'Dunno.'

Robbie held up the disc and squinted at it. 'This is real silver,' he told Kenny. 'It's probably worth a lot of money.'

Kenny eyed it greedily.

'It was scruffy,' he said, 'and it had a white bit on its tail. Can I have my money back now?'

'Come on, Kenny, for goodness sake!' his mother shouted.

Robbie gave the disc to Kenny who grabbed it and ran off after his mother before the strange boy on the bench could change his mind.

When Robbie got home his mother was sitting at the kitchen table looking upset.

'It's Mr Spatchley,' she said sadly, 'his wife sent me a letter from Canada where they went on their holiday.'

Robbie frowned and sat down next to her. 'So?'

'He died on Tuesday.'

'Oh.'

Robbie, who had never met Mr Spatchley, felt a little bit surprised. He wasn't upset though. All he could think of was Jasper. At least Mr Spatchley would never find out about the accident with the hoover now.

'Mrs Spatchley wants me to go and help pack up the office and ship the things over there. She's not coming back, not with the funeral and everything. Besides, I think they have family in Canada. She probably won't come back at all now.' Robbie's mum sniffed and looked even sadder. She had really been very fond of Mr Spatchley. 'He was a lovely old gentleman,' she said and sighed. 'I was hoping you'd come and help me tomorrow.'

'OK,' said Robbie, who didn't mind the thought of wrapping all those wretched ducks in newspaper and packing them into boxes. In fact he decided he'd quite enjoy it.

The next day Robbie and his mother walked to Mr Spatchley's office. The phantom dog was not with them, but then that didn't surprise Robbie. He never felt it walking beside him when he was with anybody else.

The office was exactly the same as Robbie remembered it. The duck with the beady eyes still watched him from its glass case on the wall above the fireplace and the three flying ducks were still flying nowhere on the wall opposite. Perhaps they were flying away from Jasper.

'All right, Robbie, here's some paper. Let's get on with it.'

Robbie noticed that the urn was still where he had left it, standing on the little table under the window. His mother started picking up things from the desk and handing them to Robbie.

They worked on for half an hour or so, Robbie's mum murmuring and sighing to herself about how awful it all was. At one point she was so overcome that she had to sit down for a bit on Mr Spatchley's chair. There was a tap at the door and a tall man with ginger hair and a beard popped his head round.

'Aah, Mrs Buckley,' he said warmly when he saw her. 'So kind of you to come. Is this your son?' The man smiled thinly at Robbie.

'Mr Cornwall! Yes, that's Robbie come to help me. I was so sad when I heard. Mr Spatchley was such a nice man.'

Mr Cornwall nodded grimly. 'Aah, yes, terrible business indeed. Mrs Spatchley phoned me last night and asked me to collect something, an urn or something, with some ashes in . . .' Mr Cornwall's eyes swept around the room.

'Do you happen to know where it—I see it!' He came in and walked over to the little table under the window. 'Apparently they're the ashes of a favourite dog they used to have. Mrs Spatchley wants me to scatter them in the park, she said something about that was where they used to take it for walks . . . I think Bill used to take it there, it was very special to him I believe . . . aaah, there's a picture of it.' Mr Cornwall squinted at the picture of Jasper. 'Funny looking thing, I must say. Mmmm,' he reached out for the urn.

'I'll do it!' said Robbie quickly. He had suddenly realized that if Mr Cornwall took the urn his secret would be discovered.

Mr Cornwall turned round in surprise. 'Would you?' He was looking very relieved. 'I'd be very grateful if you did. I can't say I was particularly looking forward to it. I've got so many other things to take care of. Well, that's that, then. I'll go back to my office. Thank you most kindly, Raymond—er, Robbie, I mean. You know where the park is?'

Robbie nodded. Mr Cornwall was not the only one who felt relieved.

'Oh, he's mad about dogs!' said Robbie's mum beaming at him proudly. 'Even dead ones.'

'Good show,' said Mr Cornwall as he left the room.

When Robbie walked out on to the street clutching the urn he was expecting the ghost dog to be there, waiting for him. It wasn't. He walked slowly down Axminster Road and into Bath Street, but there were no soft footfalls beside him, no pad-pad of dog paws, only his own footsteps that sounded strangely loud and unnatural. At the bottom of Bath Street was Turner Street and at the bottom of Turner Street was Turner Park. What was he going to do with the urn? There weren't any ashes so he didn't have to go all the way to the park. He could just as well toss it into the skip outside one of the new flats they were building in Dudley Row, or bury it in someone's dustbin. He carried on.

Perhaps he had only imagined the ghost dog. Perhaps all those feelings and noises weren't anything, just his mind playing tricks on him. Maybe he had imagined them because he had felt so bad about Jasper, so guilty about hoovering him up and not telling anyone. No, that wasn't it. And what about the little boy in the park and the name disc that said Jasper? Maybe the little boy had just seen a dog that looked like Jasper, there were plenty of them around, and maybe . . . yes, maybe the name tag was Jasper's, but one he had lost ages ago, years ago even, when Mr Spatchley had taken him on one of his duck-chasing walks in the park. That explained why it looked so old and battered.

Robbie reached the gates of the park and went in. He started walking up the path to the lake. Its glassy surface shone in the sun. When he got nearer he could see there were ducks, lots of them, paddling contentedly around and around in circles. Robbie lifted the urn above his head and sent it hurling up, up, up into the air, then watched as it came down in an arc, down, down, down, splash! right into the middle of the lake sending ducks flying and quacking and paddling frantically for cover in all directions.

When Robbie walked away from the lake he knew Jasper was beside him. It was as if he had been sitting there waiting for him, just like a real dog. He could hear his paws distinctly now, swish, swish through the long grass. Robbie felt happy, as if he had found an old friend again, or at least that an old friend had found him. Jasper stayed close to Robbie all the way home.

Alicia

LOUISE FRANCKE

S anderford is a yellow cat with yellow eyes and he is never
allowed in the attic. But Elizabeth Ann had seen him go
up, so she went after him.

She stopped five steps from the top of the stairs. The step that
put her eyes just above attic-floor level. She stood quietly
for a moment and looked along between boxes and bureau legs
for a patch of yellow fur. 'Here, Sandy; here, Sandy,' she called
softly.

The attic door had been standing open a little. That's strange,
she thought. She had seen Sandy's tail disappearing into the darkness, so she knew he was here. 'Here, Sandy; here, Sandy.'

He wasn't allowed in the attic. Ever.

'Here, Sandy; here, Sandy.'

'Here, dear. He's over here, dear Alicia,' a sweet, soft voice
answered. Elizabeth Ann froze. Her mouth dropped open slightly

and her eyes grew wide with astonishment as they turned in the direction of the gentle but terrifyingly unexpected voice.

In the chair. In the dainty great-great-grandmother rocker. A pale, pretty, white-haired woman in a delicate blue dress. Right next to the chair sat Sanderford with his tail curled neatly around him. Both of them were looking at her.

'Here, dear.' The woman's hand drifted down slowly to touch the top of Sanderford's head. 'Here's your kitty. With me. You see? Your kitty is my friend, dear Alicia.' She was smiling. But her eyes didn't smile. They seemed hard and brilliant in the dim light.

'My name is not Alicia,' said Elizabeth Ann in a faintly choked voice.

'I know. I know, my dear.' She spoke softly but quickly. 'But you do look like Alicia. You look so very much like Alicia I really don't believe I can call you anything else. You won't mind if I call you Alicia, will you? I have thought of you as Alicia for so long. Ever since I started watching you play in the garden. Right from this window.' She motioned towards the small window and her hand looked nearly transparent. 'I was hoping you would come. Today. Especially today. Because today you are eleven.' Again she smiled sweetly.

Today was, in fact, Elizabeth Ann's eleventh birthday.

'But don't just stand there on the stairway, dear Alicia. Come up, come up.' Her voice was soft but urgent. 'I've been waiting so long to talk with you.'

Elizabeth Ann didn't want to go up. She thought she should go down and tell her mother about this woman sitting in the attic.

'Come,' insisted the woman. 'Let me show you the picture of my beautiful Alicia. You'll see. You'll see how much you look like her.'

'No thank you. Not right now.' Elizabeth Ann knew that this woman should *not* be sitting in the great-great-grandmother chair in the attic. 'I must go now.' Then she remembered why she had come to the attic. 'Here, Sandy; here, Sandy,' she called, but Sanderford's tail remained curled around his paws. 'Here, Sandy; come, Sandy.' The pale woman had reached into a blue pocket and was holding a small picture out towards her.

'Come and see Alicia first, my dear, and then I will let your Sanderford go with you.' What did she mean, *let* him go, wondered Elizabeth Ann. Did she have the power to make him stay there?

No, Elizabeth Ann didn't want to go up. But she put her foot on the fourth step from the top, slowly. Perhaps she would just look at the picture quickly, then take Sandy downstairs. Her foot moved to the third step.

'Yes, yes, come dear. Here it is.'

Elizabeth Ann had reached the top and was walking cautiously towards the woman in the chair. Then, with a wave, the picture came fluttering through the air.

As she bent to pick it up from the floor, Sanderford uncurled his tail, walked across the attic and down the stairs.

Elizabeth Ann followed. On the fifth step from the top she turned her head to look at the woman once more, but the great-great-grandmother chair was empty. Quite empty.

Elizabeth Ann shut the attic door firmly.

Silly, she thought. Silly! Silly imagination. Yes, it is. Yet she had the picture in her hand.

She looked at the pale, reddish-brown portrait. At the small face looking back at her. It's *me*, she thought. It really does look like *me*.

She turned the picture over and read the pencilled inscription: 'Alicia Frost, Aged 11.' Then she walked into her room and slipped the picture, face down, into her dressing-table drawer.

Elizabeth Ann waited until after dinner. Until she and her mother were alone. She had made her wish, blown out the eleven birthday candles . . . and they had had ice-cream, too.

Now she was drying dishes as her mother washed.

'Who was Alicia, mother?'

Her mother was slipping more plates into the dishwater and hardly seemed to notice the question. 'I don't know, dear. Who was she?'

'I don't know either,' answered Elizabeth Ann. 'But she was somebody. I found her picture in the attic. On the back it says she's Alicia Frost, aged eleven. That's my age now. And she looks just like me.'

'Alicia Frost?' her mother thought a minute. 'Attic? Well, there are some old things in the trunk up there, I think, but I don't remember any pictures. Frost,' she repeated. 'That was your great-grandmother's name. Yes ... yes ...' She frowned thoughtfully. 'Alicia Frost was your great-grandmother's sister. She died when she was a little girl.'

Elizabeth Ann picked up another plate and rubbed it with the linen towel.

'But ...' her mother continued, 'I don't remember ever seeing a picture of her. Where did you find it? In the trunk?'

'I picked it up off the floor.' There, thought Elizabeth Ann. That's the absolute truth. There's no imagination about that.

'Where's the picture now, dear?'

'In my room.'

When the dishes were finished, Elizabeth Ann brought the picture down to show her mother. She was almost sorry that she had mentioned it, because now she wanted to tell her mother about the woman in the chair. Yet she knew it would sound foolish. Of course there was no woman in the attic. Even Elizabeth Ann knew that. She had simply imagined it. Hadn't she?

'Yes,' said her mother. 'That would be your great-grandmother's sister. She must have died right after this picture was taken. It was said that *her* mother—and that would be your great-*great*-grandmother, Elizabeth Ann—went quite mad after her little girl died. And that she wandered around the house for years, searching and calling for her daughter Alicia.'

'And that's her chair—my great-great-grandmother's chair—in the attic, isn't it, mother?'

'Yes, that's right. Just think, it has been in the family all these years.'

'Do you think I look like Alicia?'

'Well, I think you do.' Elizabeth Ann's mother had put on her glasses and was studying the faded picture.

She handed the picture back to Elizabeth Ann. 'Yes, I think you look a lot like Alicia.' Then she patted her daughter's hair softly and said, half to herself, 'Both very pretty girls, very pretty indeed.'

The matter was thus dismissed, and Elizabeth Ann didn't really think much about it again until the next afternoon when she

Then it happened.

Elizabeth Ann was jolted awake by a hard, hurting jerk on her left leg. So hard, it pulled her right off her pillow and her head thumped back on the bed.

Instinctively, she twisted slightly to pull her leg towards her and there, at the end of the bed, was the woman, smiling sweetly, ever so sweetly, with her eyes burning bright in the dark. Both of the woman's hands held Elizabeth Ann's ankle tightly.

Sanderford stood, arched, on the bed, puffed and huge, nearly double his normal size. His mouth was open in a near grin, his eyes furious and glowing.

She heard the hissing whispers . . . 'It's time now, Alicia-a . . . time to come. You broke your promise to me . . . you promised me . . . you promised to come . . . but you broke your promise . . . you made me come to get you . . . so I'll take you . . . with me . . . now . . .'

Elizabeth Ann struggled, but she was being pulled slowly towards the foot of the bed.

'I'll teach you . . . you'll come with me . . . you can't break your promise to me . . .'

Elizabeth Ann tried to scream, and tried again, but her breath was coming in short gasps as she fought to free her ankle.

'We'll go together now . . . the three of us . . . forever together my dearest, my darling . . . my own . . . Alicia-a.'

Elizabeth Ann pushed, but slipped on the smooth sheet. There was nothing for her hands to grasp. The eiderdown bunched and puffed and turned into soft nothingness in her fingers. She pulled and twisted and hunched her shoulders, but slowly, slowly she was being drawn towards the old woman.

Suddenly, Elizabeth Ann pulled herself upright and grabbed at the hands holding her ankle. She prised at the fingers of one bony hand and felt them weaken, slowly . . . slip . . . let go . . . *her hair*! The woman had seized her hair! One strong hand still held her ankle fast, but the other now gripped her hair and was pulling her head . . . ouch . . . ouch . . . ow-w-w-w . . . In her pain, Elizabeth Ann clenched both hands into fists and punched out into the middle of the not-so-fragile old woman. She heard a loud *hi-s-s-s-s* of breath as the woman doubled up. The hands let go.

Quickly, Elizabeth Ann rolled off the bed and, as her feet touched the floor, Sanderford's puffed, furry, yellow mass hurled itself towards her, claws digging into her shoulder. Her mouth dropped open and, this time, a piercing scream came out . . . a scream of pain as the cat's claws slid off her shoulder and down her back.

A hand clamped on to her wrist as Sanderford hit the floor with a thud. Elizabeth Ann whirled to face the woman and to prise, again, at the fingers holding her. In the distance there was a pounding on the door, and her mother's voice called, 'What's the matter, Elizabeth Ann? What's the matter? Why have you locked the door? . . . Elizabeth Ann?'

Her arm was being twisted and she was being pulled now, towards the window. The pounding turned to heavy thuds as Elizabeth Ann shrieked again. The woman's voice was still hissing in her ears, louder now, more cracking. 'You'll come . . . I have you . . . you're mine now, Alicia-a . . . you're mine . . .'

An agonizing twist of her arm and Elizabeth Ann fell against the window. So hard, the latch gave way and the window swung open. She felt herself being pulled out . . . out . . . out into the night. She grabbed the side of the window frame with her free hand, grabbing hard . . . for her life.

The bedroom door crashed open, the lights flashed on and, instantly, all was quiet except for Elizabeth Ann's choked sob as she slid to the floor by the window.

She heard her mother cry out and felt her father pick her up and carry her downstairs.

She couldn't answer the questions as they cleaned the blood from the claw marks on her shoulder and back, but she shook her head and mumbled, 'No . . . no . . . it's not his fault . . .' as horrified accusations were hurled at Sanderford, wherever he was hiding.

Then Elizabeth Ann took a deep, trembling breath and said, 'The chair. The great-great-grandmother chair in the attic . . . Burn the chair . . .' and the whole strange story came tumbling out.

By the time the story was finished, Elizabeth Ann's shoulder and back were softly wrapped in a clean, white bandage. They were all gathered in the kitchen and it was beginning to get light outside.

Elizabeth Ann stopped talking. She was exhausted. Her mother and father had listened and now sat with her in silence. After a few long minutes, her father rose. He went upstairs to the attic and brought down the dainty, dusty rocking-chair.

He carried it across the kitchen and out through the back door to the garden, where he put it down. Then he brought old newspapers out of the garage and, one by one, crumpled the sheets and tucked them under the chair.

Mother and daughter stood together, holding hands as they watched through the doorway. Elizabeth Ann's father struck a match and lit the papers in several places. The tiny flames licked around the seat of the great-great-grandmother rocker. It was very old, very dry, and the flames leaped on it, consuming it quickly as the three of them stood, transfixed, watching the smoke curl into the morning sky.

Elizabeth Ann felt a soft tickle on her leg and looked down. Sanderford was with them, watching too, rubbing himself gently against Elizabeth Ann's leg and rumbling loudly with loving purrs.

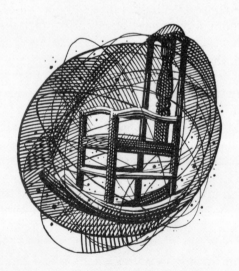

Florinda

SHAMUS FRAZER

D id you and Miss Reeve have a lovely walk, darling?'
Clare asked of the child in the tarnished depths of glass
before her.

'Well, it was lovely for me but not for Miss Reeve, because
she tore her stocking on a bramble, and it bled.'

'The stocking?'

'No, that ran a beautiful ladder,' said Jane very solemnly. 'But
there were two long tears on her leg as if a cat had scratched
her. We were going along by the path by the lake when the
brambles caught her. She almost fell in. She *did* look funny,
Mummy, hopping on the bank like a hen blackbird a cat's
playing with—and squawking.'

'*Poor* Miss Reeve! . . . Your father's going to have that path
cleared soon; it's quite overgrown.'

'Oh, I hope not soon, Mummy. I love the brambly places, and what the birds and rabbits'll do if they're cut down I can't imagine. The thickety bushes are all hopping and fluttering with them when you walk. And the path wriggles as if it were living, too—so you must lift your feet high and stamp on it, the way Florinda does . . .'

But Clare was not listening any more. She had withdrawn her glance from Jane's grave elfin features in the shadowed recesses of the glass to fix it on her own image, spread as elegantly upon its surface as a swan.

'And if Daddy has the bushes cut down,' Jane went on, 'what will poor Florinda do? Where will she play? There will be no place at all for the little traps and snares she sets; no place for her to creep and whistle in, and tinkle into laughter when something funny happens—like Miss Reeve caught by the leg and hopping.' This was the time, when her mother was not listening, that Jane could talk most easily about Florinda. She looked at her mother's image, wrapt in the dull mysteries of grown-up thought within the oval Chippendale glass—and thence to the rococo frame of gilded wood in whose interlacing design two birds of faded gilt, a bat with a chipped wing, and flowers whose golden petals and leaves showed here and there little spots and tips of white plaster like a disease, were all caught for ever.

'That's how I met Florinda.' She was chattering quite confidently, now that she knew that it was only to herself. 'I had been down to the edge of the lake where there are no brambles—you know, the *lawn* side; and I knelt down to look at myself in the water, *and there were two of me*. That's what I thought at first—two of me. And then I saw one was someone else—it was Florinda, smiling at me; but I couldn't smile back, not for anything. There we were like you and me in the glass—one smiling and one very solemn. Then Miss Reeve called and Florinda just *went*—and my face was alone and astonished in the water. She's shy, Florinda is—and sly, too. Shy and sly—that's Florinda for you.'

The repeated name stirred Clare to a vague consciousness: she had heard it on Jane's lips before.

'Who is Florinda?' she asked.

'Mummy, I've told you. She's a doll, I think, only large, large as me. And she never talks—not with words, anyway. And her eyes can't shut even when she lies down.'

'I thought she was called Arabella.'

'That's the doll Uncle Richard gave me last Christmas. Arabella *does* close her eyes when *she* lies down, and she says "Goodnight, Mamma," too, because of the gramophone record inside her. But Florinda's different. She's not a house doll. She belongs outside—though I *have* asked her to come to tea on Christmas Eve.'

'Well, darling, I've lots of letters to write, so just you run along to the nursery and have a lovely tea.'

So Florinda was a doll—an ideal doll, it seemed, that Jane had invented in anticipation of Christmas. Nine in the New Year, Jane was growing perhaps a little old for dolls. A strange child, thought Clare, difficult to understand. In that she took after her mother—though in looks it was her father she resembled. With a sigh Clare slid out the drawer of the mahogany writing-desk. She distributed writing-paper and envelopes, the Christmas cards (reproductions of Alken prints), in neat piles over the red leather—and, opening her address-book, set herself to write.

Roger came in with the early December dusk. He had been tramping round the estate with Wakefield the agent, and the cold had painted his cheeks blue and nipped his nose red so that he looked like a large, clumsy gnome. He kissed Clare on the nape, and the icy touch of his nose spread gooseflesh over her shoulders.

'You go and pour yourself some whisky,' she said, 'and thaw yourself out by the fire. I'll be with you in a minute.' She addressed two more envelopes in her large clear hand, and then, without looking round, said: 'Have we bitten off rather more than we can chew?'

'There's an awful lot to be done,' said her husband from the fire, 'so much one hardly knows where to begin. The woods are a shambles—Nissen huts, nastiness, and barbed wire. One would have thought Uncle Eustace would have made some effort to clear up the mess after the army moved out . . . .'

'But, darling, he never came back to live here. He was too wise.'

'Too ill and too old—and he never gave a thought to those who'd inherit the place, I suppose.'

'He never thought we'd be foolish enough to come and live here, anyway.'

Roger's uncle had died in a nursing-home in Bournemouth earlier in the year, and Roger had come into these acres of Darkshire park and woodland, and the sombre peeling house, Fowling Hall, set among them. At Clare's urging he had tried to sell the place, but there were no offers. And now Roger had the obstinate notion of settling here, and trying to make pigs and chickens pay for the up-keep of the estate. Of course, Clare knew, there was something else behind this recent interest in the country life. Nothing had been said, but she knew what Roger wanted, and she knew, too, that he would hint at it again before long—the forbidden subject. She stacked her letters on the desk and went to join him by the fire.

'There's one thing you *can* do,' she said. 'Clear that path that goes round the lake. Poor Miss Reeve tore herself quite nastily on a bramble this afternoon, walking there.'

'I'll remind Wakefield to get the men on the job tomorrow. And what was Jane doing down by the lake just now as I came in? I called her and she ran off into the bushes.'

'My dear, Jane's been up in the nursery for the last hour or more. Miss Reeve's reading to her. You know she's not allowed out this raw weather except when the sun's up. The doctor said—'

'Well, I wondered . . . I only glimpsed her—a little girl in the dusk. She ran off when I called.'

'One of the workmen's children, I expect.'

'Perhaps . . . Strange, I didn't think of that.'

He took a gulp of whisky, and changed the subject: 'Clare, it's going to cost the earth to put this place properly in order. It would be worth it if . . . if . . .' He added with an effort, 'I mean, if one thought it was leading anywhere . . .'

So it had come out, the first hint.

'You mean if we had a son, don't you? . . . Don't you, Roger?' She spoke accusingly.

'I merely meant . . . Well, yes—though, of course—'

She didn't let him finish. 'But you know what the doctor said after Jane. You know how delicate she is . . . You can't want—?'

'If she had a brother—' Roger began.

Clare laughed, a sudden shiver of laughter, and held her hands to the fire.

'Roger, what an open hypocrite you are! "If she had a brother," when all the time you mean "if I had a son." And how could you be certain it wouldn't be a sister? No, Roger, we've had this out a thousand times in the past. It can't be done.' She shook her head and blinked at the fire. 'It wouldn't work out.'

Roger went into the nursery, as was his too irregular custom, to say goodnight to Jane. She was in her pink fleecy dressing-gown, slippered toes resting on the wire fender, a bowl emptied of bread and milk on her knees. Miss Reeve was reading her a story about a princess who was turned by enchantment into a fox.

'Don't let me interrupt, Miss Reeve. I'll look in again later.'

'Oh, do come in, Mr Waley. We're almost ready for bed.'

'I was sorry to hear about your accident this afternoon.'

'It was such a silly thing, really. I caught my foot in a slip-noose of bramble. It was as if somebody had set it on the path on purpose, only that would be too ridiculous for words. But it was a shock—and I tore myself painfully, trying to get free.'

There was still the ghost of that panic, Roger noticed, in Miss Reeve's pasty, pudgy features, and signalling behind the round lenses of her spectacles. 'It's not a very nice path for a walk,' she added, 'but one can't keep Jane away from the lake.'

'I'm having all the undergrowth cleared away from the banks,' said Roger; 'that should make it easier walking.'

'Oh, that'll be ever so much nicer, Mr Waley.'

Florinda won't like it, thought Jane, sitting stiffly in her wicker chair by the fire. She won't like it at all. She'll be in a wicked temper will Florinda. But she said aloud in a voice of small protest—for what was the use of speaking about Florinda to grown-ups—'It won't be nice at all. It will be quite horribly beastly.'

The men didn't care for the work they had been set to do. It was the skeletons, they said—and they prodded suspiciously with their implements at the little lumps of bone and feather and fur that their cutting and scything had revealed. There was a killer somewhere in the woods; owls said one, stoats said another, but old Renshawe said glumly it was neither bird nor beast, that it was Something-that-walked-that-shouldn't, and this infected the others with a derisive disquiet. All the same, fifty yards of path were cleared during the morning, which took them beyond the small Doric pavilion that once served as boathouse and was reflected by a stone twin housing the loch mechanism on the eastern side of the lake.

Miss Reeve took Jane out in the afternoon to watch the men's progress. Jane ran ahead down the cleared path; paused at the pavilion to hang over the flaking balustrade and gaze down into the water: whispered something, shook her head and ran on.

'Hullo, Mr Renshawe—*alone?*' she cried, as rounding a sudden twist in the path she came upon the old man hacking at the undergrowth. Renshawe started and cut short, and the blade bit into his foot. This accident stopped work for the day.

'It wasn't right, Miss Jane, to come on me like that,' he said, as they were helping him up to the house. 'You gave me a real turn. I thought—'

'I know,' said Jane, fixing him with her serious, puzzled eyes. 'And she *was* there, too, watching all the time.'

Whatever the killer was, it moved its hunting-ground that night. Two White Orpingtons were found dead beside the arks next morning, their feathers scattered like snow over the bare ground.

'And it's not an animal, neither,' said Ron, the boy who carried the mash into the runs and had discovered the kill.

'What do you mean, it's not an animal?' asked Wakefield.

'I mean that their necks is wrung, Mr Wakefield.'

'Oh, get away!' said Wakefield.

But the following morning another hen was found lying in a mess of feathers and blood, and Wakefield reported to his master.

'It can't be it's a fox, sir. That head's not been bitten off. It's been pulled off, sir . . . And there was this, sir, was found by the arks.' It was a child's bracelet of blackened silver.

The path was cleared, but on the farther side of the lake the shrubberies that melted imperceptibly into the tall woods bordered it closely. Here Jane dawdled on her afternoon walk. At the bend in the path near the boathouse she waited until her governess was out of sight—and then called softly into the gloom of yew and rhododendron and laurel, 'I think you're a beast, a *beast*! And I'm not going to be your friend any more, d'you hear? And you're *not* to come on Christmas Eve, even if you're starving.'

There was movement in the shadows, and she glimpsed the staring blue eyes and pinched face and the tattered satin finery. 'And it's no use following us, so there!' Jane stuck her tongue out as a gesture of defiance, and ran away along the path.

'Are you all right?' asked Miss Reeve, who had turned back to look for her. 'I thought I heard someone crying.'

'Oh, it's only Florinda,' said Jane, 'and she can sob her eyes out now for all I care.'

'Jane,' said Miss Reeve severely, 'how many more times have I to tell you Florinda is a naughty fib, and we shouldn't tell naughty fibs even in fun?'

'It's no fun,' said Jane, so low that Miss Reeve could hardly catch a word, 'no fun at all being Florinda.'

A hard frost set in overnight. It made a moon landscape of the park and woods, and engraved on the nursery window-panes, sharply as with a diamond, intricate traceries of silver fern. The bark of the trees was patterned with frost like chain-mail, and from the gaunt branches icicle daggers glinted in the sun. Each twig of the bare shrubs had budded its tear-drops of ice. The surface of the lake was wrinkled and grey like the face of an old woman. 'And Wakefield says if it keeps up we may be able to skate on it on Boxing Day . . .' But by mid-day the temperature rose and all out-of-doors was filled with a mournful pattering and dripping.

Towards evening a dirty yellow glow showed in the sky, and furry black clouds moved up over the woods, bringing snow. It snowed after that for two days, and then it was Christmas Eve.

'You *look* like the Snow Queen, but you *smell* like the Queen of Sheba. Must you go out tonight, Mummy?'

'Darling, it's a bore. We promised Lady Graves, so we have to.'

'You should have kept your fingers crossed. But you'll be back soon?'

'In time to catch Father Christmas climbing down the chimneys, I expect.'

'But earlier than that—promise . . . ?'

'Much earlier than that. Daddy wants to get back early, anyway. He and Wakefield had a tiring night sitting up with a gun to guard their precious hens . . .'

'But she . . . it never came, did it?'

'Not *last* night. And now you go to lovely sleeps, and when you wake perhaps Father Christmas will have brought you Florinda in his—'

'No,' cried the child, 'not Florinda, Mummy, *please.*'

'What a funny thing you are,' said Clare, stooping to kiss her; 'you were quite silly about her a few days ago . . .'

Jane shivered and snuggled down in the warm bed.

'I've changed,' she said. 'We're not friends any more.'

After the lights were out, Jane imagined she was walking in the snow. The snowflakes fell as lightly as kisses, and soon they had covered her with a white, soft down. Now she knew herself to be a swan, and she tucked her head under a wing and so fell asleep on the dark rocking water.

But in the next room Miss Reeve, who had gone to bed early, could not sleep because of the wind that sobbed so disquietingly around the angles of the house. At last she put out a hand to the bedside table, poured herself water, groped for the aspirin bottle and swallowed down three tablets at a gulp. It was as she re-screwed the top, she noticed that it was not the aspirin bottle she was holding. She could have sworn that the sleeping-tablets had been in her dressing-table drawer. Her first thought was that someone had changed the bottles on purpose, but that, she told herself, would be too absurd. There was nothing she could do about it. The crying of the wind mounted to shrill broken fluting that sounded oddly like children's laughter.

The first thing they noticed when the car drew up, its chained tyres grinding and clanking under the dark porch, was that the front door was ajar. 'Wait here,' said Roger to the chauffeur, 'there seem to have been visitors while we were away.'

Clare switched on the drawing-room lights, and screamed at the demoniac havoc they revealed, the chairs and tables over-turned, the carpet a litter of broken porcelain, feathers from the torn cushions, and melting snow. Someone had thrown the heavy silver inkwell at the wall glass, which hung askew, its surface cracked and starred, and the delicate frame broken.

'No sane person—' Roger began.

But already Clare was running up the stairs to the nursery and screaming, 'Jane! . . . Jane!' as she ran.

The nursery was wrecked, too—the sheets clawed in strips, the floor a drift of feathers from the ripped pillows. Only the doll Arabella, with a shattered head, was propped up in the empty bed. When Clare touched her she fell backwards and began to repeat, 'Goodnight, Mamma!' as the mechanism inside her worked.

They found Jane's footsteps in the snow, leading over the lawn in the direction of the lake. Once they thought they saw her ahead of them, but it was only the snowman Roger had helped her to build during the afternoon. There was a misty moon, and by its light they followed the small naked footprints to the edge of the lake—but their eyes could make out nothing beyond the snow-fringed ice.

Roger had sent on the chauffeur to a bend in the drive where the car headlights could illuminate the farther bank. And now, in the sudden glare, they saw in the dark centre of ice the two small figures, Jane in her nightdress, and beside her a little girl in old-fashioned blue satin who walked oddly and jerkily, lifting her feet and stamping them on the ice.

They called together, 'Jane! . . . Jane! Come back!'

She seemed to have heard, and she turned, groping towards the light. The other caught at her arm, and the two struggled together on the black, glassy surface. Then from the stars it seemed, and into their cold hearts, fell a sound like the snapping of a giant lute-string. The two tiny interlocked figures had disappeared, and the ice moaned and tinkled at the edges of the lake.

Rowena Ballantyne

ADÈLE GERAS

Have you ever wondered what brings a ghost back to a certain place at a particular time? I never used to, but I've been thinking about this ever since I summoned Rowena Ballantyne back from the dead to haunt the corridors of her old boarding-school. I did it without meaning to. I found Rowena's rough book under a loose squeaky floorboard in the bedroom I share with two other girls. I'm nosy, and one day I nearly tripped up on this bit of wood as I was on my way from my bed to my cupboard. I lifted it up and there was the book: exactly like the ones we still use, for making notes about home-work and so forth, only with a royal blue cover instead of a red one. The pages were all curled up and dusty at the edges, so I knew at once that it had been lying buried for years and years, and sure enough there was the date on the first page. 1962. I opened it. Wouldn't you have done the same thing? And as I began to read, I could almost feel Rowena taking shape in the air, though of course I didn't see her until some time later.

But I'm plunging straight into the narrative without any kind of introduction. Miss Baldstone, our English teacher, would not approve. Stories should have, she says, a beginning, middle, and end, and I think finding the rough book is probably the middle. Let me start again.

My name is Vanessa. I'm thirteen years old and I go to school in a traditional boarding-school for girls. There are still some around outside the pages of an Enid Blyton book, for children of parents who aren't short of a pound or two. But we have all the problems you'd find in a comprehensive and we also have all sorts coming here. There are sporty types, fashion victims, jolly bouncy sorts, and swots, which I suppose is what I am. We have the same posters up on our walls, and admire the same footballers and pop stars.

The school is called Staghurst College. I've just moved into the Senior School. We live in four different 'houses' and mine is Nelson. The others are Wellington, Churchill, and Raleigh. Prefects have studies, and the rest of us make do with a Common Room. We sleep in bedrooms, not dormitories, and we can choose to share with one, two, or three girls. Some of our customs and pastimes are quaint. For example, one of the things that happens quite a lot is this: people are invited in from the outside world to talk to us and tell us about their fascinating lives, etc. We call these talks Lectures and what we do is: we all troop into the Hall. We listen if the talk is interesting and daydream if it isn't. One poor soul, though, always has to pay attention and that is the unfortunate creature who's been chosen to give the vote of thanks. The list of lectures goes up at the beginning of term and it's easy to spot the ones that are just Careers Advice in disguise: *Ten things you never knew about Merchant Banking*; *My happy days as a Veterinary Nurse* . . . you know the sort of thing I mean.

I noticed Jemima Westman's lecture at once (*Helping young offenders—the gentle way*) because I want to be a social worker when I leave school, or an investigative journalist. I think I'd be good at that, because I'm nosy, as I said, and I also like helping people. I suppose being an Agony Aunt would be fun . . . I'm getting carried away. Miss Baldstone would be scribbling in the margin like mad by now, if I were to hand this in. She often writes things like 'irrelevant' beside my work. I'm not sure if all this is relevant or not, but surely you have to know a little about what sort of person I am, before you'll believe me, right? I'm honest, then, and curious and kind-hearted.

I found Rowena's rough book in October. It was nearly time to go down to Prep, and I put it straight into my sack (another quaint custom: we don't have school bags but large canvas sacks to carry our stuff around in). Something, I'm not sure what, told me to say nothing about the book to anyone. There was a musty smell on the pages and I felt like some kind of archaeologist, even though 1962 isn't a very long time ago.

I decided to read it during Prep. We all sit at desks, and there's a Prefect sitting at the front to make sure we're all silent and getting on with our work. I waited till I was certain that Jacky and Hetty on either side of me were lost in the wonders of quadratic equations and then I started to read.

Rowena had spiky writing, and she wrote in black fountain pen, which is not surprising. It's just one other strange thing at this school: many of the older teachers won't hear of you doing any work in biro . . . they say it ruins the handwriting. The letters had faded to a sort of brown and they were quite hard to make out sometimes, but I managed to read what there was. It wasn't very much. Most of the pages didn't have anything more thrilling on them than things like: *Geog. Glaciated valleys. p.35*, but there were some near the end which made shivers run down my spine. Reading those, I felt I knew what she was feeling. I was bringing her to a kind of life. That sounds ridiculous, I know, but as Miss Baldstone is forever pointing out, words are powerful. They can hurt, and move, and startle, and make you laugh and cry. This is why you have to be so careful about which ones you choose.

I don't think Rowena was worried about fine writing. It was more as though she were using the pages as a shoulder to cry on. That's the only way I can put it. Here are some of the things she wrote.

They hate me. They all do. I wish I could disappear . . . just walk away and never come back. They stare at me. J.W. is the worst. She says only witches have red hair like mine, so am I a witch, and when I said no, she turned to Babs and said: we don't want fat, red-headed witches in our gang, do we? And they both had hysterics. After they'd gone, I started crying, and then I was late for Physics because I had to wait in the cloakroom for ages afterwards till my eyes stopped being red. My eyes were all right when I went in, but my whole body hurt from being sad, and they all looked at me, and J. and Babs specially smirked and when I went to sit down they sort of moved up the bench, and pulled all their stuff away, so that it shouldn't touch any of my stuff. I pushed down all the tears, but later in bed I cried so much that my pillow was wet and I had to turn it over.

Later on, she wrote:

*M and D spend tons of money to send me here. I wish I could
tell them I want to leave, but they'd be disappointed. D likes
boasting about me being here. I wish I could do better. I'm good
at swimming, but changing is awful. They all laugh. Fat, fat,
they say. And wobbly. J.W. is so thin. She's always going on about
me being a witch, and will I turn her into a frog? More hysterical
laughter. Every night when I go to bed, I wish the morning
would never come. I hate it here. I hate myself.*

The last entry in the book was:

*I've decided what to do. It's easy and I don't know why I
haven't thought of it before. Who'd care? No one, that's who.
M and D maybe, but they've got Sheila and Donald to cheer
them up. Everyone else will be glad to be rid of me. Me more
than anyone else. I just wish it was all finished. All over. Well, it
soon will be. I'm never going to cry again. Never.*

Even though it was warm in the Prep Room, I shivered. It was as though Rowena had been whispering in my ear, and I could hear the full misery of her voice. She meant to kill herself, but did she do it? Who could I ask? Even though our teachers were old, they didn't go back that far, surely? Also, if Rowena *had* committed suicide, they wouldn't be in a hurry to tell anyone. Death isn't the kind of thing you want on your prospectus, if you're a posh girls' school. I decided to think about it. I hid Rowena's rough book in my pyjama case which was a babyish, fluffy-cat thingie I've had since I was a Junior.

I began to dream about Rowena Ballantyne every night, wandering through the corridors, and then one day, I saw her. We were all in Chapel. I caught sight of someone in the Choir, standing at the far left of the second row. I recognized her at once. She was a big girl, and you could see why some people (horrible J.) would call her fat, but she wasn't really . . . just big and healthy-looking with a wide, pale, freckled face that should have been smiling and wasn't. And the hair . . . there wasn't anyone I knew in school who had hair like that: bright, clear red that glittered as though each strand was touched with gold.

Red red, that could not have come from any bottle, but which flared like a lit torch in the dimness of the Choir gallery.

'Who's that?' I asked Jacky. 'Up there next to Valerie Smyth in the second row.' Jacky looked at me as though I'd taken leave of my senses.

'There's no one standing next to Val. She's on the end of the row.'

I looked again and Rowena had disappeared. That was the first sighting. I thought of the notebook and how I had opened it, and read it, and—this is how I put it to myself—brought the ghost of Rowena back to where she had been so unhappy. I felt guilty. I wished I'd never lifted that dratted floorboard. What I had done, I felt, was condemn her to wander through this place that she loathed for all time. I wondered if one could talk to a ghost, and if you could, would it listen? There was also the possibility, the distinct possibility, that the whole thing was in my head. I could have been imagining it.

But then I saw her over and over again: running up from the playing fields at the end of Games, in a crowd of people, her hair streaming behind her like a banner; in the back row of the Prep Room, peering at me from behind a desk; and also, quite often, hanging about outside Study Two on the Prefects' Corridor almost as though she were looking for someone. Every so often, I asked one of my friends if they could see her, and they never could. They didn't know about her rough book because I'd kept it secret, so I suppose it wasn't surprising that they began to think I was mad, in a jokey way, of course.

The days and weeks went by, and one Sunday in November, there we all were, on our chairs in the Hall, ready to listen to Jemima Westman talking about her brilliant career as a Social Worker. The first surprise was how glamorous she was, even though she was old . . . at least fifty, I should think. The second surprise was: she was an Old Girl. I'm sure no one had ever told me that, so it came as a bit of a shock when she mentioned that she'd been in Nelson House.

'And when I was a prefect, I had Study Two . . . I've just been down to have a look at it, and it's made me feel very strange. It is the things that happened to me while I was at Staghurst . . . things that I did . . . which led directly to my work with teenagers.

I'm concerned with the fact that so many of them have such low self-esteem, and put up with dreadful things like bullying which no one, no one, should ever have to cope with at any age. My job is to try and help them as much as I can.'

Jemima Westman looked down, and blushed.

'I have', she said, 'a confession to make. I've never told anyone this before, but now that I'm here, in the old school Hall, I feel as though there are certain people looking at me, and listening, and I'd like to apologize, publicly, for something I did. Or rather, for something I didn't do.'

She gazed all round the Hall, and suddenly her mouth fell open, and her skin turned the colour of pale cheese. She took a mouthful of water from the glass on the table beside her, and looked towards the back of the Hall again. I glanced at the place I thought she was looking at, and I think I knew even before I saw her that Rowena would be there, sitting on a chair at the back. Jemima Westman had seen her too. I was sure of it. Jemima Westman. J.W. Was she the J.W. of the rough book? My heart began to beat fast, and I decided that I would ask her when the time came for questions. *Did you ever know a red-headed girl called Rowena Ballantyne?* I would say. I was trembling all over at the thought of saying it out loud in front of everyone like that, but I needed to know. I thought I knew now why Rowena had been wandering all around school. She'd been looking for her, for J.W. her tormentor, and now she'd found her.

Up on the stage, Jemima Westman was speaking again. She was still pale, but quite composed now. And she was addressing her words to the back of the Hall.

'When I was fourteen, I was the leader of a gang. We were vile. Conceited, arrogant, smug. We called ourselves the Beauties . . . can you believe it?'

There was much polite laughter, and you could see the teachers looking at one another and thinking: this isn't terribly helpful for those of our girls who are anxious to be social workers . . .

'There was one girl in Nelson House who was not one of the Beauties. Her name was Rowena Ballantyne, and she was completely ordinary, except for her hair, which was like flames growing out of her head. Her hair was a wonder of nature, and we tortured her for it.'

Jemima had tears in her eyes. I could see them quite plainly from where I was sitting in the second row. She went on, 'She would have done anything we asked, because she wanted to be in our gang. We . . . I . . . wouldn't share her chocolates, and we wouldn't let her help us with our Latin homework, even though she was brilliant, and we told her that her hair was ugly, and that she must be a witch, because only witches had hair that colour.'

By now, Jemima's voice had faded to a whisper.

'When we became prefects, we were allowed to invite younger girls to tea in our studies on Sundays. For weeks and weeks, no one invited Rowena. The list would go up on the noticeboard, and week after week she was ignored. Then one day I asked her to come to Study tea, and . . . I was horrible to her in front of everyone. Horrible in the way thin people are to those who are not so thin. *No teacakes for you, Rowena. You stick to fruit . . . look, there's an apple here.* She was found face down in the swimming-pool next morning. She was a very good swimmer. It couldn't have been an accident. She just didn't want to live any more, and we were the ones . . . I was the one . . . who had driven her to it. I killed her.' Jemima spoke in a whisper and her eyes were filled with tears. Then she pulled herself together and said:

'I really didn't mean to mention this today, but coming back here has reminded me, and I feel I owe her this apology, after all these years.' She stared at the back of the Hall. 'Rowena, I'm so sorry. It won't help you now, but I'm sorry. Forgive me.'

She smiled, and looked at us again.

'That's why I've spent my life trying to help young people. Because of Rowena. May she rest in peace.'

After that, the lecture went on as you would have expected it to. Jemima Westman relaxed and told us all about her brilliant career, and how we, too, could have one if we wanted one. I looked at the back of the Hall, and Rowena Ballantyne had gone. I never saw her ever again. I moved the rough book from my pyjama case into the small, locked box where I keep my treasures. Sometimes I take it out and look at her spiky, faded brownish words, still powerful after all this time. Rowena herself is, I think, I hope . . . resting in peace at last.

If She Bends,
She Breaks

JOHN GORDON

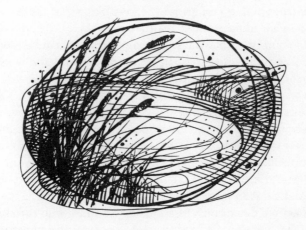

Ben had felt strange ever since the snow started falling. He looked out of the classroom window and saw that it had come again, sweeping across like a curtain. That was exactly what it seemed to be, a curtain. The snow had come down like a blank sheet in his mind, and he could remember nothing beyond it. He could not even remember getting up this morning or walking to school; yesterday was only a haze, and last week did not exist. And now, at this moment, he did not know whether it was morning or afternoon. He began to get to his feet, but dizziness made him sit down.

'I know it's been freezing hard.' Miss Carter's voice from the front of the class seemed distant. He wanted to tell her he felt unwell, but just for the moment he did not have the energy. She had her back to the stove as usual, and the eyes behind her glasses stared like a frightened horse's as they always did when she was in a passion. 'It's been freezing hard,' she repeated, 'but the ice is still far too dangerous, and nobody is to go anywhere near it. Do you understand?'

Tommy Drake, in the next desk to Ben, murmured something and grinned at somebody on Ben's other side. But he ignored Ben completely.

'Tommy Drake!' Miss Carter had missed nothing. 'What did you say?'

'Nothing, Miss.'

'Then why are you grinning like a jackass? If there's a joke, we all want to hear it. On your feet.'

As Tommy pushed back his chair, Ben smiled at him, weakly, but Tommy seemed to be in no mood for him and winked at somebody else as though Ben himself was not there.

'Well?' Miss Carter was waiting.

Tommy stood in silence.

'Very well. If you are not going to share your thoughts with the rest of us, perhaps you will remind me of what I was saying a moment ago.'

'About the ice, Miss?'

'And what about the ice?'

'That it's dangerous, Miss.' Then Tommy, who did not lack courage, went on, 'What I was saying was that you can always tell if it's safe.'

'Oh you can, can you?' Miss Carter pursed her lips, and again waited.

'If she cracks, she bears,' said Tommy. 'If she bends, she breaks.' It was a lesson they all knew in the flat Fenland where everybody skated in winter. A solid cracking sound in the ice was better than a soft bending. But it meant nothing to Miss Carter.

'Stuff and nonsense!' she cried.

'But everybody knows it's true.' Tommy had justice on his side and his round face was getting red.

'Old wives' tales!' Miss Carter was not going to listen to reason. 'Sit down.'

Ben saw that Tommy was going to argue, and the sudden urge to back him up made him forget his dizziness. He got to his feet. 'It's quite true, Miss,' he said. 'I've tried it out.'

She paid no attention to him. She glared at Tommy. 'Sit down!'

Tommy obeyed, and Miss Carter pulled her cardigan tighter over her dumpy figure.

'Listen to me, all of you.' Her voice was shrill. 'I don't care what anybody says in the village; I won't have any of you go anywhere near that ice. Do you hear? Nobody!' She paused, and then added softly, 'You all know what can happen.'

She had succeeded in silencing the classroom, and as she turned away to her own desk she muttered something to the front row who began putting their books away. It was time for Break.

Ben was still standing. In her passion she seemed not to have seen him. 'What's up with her?' he said, but Tommy was on his feet and heading towards the cloakroom with the rest.

The dizziness came over Ben again. Could nobody see that he was unwell? Or was his illness something so terrible that everybody wanted to ignore it? The classroom had emptied, and Miss Carter was wiping her nose on a crumpled paper handkerchief. He would tell her how he felt, and perhaps she would get his sister to walk home with him. He watched her head swing towards him and he opened his mouth to speak, but her glance swept over him and she turned to follow the others.

A movement outside one of the classroom's tall, narrow windows made him look out. One boy was already in the yard, and the snow was thick and inviting. Beyond the railings there was the village, and through a gap in the houses he could see the flat fens, stretching away in a desert of whiteness. He knew it all. He had not lost his memory. The stuffiness of the class-room was to blame—and outside there was delicious coolness, and space. Without bothering to follow the others to the cloakroom for his coat, he went out.

There was still only the boy in the playground; a new kid kicking up snow. He was finding the soft patches, not already trodden, and as he ploughed into them he made the snow smoke around his ankles so that he almost seemed to lack feet.

Ben went across to him and said, 'They let you out early, did they?'

The new kid raised his head and looked at the others who were now crowding out through the door. 'I reckon,' he said.

'Me an' all,' said Ben. It wasn't strictly true, but he didn't mind bending the truth a bit as he had been feeling ill. But not any more. 'Where d'you come from?' he asked.

'Over yonder.' The new kid nodded vaguely beyond the railings and then went back to kicking snow. 'It's warm, ain't it?' he said, watching the powder drift around his knees. 'When you get used to it.'

'What do your dad do?'

'Horseman,' said the kid, and that was enough to tell Ben where he lived and where his father worked. Only one farm for miles had working horses. Tommy's family, the Drakes, had always had horses and were rich enough to have them working alongside tractors, as a kind of hobby.

'You live along Pingle Bank, then,' said Ben. The horseman had a cottage there near the edge of the big drainage canal, the Pingle, that cut a straight, deep channel across the flat fens.

'That's right,' said the kid, and looked up at the sky. 'More of it comin'.'

The clouds had thickened over the winter sun and, in the grey light, snow had begun to fall again. The kid held his face up to it. 'Best time o' the year, winter. Brings you out into the open, don't it?'

'Reckon,' Ben agreed. 'If them clouds was in summer we should be gettin' soaked.'

'I hate gettin' wet.' The kid's face was pale, and snow was resting on his eyelashes.

'Me an' all.'

They stood side by side and let the snow fall on them. The kid was quite right; it seemed warm.

Then the snowball fight rolled right up to them, and charging through the middle of it came Tommy pulling Ben's sister on her sledge. Just like him to have taken over the sledge and Jenny and barge into the new kid as though he was nobody. Ben stooped, rammed snow into two hard fistfuls and hurled them with all his force at Tommy's red face. He was usually a good shot but he missed, and Tommy was yelling at Jenny as she laboured to make snowballs and pile them on the sledge.

'They ain't no good! Look, they're fallin' apart.' Tommy crouched and swept them all back into the snow.

Jenny had no height but a lot of temper. She was on her feet, her face as red as his, and yanked her sledge away.

'Bring that back!' he yelled, but Ben was already charging at him.

Tommy must have been off-balance because it took no more than a touch to push him sideways and send him into the snow flat on his back.

'You want to leave my sister alone.' Ben sat on his chest with his knees on Tommy's arms. 'Tell her you're sorry.'

He and Tommy were the same size, both strong, and sometimes they banged their heads together just to see who would be the first to back off. But this time, without any effort or even bothering to answer him Tommy sat up and spilled Ben off his chest as though he had no weight at all. And as he tilted back helplessly, Ben saw the new kid standing by, watching.

'Hi!' he shouted. 'Snowball fight. You're on my side.'

The kid looked pretty useful; pale, but solid. And Ben needed help.

'You done it wrong,' the new kid said to Ben, and without hurrying he stepped forward.

The kid reached out to where Tommy was still sitting and put a hand over his face, spreading out pale, cold fingers across his mouth and eyes. He seemed merely to stroke him, but Tommy fell backwards.

'You don't need no pressure,' said the kid. 'All you got to do is let 'em know you're there.'

'You got him!' Ben had rolled away to let the kid tackle Tommy alone. 'Show us your stuff!'

The kid seemed to be in no hurry, and Tommy lay where he was, one startled eye showing between the pallid fingers. Any second now and there would be a quick thrust of limbs and Tommy would send the kid flying. It was stupid to wait for it; Ben started forward to stop the massacre.

But then the kid looked up. The snow was still in his eyelashes, and a crust of it was at the corners of his mouth, like ice.

'Want me to do any more?' he asked.

In the rest of the playground, shouts of snowfights echoed against the high windows and dark walls of the old school building, but in this corner the grey clouds seemed to hang lower as if to deaden the kid's voice.

'I asked you,' he said. 'You want to see me do some more?'

Tommy stirred, gathering himself to push. In a moment the

boy would pay for being so careless, unless he had some trick and was pressing on a nerve. Ben wanted to see what would happen. He nodded.

The kid did not look away from Ben, but his hand left Tommy's face. And Tommy did not get up. He simply lay there with his eyes and mouth wide open. He looked scared.

The kid, still crouching, began to stroke the snow. He curved his fingers and raked it, dusting the white powder into Tommy's hair, then over his brow and his eyes, and then the kid's hand, so pale it could not be seen in the snow, was over Tommy's lips, and snow was being thrust into the gaping mouth. The kid leant over him and Tommy was terrified. He tried to shout, but more snow was driven into his mouth. He rolled over, thrashing helplessly.

The kid paused as though waiting for instructions. But Ben, curious to see what Tommy would do, waited.

It was then that the brittle little sound of a handbell reached them. It came from the porch where Miss Carter was calling them in. But suddenly the sound ceased, and even the shouting of the snowfights died. The whole playground had seen her drop the bell.

She started forward, pushing her way through the crowds, and then, caught up in her anxiety, they came with her like black snowflakes on the wind.

It was Tommy, jerking and choking on the ground, that drew them. It was no natural fooling in the snow. He was fighting to breathe. And the new kid stood over him, looking down.

'Tommy, what have you done!' Miss Carter was stooping over him, crying out at the sight of his mouth wide open and full of whiteness. 'Oh my God!'

Ben stared across her bent back at the new kid. He simply stood where he was, a sprinkle of white in the short crop of his black hair, and gazed back at him.

'Who did this to you?' Miss Carter had thrust her fingers into the snow-gape in Tommy's face, and rolled him over so that he was coughing, gasping, and heaving all at once. 'How did it happen?'

But he could not answer and she helped him to his feet and began walking with him.

'Who saw it? Which of you did this?' She had snow in her fur-lined boots and her grey hair was untidy. Her little red nose was sharp with the cold and she pointed it round the ring that had gathered, sniffing out the guilty one. 'You?' Her eyes were on Ben but had passed by almost before he had shaken his head. 'What about you?' The new kid was at the back of the crowd and did not even have to answer.

Denials came from every side, and the chattering crowd followed her into school.

Ben and the kid hung back, and were alone in the porch when the door closed and shut them out. Neither had said a word, and Ben turned towards him. The kid stood quite still gazing straight ahead as though the door was the open page of a book and he was reading it. He wore a long black jacket, and a grey scarf was wound once around his neck and hung down his back. Ben noticed for the first time that the kid's black trousers were knee-length and were tucked into long, thick socks. They looked like riding breeches, and he thought the kid must help his father with the horses. But his boots were big and clumsy, not elegant like a horseman's. There was something gawky about him; he looked poor and old-fashioned.

'You done all right,' said Ben. 'Tommy ain't bad in a fight.'

The kid turned towards him. There was still unmelted snow on his cheeks, and his eyelashes were tinged with white. His dark eyes were liquid as though he was on the verge of crying, but that was false. They had no expression at all. 'He ain't as good as he reckon,' said the kid, and left it at that.

'What class you in?' Ben asked.

'Same as you.'

'Didn't notice you.'

'I were by the stove.'

'Miss Carter always keep her bum to that, that's why it don't throw out no heat,' said Ben, but the kid did not smile. He led the way inside.

They had not been missed. Miss Carter was still fussing around Tommy. She had pulled the fireguard back from the stove so that he could go to the front of the class and sit close to it. But she was still angry. 'I'm going to catch whoever did that to you, and when I do . . .' She pinched in her little mouth until it was lipless and her eyes needled round the room.

Ben had taken his usual place at the back, and suddenly he realized the new kid had wandered off. He searched and found him. He was sitting at a desk no more than two paces from Miss Carter and Tommy. He had one arm over the desk lid, and the other resting loosely on the back of his chair. He was quite untroubled.

'Stand up, Tommy,' Miss Carter ordered. 'Now turn round and point out who did this terrible thing.'

Tommy, a hero now, was enjoying himself. He faced the class. Ben could see the pale curve of the new kid's cheek and guessed at the deep-water look of the eyes that were turned on Tommy.

'Tommy!' said Miss Carter, and obediently Tommy looked round the room. He smirked at several people but not at Ben. He ignored him as though angry with him for what had happened yet not prepared to betray him. But there was a real risk he would get his revenge on the kid. Yet again his glance went by as though the boy's desk was empty, and he said, 'Nobody done it. I just fell over, that's all.'

The girl next to Ben whispered to her friend, 'Maybe he had a fit. That looked like it with his mouth all white. Like he was foaming.'

'Be quiet!' Miss Carter had lost her patience. 'Sit down!' she ordered Tommy, and for the rest of the afternoon she was savage, even with him.

From time to time Ben looked towards the new kid, but he kept his head bowed over his work and Ben saw no more than the black bristles of his cropped hair. Nobody attempted to speak to him because whenever anybody moved, Miss Carter snapped.

The last half-hour dragged, but then, with a rattle of pencils and a banging of desk lids, the afternoon ended. The new kid wasted no time. He was out of the door ahead of everybody else, and Ben did not catch him until he was halfway across the playground.

'Where you going?' he asked.

'The Pingle.'

'We ain't supposed to. Because of the ice.'

'I live there.'

Then Ben remembered the horseman's cottage on the bank, but he said, 'Ain't you going to hang around here a bit? We got some good slides in the yard.'

'Ice is better.'

The others, charging out at the door, prevented Ben saying more. Jenny, with her sledge, was being chased by Tommy. He was himself again and was telling her, 'Your sledge will go great on the Pingle.'

'I don't want to go,' she said.

A bigger girl butted in. 'You heard what Miss Carter said, Tommy Drake. Ain't you got no sense?'

Tommy paid no attention. 'Come on, Jenny. I ain't got time to go home and fetch me skates, or else I would. I'll bring 'em tomorrow and you can have a go. Promise.'

She was tempted, but she said, 'I don't want to go there. And you know why.'

'I won't take a step on it unless it's rock hard,' said Tommy.

'I ain't going,' said Jenny.

At the school gate, the kid moved his feet impatiently on the step. It had been cleared of snow and the metal studs on his boots rattled.

Tommy had also lost his patience. 'If she cracks she bears, if she bends she breaks. Everybody know that's true, no matter what old Carter say. And I won't budge away from the bank unless it's safe.'

'No,' said Jenny.

Suddenly the kid kicked at the steps and made sparks fly from the sole of his boot, and Tommy looked up. The wind dived over the school roof in a howl and a plunge of snow, and the kid's voice merged with it as he yelled, 'Come on!'

He and Ben ran together, and Tommy grabbed at the sledge and made for the gate. Several others came with him.

Ben and the boy kept ahead of the rest as they rounded the corner into the lane. Traffic had failed to churn up the snow and had packed it hard, almost icy, so it would have been as good as anywhere for Jenny's sledge, but Ben ran with the boy between hedges humped and white, and the others followed.

They left the road just before it climbed to the bridge across the Pingle, and they stood at the top of the bank, looking down. They were the first to come here. The grass blades, slowly arching as the snow had added petal after petal through the day, supported an unbroken roof just clear of the ground. Below them, the straight, wide channel stretched away to left and right through the flat, white land. The water had become a frozen road, and the wind had swept it almost clear, piling the snow in an endless, smooth drift on the far side.

Tommy had come up alongside them. 'You could go for miles!' he shouted.

But Jenny hung back. 'I don't like it.' The air was grey and cold and it almost smothered her small voice. 'I want to go home.'

'It ain't dark yet.' His voice yelped as though it came from the lonely seagull that angled up on a frozen gust far out over the white plain. He began to move forward. 'Let's get down there.'

'She doesn't want to go.' Ben was close to him, but Tommy paid no heed. 'Nobody's going down that bank, Tommy.' Ben stepped forward, blocking his way. 'Nobody!'

Tommy came straight on. His eyes met Ben's but their expression did not change. His whole attention was focused on the ice below and his gaze seemed to go through Ben as though he was not there.

In a sudden cold anger Ben lowered his head and lunged with both arms. He thrust at Tommy's chest with all his force. His fingers touched, but in the instant of touching they lost their grip. He thrust with all his power, but it was air alone that slid along his arms and fingers, and Tommy was past and through and plunging down the bank.

The kid, watching him, said, 'You still don't do it right.'

Tommy had taken Jenny's sledge with him, and at the ice edge he turned and shouted to them up the bank. 'Come on, all of you!'

'No!' Ben stood in front of them. 'Don't go!' He opened his arms, but they came in a group straight for him. 'Stop!' They did not answer. Their eyes did not look directly at him. They pushed into him, like a crush of cattle, pretending he was not there. He clutched at one after another but the strange weakness he had felt earlier made him too flimsy to stop anything and they were beyond him and going down to join Tommy.

'I got to teach you a few things,' said the kid.

'I don't feel too good,' said Ben. 'I think I ought to go home.' The boy gazed at him for a moment with eyes that again seemed to be rimmed with frost, and shook his head. 'There's them down there to see to,' he said.

Slowly, Ben nodded. He had to think of Jenny.

They went down together and found Tommy still on the bank. Frozen reeds stood up through the ice and there was a seepage of water at the edge that made them all hesitate. All except the new kid. He put one foot on it, testing.

'If she cracks she bears,' he said.

Ben watched. The boy had plenty of courage. He was leaning forward now, putting all his weight on the ice.

'She cracks,' he said.

But Ben had heard nothing. 'No,' he called out. 'She bends.'

He was too late. The boy had stepped out on to the ice. Then Ben heard the crack under his boots, and the echo of it ringing from bank to bank and away along the endless ice in thin winter music.

The boy moved out until he was a figure in black in the middle of the channel. 'She bears,' he called out, and Ben, who knew he could never stop the others now, stepped out to be with him.

There was no crack this time, but the ice held. He could feel the gentle pulse of it as he walked towards the middle. There was something almost like a smile on the new kid's face. 'Both of us done it,' he said, and Ben nodded.

On the bank there was a squabble. The big girl, protecting Jenny, was trying to pull the sledge rope from Tommy. 'Let her have her sledge,' she said. 'You didn't ought to have brung her here.'

'It's safe enough.'

'I don't care whether it's safe or not, you didn't ought to have brung her. Not Jenny, of all people.'

'Why all the fuss about Jenny?' said Ben to the kid. 'I don't know what they're going on about.'

'Don't you?' The kid's eyes, darkening as the day dwindled, rested on him. Far away along the length of the frozen channel, snow and sky and darkness joined.

'Why don't they come out here?' said Ben. 'They can see us.'

'We can go and fetch 'em,' said the kid.

'How?'

'Get hold of that sledge. They'll follow.'

Ben hesitated. Perhaps he was too weak to do even that.

The kid saw his doubt, and said, 'You've pulled a sledge before, ain't you?' Ben nodded. 'Well all you got to do is remember what it feel like. That's all.'

Ben had to rely on him. Everything he had tried himself had gone wrong. He walked across to where Tommy was still arguing.

'See what you done to her,' the girl was saying. She had her arm around Jenny's shoulder and Jenny was crying, snuffling into her gloves. 'Ain't you got no feelings, Tommy Drake?'

'Well just because it happened once,' said Tommy, 'that ain't to say it's going to happen again.'

'Wasn't just once!' The girl thrust her head forward, accusing him. 'There was another time.' She lifted her arm from Jenny's shoulder and pointed up the bank behind her. 'There was a boy lived up there, along Pingle Bank; he came down here and went through the ice one winter time, and they never found him till it thawed.'

'That were a long time ago,' said Tommy. 'Years before any of us was born.'

'You ought to know about that if anybody do, Tommy Drake. That boy's father worked on your farm. Everybody know about that even if it was all them years ago. His father were a horseman and lived along the bank.'

'Hey!' Ben was close to Tommy. 'Just like the new kid.'

But even that did not make Tommy turn his way. Ben reached for the sledge rope and jerked it. He felt the rope in his fingers just before it slipped through and fell, but he had tugged it from Tommy's grasp and the sledge ran out on to the ice.

'Come on, Tommy,' he said. 'Come with me and the new kid.'

The girl was watching the sledge and accusing Tommy. 'What did you want to do that for?'

'I didn't,' he said.

'I did it,' said Ben, but nobody looked towards him.

The girl was furious with Tommy. 'Just look what you done. Now you'll have to leave it.'

Tommy had put one foot on the ice, testing it. 'I ain't frit,' he said. 'I reckon it'll hold.'

'Of course it will.' Ben encouraged him. 'We're both out here, ain't we?' He paused and looked over his shoulder to make sure, but the kid was still there, watching. 'Two of us. Me and him.'

Tommy had both feet on the ice and had taken another step. 'See,' he called to the others on the bank. 'Nothing to it.'

'Don't you make a parade out there by yourself any longer, Tommy Drake.' The girl pulled Jenny's face tighter into her shoulder and made an effort to muffle Jenny's ears. She leant forward as far as she could, keeping her voice low so that Jenny should not hear. 'Can't you see what you're doing to her? This were just the place where Ben went through the ice last winter.'

Tommy, stamping to make the ice ring beneath him, kept his back to her. 'If she cracks,' he said, 'she bears. If she bends, she breaks.'

'Can't you hear?' said the girl. 'This is just the place where Ben were drowned!'

The snow came in a sudden flurry, putting a streaked curtain between Ben and the rest of them. It was then that he remembered. He remembered everything. The kid had come up to stand beside him, and they stood together and watched.

The ice under Tommy sagged as they knew it would. They heard the soft rending as it split, and they saw its broken edge rear up. They heard the yell and the slither, and remembered the cold gulp of the black water that, with years between, had swallowed each of them. But now it was somebody else who slid under.

Then Jenny's scream reached Ben through the wind that was pushing down the channel as the night came on. She should be at home; not out here watching this. He stooped to the sledge and pushed. On the bank they saw nothing but a tight spiral of snow whipped up from the ice, but the sledge slid into the water beside Tommy and floated. He grabbed at it.

From out on the ice they saw the girl, held by the others, reach from the bank and grasp the rope, and then Tommy, soaking and freezing, crawled into the white snow and made it black. They watched as the whole group, sobbing and murmuring, climbed the bank, showed for a few moments against the darkening sky and were gone.

In the empty channel the two figures stood motionless. Their eyes gazed unblinking through the swirl as the snow came again, hissing as it blew between the frozen reeds.

Snookered

CATHERINE GRAHAM

It all started in our Civic Hall games room. The floor had to be strengthened to take the snooker tables—they're solid slate under the baize, you see—and I remember how thrilled we were, my mates and me, when it was done and we had somewhere decent to practise instead of on that tacky old table down the Youth Club.

And then along came Smithy.

He was one of those moon-faced, weedy kids, all round shoulders and glasses, and he came wandering up to the three of us that summer afternoon like a lost soul. Straight away he started talking—who was winning, did anyone want a game—we just wanted him to push off, because I was in the middle of a battle with the Ape and Franny never says much anyhow.

'Can I keep score?' he asked us, diving for a nice blue that the Ape had just put down.

'No, I'm doing that,' Franny said shortly.

'Oh, OK. Just thought I could help.' He dragged up a stool, watching the play with big round eyes goggling through his specs.

The Ape was on an unusually lucky streak. I was finding it hard to beat him and it didn't help having Smithy perched three feet from the table gawking at every shot. After the session he sort of tagged along, chattering all the way. It turned out that he and his dad had just moved into a house on the estate and he was starting at our school come autumn, that he read a lot, had a passion for snooker, and was, quite obviously, lonely.

You know how stray dogs attach themselves to you, if you let them? We got used to having Smithy around. The Regional Junior Championships weren't far off and we were all getting in as much practice as we could, so he made a useful fourth player. We used to toss a coin, and the loser played Smithy. It wasn't that he was hopeless, you understand; in fact he was the best tactician I'd ever played, but he was infuriatingly slow. I mean, Franny took his time, but Smithy would circle the table oh, half a dozen times, ducking and craning to examine every angle, settling for a shot then changing his mind—I tell you, I nearly lost my temper with him many a time and fluffed an easy shot through getting nettled. The Ape swore it was gamesmanship but it wasn't, it was just the way he played.

Very thorough, was Smithy.

The holidays went too quickly, as usual, and we were soon back into the school routine. Smithy settled down well. He had no trouble with lessons because he was bright, in spite of his gormless looks. The yobs in the school didn't give him as much stick as they usually gave new kids—he avoided them by hanging round us most of the time.

'Not long to go now before the Championships,' the Ape said as we were walking along the canal bank to the Civic Hall for our evening game. 'Tom Donaghue from St Pat's is odds-on favourite to win. Still, we'll give him a run for his money, won't we, Chris?'

'I don't know,' I said, shying a stone into the orange waters of the canal. 'Dad's been going on about my practising instead of doing school work. He doesn't like the idea of professional snooker as a career—he says it's not secure enough. I'm getting the "mis-spent youth" bit all the time.'

'Me too,' said Franny.

'I'm not.' As usual, Smithy was panting along behind us with his twine-toed trot, trying to keep up.

'Your dad spends all his time in the pub,' muttered the Ape. 'Pick your feet up, can't you?'

Smithy only grinned and went into a goose-stepping silly walk that had us laughing in spite of ourselves.

He never minded playing the fool to cheer people up. Apart from being naturally soft-hearted—he couldn't pass a beggar or a collection box without giving away half his pocket money —I suppose it was a defensive habit. You couldn't stay mad with him for long, even when he was at his most irritating. He used to analyse every game we had, you know, shot for shot.

'You should have played the brown instead of the pink, then you wouldn't have had so much trouble with those reds . . .' That sort of thing. The way we looked at it, if you've lost you're quite aware of what went wrong, and if you've won you don't particularly want to be told how you could have improved your breaks. We'd take it from Mr Simpson, our coach, but not from Smithy, though I must say Smithy was usually right. He wasn't such an accurate potter himself—he had this old one-piece cue his grandfather had given him and he thought the world of it. Mr Simpson used to say he'd do better with a straighter cue and lighter specs, but Smithy was stubborn. He'd just nod vaguely and carry on in his own sweet way.

Mr Simpson cheered me up that evening by saying I had a good chance in the Championships. The Ape was terrific on form and Franny had a better temperament for the game, but he thought I had the edge because of my technique.

'If you'd just control your nerves and impatience, Chris,' he told me, 'you'd do much better. But you must relax into the game and stop taking chances. You were hanging on to the butt like grim death when you missed that last shot, weren't you? And you hadn't bothered to get your stance right. Fatal, that, absolutely fatal.'

From which you'll gather I used to play fast and recklessly.

Mr Simpson's criticism worried Smithy. Not having entered himself, he badly wanted me to win this competition, and from then on he used to nag me when he saw me getting aggressive during a game. He was trying to help, you see, as usual.

The Championships were just a couple of months away and I was beginning to feel pressured. Mum and Dad nagged me about school work—they were afraid I was neglecting it to practise my snooker—everyone at school seemed to expect me to beat Tom Donaghue easily, and I knew he was brilliant at the game. I was almost wishing I hadn't entered the competition, and I was feeling wound up like a tight spring, on the night of Smithy's accident.

Smithy lived round the corner from me and we met Franny and the Ape on the canal bank as we always did after school, taking the short cut across the fields to the Civic Hall.

I played disastrously that evening. The balls weren't running for me and my surly mood didn't help; I was jerky and careless, incapable of thinking ahead, growing more tense and angry with myself as I lost frame after frame. Franny and the Ape looked worried and depressed. Smithy was bursting to comment but he didn't dare. I knew that they all wanted to lose to me so I'd regain some self-confidence, and that made everything worse. I should have given up, talked out my temper, and just watched them play but I kept on, tight-lipped and stubborn, making stupid mistakes increasingly often.

It was raining outside and we walked home in gloomy silence, parting company with Franny and the Ape at the canal bank. We were approaching the wooden bridge over the canal when Smithy couldn't contain himself any longer:

'You didn't have much luck tonight, Chris.'

I didn't answer.

'Of course, if you'd played a safety shot in that last frame when Franny missed the blue, you could have snookered him easily. Do you know you moved on the shot five times in the frame before that one? I counted. You need to think harder about tactics, as well. It's very important, that is, and so is your attitude to the game, you know what I mean? If you could just relax a bit more, keep calm and—'

That did it; I turned on him.

'Don't tell *me* how to play, you lame brain! You and that stupid bent cue of yours!'

We were standing on the bridge by now; I grabbed Smithy's cue off him and hurled it as far as I could into the turgid waters of the canal.

There was a heart-rending cry from Smithy:

'My cue! That was my grandad's cue!'

I stamped off home. I remember hearing a distant splash and feeling a twinge of alarm, then thinking that not even Smithy would be thick enough to fall into the canal and what I wanted most was a hot drink and a lot of sleep.

They found his body next morning, the cue clutched in his hand. I couldn't believe he was dead, for Smithy had been a strong swimmer. But it was discovered that he'd had an abnormally thin skull; the odds had been against his living very long. He'd tapped his head against the concrete side of the canal in the dark and that had been enough to finish him.

Everyone was very kind to me, including Smithy's father, and said I mustn't blame myself, but you can imagine how I felt. If I hadn't thrown away his cue in a flash of spiteful anger, Smithy would still be alive. I forgot his infuriating habits and only remembered how cheerful and good-natured he'd been, cracking his corny jokes and always insisting on helping people, whether they wanted his help or not. I missed Smithy, but not for long . . .

A few days afterwards I had a nightmare. I dreamed I was standing on the canal bridge watching the moonlight in the slow, polluted water. It was raining lightly. There was no sound, only a sad, wandering breeze that made me shiver as it touched me.

A dark and shapeless thing was floating downstream. I watched it idly until it drifted out of sight under the bridge. There was a ripple of water and then the sound of laboured footsteps crossing behind me. They stopped. A hoarse, choking voice began to whisper in my ear:

'*Don't worry, Chris. I found my cue. Everything's all right. I've forgiven you, see? I'm going to help you, Chris. I'm going to help you win.*'

In my dream I turned slowly, reassured by the soothing words. And then I saw what was behind me.

I screamed and ran, the nightmare footsteps stumbling and thudding behind me. I managed to reach home and bolted the door against the thing outside . . .

When I woke up I was lying on my bedroom floor. Relief flooded me as I realized it had all been a bad dream; I'd fallen out of bed. And then I saw, with a growing sense of horror, that my pyjamas were wet with rain and my feet grimy with mud.

In the days leading up to the Final I pushed the memory of that night out of my mind. It was just a dream, I reasoned, I must have been sleepwalking because I was disturbed about Smithy. I'd privately vowed never to lose my temper again and every evening I worked hard to improve my game and get on top of my 'highly-strung temperament,' as Mr Simpson called it.

I felt reasonably calm on the day of the match and determined to play as well as I could. My parents offered me a lift to the Civic Hall but I refused, thinking that a walk along the banks of the canal would clear my head, though I'd avoided that route since Smithy's death.

I took the short cut across the fields behind our estate. Over the sluggish water of the canal the bridge stood stark and sinister in the gathering dusk. As I crossed it a strong breeze began to blow. I shuddered, my shoulders hunched against the fear that something was following me. That's what it felt like, anyway. I even thought I could hear a faint, halting voice close to my ear:

'It's all right, Chris. This is your big night and you're going to win. I'm with you, all the way.'

I walked faster; the soundless footsteps behind me broke into a shambling trot. I kept telling myself that this ghostly presence was all down to pre-match nerves and imagination but still I couldn't bring myself to look round, just made blindly for the neon-lit bulk of the Civic Hall, which stood like a haven just a few minutes' walk away . . . and then I was inside, leaning on the wall of the foyer, gasping for breath and waiting for my heartbeat to slow down.

Everything looked bright and real and normal. When I'd pulled myself together I went down to the dressing rooms to get ready. Mr Simpson was there, being reassuring, and so was Tom Donaghue, looking far more confident than I felt. We had a few practice shots before the audience arrived—there was a tense wait as they settled—and then the referee announced us and I was walking into the brightly-lit auditorium to loud applause. For a moment I wanted to turn and run. Then I saw Mum and Dad smiling at me from the front row, Franny and the Ape giving me the thumbs-up sign, and as the lights dimmed I suddenly felt very calm, as if the rest of the world had faded and there was only me and my cue and the battle for the vivid pattern on the baize.

I won the first frame easily. Tom, for all his skill, had a struggle to beat me in the second. It was the best of three frames, and I had no worries about the third. I was on the top of my form, the atmosphere excited and friendly; I was leading 34 to 30, when my concentration was shattered by a stupid incident. As I leaned over the table for an awkward red my shirt cuff touched another red close to the cushion. It was a foul, of course, four away, which made the score even with three reds left. I stamped off to my seat, angry with myself and worried for the first time in the match.

Tom played a mediocre safety shot and I foolishly went for a very difficult red. I missed it by a mile and only just avoided potting the cue ball. Four more away. Tom hadn't bothered to sit down, he'd sensed I was rattled. He circled the table a couple of times, chalking his cue, looking as relaxed as if he were about to knock off a few practice shots on a Sunday morning. Then he settled in with catlike concentration and steadily potted a blue, a very good pink, and all the reds. I could only sit and watch as his score rose to 52, and my chances of winning began to slip away. If his break continued I would be in serious trouble and needing snookers pretty soon.

I've blown it, I told myself; as soon as the thought entered my head a door banged violently at the back of the hall and a cold draught wafted downwards through the tiered, crowded auditorium towards the table. People shivered, moving restlessly in their seats. Somebody went to close the door. Tom Donaghue waited for the disturbance to pass, surveying the table patiently, and then a nervous shudder ran through him and his hands tightened convulsively on the cue, as if he were suddenly chilled through. I shuddered too; but then, I could see the ghost of Smithy hovering eerily at his shoulder.

The image was translucent and glistened in the light, as if the oily canal water still clung to the thin frame. The mouth was stretched into a pathetic, ingratiating, unchanging grin and his red-rimmed eyes stared eagerly into mine.

Tom, with an obvious effort, resumed his play. The cue ball bounced, hitting the black he was aiming for only by a fluke, and rolled sulkily into what was, for me, a perfect position on the yellow. Tom had badly miscued.

'*But that's not going to happen to you, is it, Chris?*'

I sat stunned, trying to absorb the fact that nobody else in the hall could see or hear the apparition.

'*This is your chance, Chris. I'm here to help you to win.*'

The voice seemed to be whispering right inside my head, filling my brain, taking me over.

'*On your feet, Chris. That's right. The yellow in the top pocket. The yellow, Chris, screw back for the green . . . that was good, Chris, very good. Now we want the green, don't we? Play a stun shot and you'll be just right for the brown.*'

I played like a robot programmed by the soft, insistent voice. I felt numb and terrified at the same time, not daring to look up from the table into the eyes of the weird, wavering spectre whose will was controlling my own . . .

'*You're getting tense, Chris, much too tense. Chalk your cue. Walk round the table. Slow down. That's better. We need every one of the colours, don't we? It's the blue next, Chris, and then we're nearly there.*'

I obeyed, moving in a daze, seeing only the death-white hand which pointed continuously to the dazzle of colour on the table. Some part of my mind was desperately trying to throw off Smithy's influence, to think and play out my own game. I couldn't; I was mesmerized by terror, guilt, and an awful kind of pity . . .

'*Well done, Chris, you've nearly caught up with him now. Just the pink, a long shot into the middle pocket. No, not the rest. No rest, we don't need it . . . Good. Never mind that, it's only applause. We'll get the black safe now, won't we? Won't we, Chris?*'

Like a blinkered racehorse I could sense the excitement, movement, noise, all around me. My family and friends are here, I thought, they all want me to win, and there's nothing to stop me winning if I do what Smithy tells me. I've wanted to win for ages . . . But not like this. Not like this.

'*Come on, Chris, concentrate, you're wandering. We're nearly home and dry, right? Just the black for the game. Steady. That's it. You're going to be the Champion, Chris . . .*'

NO!

I shot wildly, with a force that split the end of my cue and sent the black hurtling senselessly round the table.

Smithy's ghost began, instantly, to fade. I was hardly aware of Tom's winning shot for Smithy's sad eyes were fixed on mine, his voice whispering feebly,

'Next time, Chris. Next time we'll do it.'

And then the black was down and the cheering began.

Tom had won the frame by five points, 59 to 54. I felt no disappointment, only a tremendous relief that my ordeal was over. During the flattering speeches and presentation of our cheques and trophies I calmed down, and everyone said it was the most exciting Junior Final they'd ever seen, and made as much fuss of me as if I'd actually won.

People said my nerve broke. They said I couldn't play under real pressure and I should forget my ambition of becoming a professional snooker player. Well I have, but not for the reasons they imagine. 'Smithy's Revenge', I call it—not that Smithy wouldn't feel very hurt at being thought revengeful—but I know I can never play snooker seriously again. You see, Smithy wouldn't be able to rest; his terrible presence would be at my elbow during every important game, invading my mind, controlling my hands, trying to force me to win. And I couldn't take that, see? I couldn't stand that.

The night of the tournament I sneaked out of the house at midnight and made for the bridge over the canal. I took my cue and broke it in two, throwing the halves as far as I could into the murky, gingery waters of the canal. As they floated downstream I heard a long, faint sigh behind me, and the air became very peaceful.

Mum still keeps my semi-finalist's trophy on the sideboard, but my prize money I sent to a sports charity.

I thought Smithy would approve of that.

Incident on the
Atlantic Coast Express

DENNIS HAMLEY

Percy Padlow was forty-two and lived with his mother most of the time. The rest he spent on railways—old steam lines for weekends and holidays, modern electric and diesel trains to get there. He ate, drank, lived, and slept railways and would pass his whole life on them if he could.

But he couldn't. Mother came first. So mother always told him. Her friends, on the few occasions they came round, would say, 'You are lucky, Mrs Padlow, to have a fine son like Percy to look after you now Arthur's gone.'

And Mrs Padlow would sit up straight in her wheelchair and say, 'Yes, I know. That's why you have three children. A son to carry on the family name, a daughter to give you grandchildren, and a third, doesn't matter what it is, to look after you when you're old. Of course, it might have been better if Percy had been a girl.'

When he heard this, Percy winced. *You could look after yourself, you old bat*, he thought but daren't say. *You could get up out of that wheelchair for a start*. He ground his teeth, put the kettle on and arranged teacups on a tray so the old crones couldn't say how ungrateful he was. Then he looked out of the window and imagined 'Princess Elizabeth', pouring out smoke as she pounded up Shap Fell with The Royal Scot. The massive maroon engine with its huge driving wheels and flashing connecting rods followed by twelve maroon coaches seemed real in the back garden. Then the train passed, Shap's purple horizons passed with it and only the back fence and weedy patio were left.

'Four teabags, mother? One for each of you and one for the pot?' Percy called out.

He took a last wistful look through the window. The empty track over which The Royal Scot had just passed appeared again. A squashed and twisted wheelchair lay on it.

Enthusiasts' Steam Weekend at the Moors and Tors Railway was coming up. Once part of the London and South Western line to Devon and Cornwall, it had been closed west of Exeter, only for part of it to reopen as a preserved railway ten years later. Twelve miles of track across the moors. And what a weekend was offered! All the steam engines based on the line would run: others were visiting from other preserved lines. 'Clun Castle', a big express engine from the old Great Western Railway. 'Sir Lamiel' of the King Arthur class from the Southern Railway. 'Kolhapur', a Jubilee class locomotive from the London Midland and Scottish and, pride of place for the weekend, an A4 from the London and North-Eastern, 'Sir Nigel Gresley'. A British Railways 9F 2-10-0 freight locomotive. Thomas the Tank Engine for the kids. Tank and shunting engines galore. Special trains all day and half the night. Photographers' Specials, so keen cameramen could take wonderful atmospheric shots to recreate times past. All staff wearing old-time uniforms. And perhaps the ghost might come again.

Fantastic.

Well, that's what Percy thought when he read about it in his *Railway Magazine*. *I'm going to that*, he thought.

'Mother,' he said. 'I'd like to go away for the weekend in a fortnight's time, if that's all right with you. I'll go Friday and come back Sunday night. I'll make arrangements with Mrs Larkin next door to pop in and look after you.'

Mother drew a weary hand across her forehead, just brushing her eyebrows with her fingertips. 'Of course you must, Percy,' she said. 'It's terrible for a young man like you to have to stay at home to look after his old mother.'

Percy said nothing, but looked at her long and hard. *Don't you dare be ill*, he thought.

As the fortnight passed, Percy got his gear ready. He bought four films. One he loaded in his camera, the others he packed away. He was going to make whole albums out of this weekend. He booked bed and breakfast near the railway, then rang up for

Advanced Super Saver tickets. The first stage of his journey would take him to London, down the old North Western line. To Exeter, he could go from Paddington by Great Western or from Waterloo by South West Trains. He had his own reasons for going from Waterloo.

The postman delivered his ticket. Four days to go. Wonderful engines—Castles, King Arthurs, Jubilees, and A4s—paraded up and down in his brain. And what was that ghost, he wondered.

Friday came. He'd leave at 10.30 a.m. His hold-all was packed. He'd bought a new purple and red anorak. He would allow himself ten minutes to walk to the station and twenty minutes to wait on the platform—always a joy of anticipation.

10.15. He'd stick to his timetable. Every moment of this weekend was to be savoured.

10.25. 'Percy.' A quavery call.

'Yes, mother?' He ran to her. She was on her bed, sprawled awkwardly over the duvet cover.

'Percy, I'm not well.'

Sudden horror. 'Yes you are, mother. You only think you're not.'

'No, Percy, I'm ill. I think I could die this weekend, I feel so bad.'

'Mother, you're only saying this because I'm going away. You don't want me to have any pleasure, that's why.'

'Percy, how could you say such a thing? You *know* I always want you to enjoy yourself. But this time . . .'

'There's nothing wrong with you, mother. I'll get Mrs Larkin to come round early.'

'I don't want Mrs Larkin. I want *you* here when I'm dying.'

'Mother, you're not dying. You're fine.'

She clamped her mouth shut in a straight line. Percy left the room, put his purple and red anorak on, and picked up his hold-all.

'I'm going now, mother,' he called.

No answer.

'Yes, I'm on my way. See you Sunday night.'

He listened. Nothing. He opened the front door.

Should he go?

He turned back. No, he couldn't leave her.

Then he remembered: 'I think I'm going to die this weekend.' That whining voice. 'You've done this to me before, you old fraud,' he said out loud, stepped out of the house and closed the door behind him.

He strode down the drive and into the road. He called on Mrs Larkin, who didn't mind going round early, then made it to the station by 11.00.

Castles, Jubilees, and A4s. And a ghost on the line. Who could ask for more?

*

'Percy?' Mrs Padlow called. No answer.

Was that the front door she heard then? She stepped out of bed, ready to dash back if necessary, and looked through the window. Percy was just turning the corner at the end of the road.

'How *could* he?' she cried. 'Putting those dirty trains before his mother. I *hate* trains.'

Yes, she did. Ever since . . .

That awful memory came back to her, vivid as if it were happening now, of when she'd married Arthur all those years ago and they set off on their honeymoon by the sea. To London, a big, echoing terminus and a train which went slower and slower and got later and later until the darkness of the lonely country outside seemed to pour in through the window. They should have been in their hotel by the sea hours before.

Then, miles from anywhere, a few minutes after crawling away from yet another deserted, dark station, the train stopped altogether. Why?

Arthur went to find out. 'The guard says there's been an incident on the line ahead,' he said when he came back.

'What's that?' she asked.

'Oh,' he said vaguely. 'Just an incident.'

She was angry. 'Why don't you tell me properly?'

'Because it's only an incident.'

She looked at him with sudden dislike. 'Who do you think I am, Arthur?' she said. 'You'll tell me the truth in future or you'll just shut up.'

'All right,' Arthur replied. 'I only repeated what the guard said. It seems a man's been killed on the line ahead.'

'There, that was easy enough to say, wasn't it?'

'I didn't want to upset you.'

'I'm a big girl now, Arthur.'

Arthur hung his head and was silent.

'Did the engine run over him?' she asked. If there were some gory details, she'd like to know them.

'No. It seems he jumped off the train on to the rails.'

'Is that all?' She felt quite disappointed. And even angrier with Arthur. Did he *really* think so little of her that he wouldn't tell her that? By now she nearly felt like jumping off as well.

She was even more disappointed when she heard what really happened. Or rather, what didn't happen. She found it all out afterwards. The driver thought he saw a strange man appear suddenly on the footplate. He was just about to ask this intruder where he'd been hiding when, with a great cry louder even than the noise of the engine, he had jumped off into empty air. Looking back, the horrified driver saw his body sprawled broken on the sleepers. But when the train stopped and they went to look, there was nobody there.

The driver—he must have been drunk or something. No wonder he'd gone to hospital with a nervous breakdown. Yet the fireman said he'd seen the apparition too. Well, he would, wouldn't he. He was just sticking up for his friend.

But she wouldn't stick up for Arthur. No, something had gone out of her that night. He'd let her down. He didn't trust her enough to tell her the truth until she forced it out of him. She could never look at him in the same way again. She felt their marriage was somehow over before it started.

She hated all trains—and that train in particular. 'I shall never journey along this way again,' she said as the train started again with a new driver.

The front door opened. No, it wasn't Percy back.

'He thinks more of those dirty trains than he does of me,' she said.

'Pardon, dear?' said Mrs Larkin as she entered the room.

*

The red and brown Virgin train was only three minutes late into Euston. Then he took the tube to busy, echoing Waterloo. The smart diesel multiple unit to Exeter was already waiting at the platform. Why hadn't he gone from Paddington? Because Waterloo was where the Atlantic Coast Express once left from, hauled by a big Merchant Navy streamlined Pacific, belting its packed green coaches down to Exeter Central, then the long bank to Exeter St David's, then splitting into portions, part for Plymouth, the rest for seaside places all over north Devon and Cornwall—Ilfracombe, Bude, Padstow, the lot. The Moors and Tors Railway was once part of one of those Devon branches, through Barnstaple to Ilfracombe, so to go from Waterloo was as near as he could get to travelling down on the old Atlantic Coast Express.

The journey over, Percy unpacked in the guest house near the old junction station which was the Moors and Tors Railway headquarters. From his room he could clearly hear the trains, though he could not see them. But there was a glow in the sky over the engine shed, where even now engines were getting steam up for the next day.

After dinner, Percy took his first stroll down to the railway, taking his camera with him. He was not disappointed. A slight drizzle made the platform shine in the station lights. Red and green lights from signals made bright splashes in the darkness. The rails stretched away like thin, shining, straight snakes. Dozens of photographers were already snapping away. A steam engine drifted through, smoke billowing from its pistons, cab lit up from the glow of its fire. Percy took his first pictures, breathed in the magic smell of oil, smoke, steam, and sulphur, and sighed with satisfaction. The atmosphere was perfect. They were back in time forty years at least. He could well imagine a ghost train turning up.

'We'll have better than this tomorrow,' said a man standing next to him.

Percy got into conversation. Funny, he thought, how only railways loosened his tongue to strangers. The engine came through a few more times, they snapped it, then the man said, 'Let's go and have a drink.'

So they did, in the South Western Hotel just outside the station.

Percy had a question. 'What about this ghost? Will I see it?'

'You'll be lucky,' said his new friend. 'It's a ghost you mainly hear, not see. People say that often, late at night, there's the clear sound of a steam train coming through, stopping at the station, then steaming on up the line towards the North Devon coast. I've never heard it myself but I know plenty who insist they have and they're not idiots. That's all—except that some car drivers say they've seen something strange on the nights it's heard, on a crossing six miles up the line. A man seems to be falling through the air as if he's jumped off this invisible train. He hits the ground awkwardly as if the fall has smashed him to bits. He must be dead. But when the drivers look, there's never anyone there and there's not been a train either. Perhaps it's all rubbish. Some say the drivers are drunk and the noise of the train is just faraway thunder. Whether it is or not, the ghost was heard and the man was seen even when the line was closed and before the Moors and Tors started up.'

'What's the ghost supposed to be?' asked Percy.

'I've no idea. There's never been anyone killed on the crossing that I know of.'

'So I won't see it,' said Percy disappointedly. Then he brightened. 'But I might hear it.'

'You won't know,' his new friend replied. 'This is the one weekend when there'll be trains most of the night.'

It took Percy a long time to sleep properly. But had he dozed off almost at once? He wasn't sure and that was what kept him awake. He thought he suddenly sat up in bed, every nerve tingling. Somewhere far away was the deep whistle of a large steam engine and the steady beat of its exhaust. It came nearer, nearer, then clear as if he stood by the line as it passed: the locomotive, then the fourfold beat of coach wheels passing over jointed track—'da-da-da-*dum*, da-da-da-*dum*.' He dashed to the window. Here, though, the track was in a shallow cutting: apart from a drift of steam and a suspicion of passing lights, he saw nothing.

He climbed back into bed. *If it wasn't the ghost or I didn't dream it, then that was a brilliant photographers' special*, he thought. He closed his eyes—but for some reason sleep eluded him for hours until he finally drifted away through sheer exhaustion.

At 7 a.m. he got up, came down to a typical guest house fry-up of a breakfast, ate every morsel and half a loaf of toast as well, then strode down to the station, as happy as he had been at any time in his life.

*

His mother, though, was not happy, and Mrs Larkin was regretting her generosity in agreeing to look after her. At last, she couldn't bite her tongue any more. 'Look, the poor lad deserves a break. Besides, he'll be home tomorrow night.'

But she felt like saying, 'Why don't you stick pins in a Percy-shaped doll and be done with it?'

*

Percy was having a marvellous day. He used up three films during the hours of light. Every locomotive on the line was now in his camera—at rest in the engine shed, backing down on its train, making impressive smoke effects as it left the station with a rake of loaded carriages. He had photographed goods trains, passenger trains, shunting operations, signal boxes, station buildings. He had taken two separate journeys up and down the line, one behind 'Clun Castle' in a rake of vintage pre-war Great Western coaches, the other behind 'Sir Nigel Gresley' hauling eight coaches painted maroon, which made it look like the Flying Scotsman express of the 1950s. He had exchanged wonderful railway talk with dozens of enthusiasts. He was very, very happy.

Dusk was falling. He loaded his last film and fitted his flash gun. These photographs should be the best of the lot.

*

By seven o'clock, Mrs Larkin reckoned she'd done enough for the day. She'd made Mrs Padlow a lovely supper of steamed fish, green beans, and mashed potatoes which had hardly been touched. She made the old lady comfortable in bed, with the TV control and bedside lamp close at hand, left a jug of orange and a glass beside her and checked that her alarm was switched on in case anything went wrong in the night. Then she said, 'Well, I'll leave you now. My husband will be wondering where I've got to. You'll be all right until morning.'

Then she stepped outside the room, sighed with relief and thought two thoughts at once. The first was, *Percy, you're a saint to put up with her day after day*. The second was, *Please never go away for the weekend again*. There was no doubt: Percy's mother was getting worse.

But Mrs Padlow did not watch TV, nor did she drink her orange. She let the room darken and stared straight ahead, remembering her honeymoon journey. The slow, bumping train, smut in her eyes, mounting misery as they seemed no nearer journey's end, then the grinding halt which threw her from her seat. Then Arthur trying to find out what had happened, coming back with that fatuous grin that over the years she came to hate. 'There's been an incident.' Stupid word. 'An inci*dent* . . . an inci*dent* . . . da-da-da-*dum* . . . da-da-da-*dum*.' The words beat in her mind with the wheels.

*

The night was even better than the day. Every engine made a show in the station. 'Sir Nigel', 'Clun Castle', 'Kolhapur', and 'Sir Lamiel' did impressive run-throughs with full-length trains which really caught the old-time atmosphere of a busy junction on the main line. Everything was perfect: lights, sights, sounds, smells, the slight tension of journeys beginning and ending. Percy and a few hundred others were enraptured.

All the time, Percy had an odd feeling of anticipation. *The best is yet to be*. Even when enthusiasts began to drift away, he stayed on. Activity on the station slackened. It was late: even old-time railwaymen had to sleep. But Percy had more shots to take. He still hung around, convinced there would be a grand finale. What about the train he heard last night? Would they run it again?

*

'Incident . . . incident . . . *stupid* word. And besides, there *wasn't* one.'

*

The station was almost deserted. A tank engine simmered at the end of the opposite platform. In the distance, signal lights glowed red and green. The signal box was lit up and Percy could see a signalman leaning to the levers. There was a tiny metallic thud as the arm of the signal at the end of the platform swung upwards and the light changed from red to green. Porters in old Southern Railway uniforms were waiting. The night was suddenly colder. From away to the east came the same deep engine whistle he had heard last night. A train hauled by a large locomotive was approaching. He saw lights as it rounded the bend, smoke billowing grey against the darkness. It slowed as it passed the signal box and cleared the far end of the platform.

Percy felt the greatest elation even of this wonderful day. What a marvellous run-through for the Moors and Tors Railway to organize right at the very end! For the engine was a superb streamlined Merchant Navy Pacific in bright Southern Railway green. Behind it was a line of green Southern coaches. And at the front end of the Pacific's streamlined body was a headboard—ATLANTIC COAST EXPRESS.

They've really done us proud, thought Percy as he snapped and snapped and snapped. The green coaches passed slowly in

front of him. Behind the lighted windows passengers sat. Percy was dumbfounded with admiration. Somehow the Moors and Tors Railway had managed to fill it with people wearing old-fashioned clothes, just like those he saw his parents wearing in family photographs taken before he was born. And, in one compartment—why, there was a young couple, the woman in a white two-piece suit and the man in a dark suit with a white carnation is his lapel buttonhole, a newly married couple on their honeymoon. They appeared to be having an argument. How realistic! Oh, this was wonderful. This was the way to recreate the old railway atmosphere all right. Flash! flash! flash! went his camera and the film filled with shots that would be priceless.

The massive green engine drew to a halt with a metallic squeal of brakes and let off steam deafeningly. Percy ran back along the train to stand just below the footplate. He saw the fireman bending to his fire and the driver, his hand on the regulator, leaning out of the window watching the signal.

'Do you finish here or go on up the branch?' Percy shouted.

The driver turned an indistinct face towards him. 'We go on,' he said. It was amazing how clear his voice sounded above the noise without need to shout.

Percy suddenly felt filled with a wild rush of power. After all, here was the day's best event and there was hardly anyone left to see it. Didn't they know what they were missing? If it was his good fortune, why not take it further? This wasn't cheeky: they ran steam engine driving courses here and he was just getting an idea of what it would be like before he enrolled on one.

Before he had second thoughts, he swung himself up to the footplate and braced himself for the blast of heat from the firebox. As he did so, the driver pulled the regulator and the Merchant Navy slowly began to move.

The moment it did so, Percy's delight was replaced by pure terror.

*

Mrs Padlow slept now, but her dreams were shot through with sights and sounds which made her whimper aloud. When she woke next morning she had no memory of the nightmares which pursued her.

*

He had braced himself needlessly: there was no heat from this firebox. Nor was there any defeaning clang of steel or blast of steam. There was just a quiet, echoing beat which seemed in his mind rather than in his ears. The driver and fireman were very close, so he could see every detail on their dirty blue overalls, every streak of sweat on the fireman's face. Yet they were somehow far away, like tiny mechanical dolls in a puppet theatre. Outside, steam and smoke drifted by, yet he could make out nothing beyond. It was as if the Atlantic Coast Express flew through cloudy darkness, fell free into bottomless pits of nothing.

Overwhelmingly, Percy wanted to be off, back on the platform with comforting stone beneath his feet. How could he stop this thing? What was that lever by the driver's head? The regulator? Or the wheel on that pipe, like the stopcock on the water pipes at home? Percy thought he knew a locomotive cab's layout, but these levers, wheels, pipes and dials stared back like the denizens of a steel serpent-house.

And still the Atlantic Coast Express drove remorselessly on.

The driver turned to him. His face was still indistinct. 'So you want to get off?' he said.

'*Yes!*' Percy shrieked.

'So you will. But not yet,' said the driver.

Percy stood still for a moment. What did this man mean?

And then, suddenly, clear as a bell in his mind, he heard a voice. 'An inci*dent* . . . An inci*dent*.'

He knew that voice. He'd heard it often enough, nearly every day of his life, once clear and high and young, then older and older until it became a succession of grudging grunts. His mother's.

And she meant what she said. He knew it with every sense that he possessed. An incident . . . an *acc*ident! Someone was going to be killed. There was only one thing left. He *had* to get off. *Now.*

He lurched to the edge of the swaying footplate, held on to the rail for an instant, and then let go. For a split second he saw wooden sleepers flying beneath and knew the shiny steel flanks of the locomotive were leaving him for ever. Then the ground rose and met him and that was the last Percy Padlow ever knew.

The police found the car driver in a state of shock. His story was extraordinary. 'I was just coming up to the old crossing when I saw this figure,' he told them. 'I thought I was seeing the ghost people talk about. You know—the one who jumps off an invisible train. But when I stopped and went to see for myself I got the fright of my life. You see, after all those stories, I didn't think I'd find anything there. But I did. This man, sprawled out dead, all his limbs twisted and broken. So I rang 999 on my mobile. It wasn't me who killed him and I haven't had a drop to drink all night. You can breathalyse me if you like.'

The sergeant looked at him sympathetically. None of those things had occurred to him. He knew fear when he saw it.

Before news of a dead man at the crossing reached the junction, everybody was full of something else.

'Did you hear it last night?' was the question.

'What, that train coming in and then leaving again?'

'That's it. Pity no one ever sees it.'

'Still, trust the ghost to turn up for the enthusiasts' weekend.'

'You're right. It's got a great sense of timing. Good old ghost.'

Who Is Emma?

KENNETH IRELAND

G oodnight,' she called down the stairs.
        'Goodnight, Emma,' called her father. She could hear
        the television playing in the living room.

She closed her bedroom door, got into bed, and pulled the cord hanging over her bed to turn out the light. The room was in darkness.

It took several minutes before she realized that something was wrong. First she could hear the sound of quiet breathing, and at once lay still, listening, trying to make out where it was coming from.

It was unlikely to be inside the room, she thought. There was no way any stranger could have got into the house without everyone knowing about it. And since the house was detached, she wasn't hearing the breathing sound coming through the wall from the house next door, either.

Then there was a definite movement, just a slight rustling as if something was touching the bedclothes. At once Emma thought of some kind of animal, and that was just as scaring. They had no pets, so if it was an animal it must have entered through a half-open door some time during the day and found its way upstairs. And it could be any sort of animal, if that's what it was.

For the moment the rustling was still on the far side of her bed. She eased the bedclothes free on her side, as quietly as she could, ready to be able to jump out quickly and run for the bedroom door, then half-raised her head from the pillow to make sure.

Suddenly she found herself accidentally touching something —in bed with her! She sat upright at once, and jumped out of bed almost in the same movement. And now that her eyes were becoming more accustomed to the darkness, she could tell that whatever it was was now upright as well.

Before she had time to get the door open and run, the light came on. Sitting up in her bed, still with her hand on the cord of the pull-switch, was another girl, of about the same age as herself.

'Who are you?' this other girl asked. 'Where did you come from?'

Emma stared at her in surprise now, rather than fear. She was just an ordinary girl, wearing a pink nightie.

'More to the point, how did *you* get here?' Emma demanded. 'This is where I live. It's my house . . .'

Then she realized that it was not. Looking quickly round the room she saw that the curtains had a flowered pattern on them, when they should have been a plain fawn colour. The wardrobe was in the wrong place, and there was a mirror on it, while hers had no mirror.

She glanced cautiously into that mirror, and could see distinctly the reflection of this strange girl, whoever she was. So at least she had to be real. The carpet, now she noticed, was pink as well, while hers had been brown.

The girl was climbing out of bed equally cautiously, remaining on the far side of it. Emma glanced at the clock to find the time. That had vanished, though, and instead was a clock-radio—on a table alongside the bed, not on the dressing table where she had kept her alarm-clock. It was all wrong.

'This doesn't make sense,' was all she could find to say. 'I just don't know what's happened.'

She had gone to bed normally, with everything in its usual, comfortable place, and now it had all changed. She didn't think she had even been asleep, but perhaps she had been—the display on the clock-radio was reading half an hour later than when she had first got into bed.

Then it came to her—this had to be her own house. The size and shape of the bedroom were the same, for one thing. And outside was the landing at the top of the stairs, and next on her left would be her parents' bedroom, and on her right the door to the small bedroom which was used only for storage.

She moved at once to open the bedroom door. Then she felt round the edge of the wall outside for where she knew the light switch to be, found it at once and switched it on. It was the same landing. Only the wallpaper was different, and the stair carpet had somehow changed colour. At least the woodwork was still painted white.

Then a face appeared at the foot of the stairs as she stood looking down. 'Why is the light on? Is something wrong, Hannah?' asked a man whom she didn't recognize. Then after a brief pause: 'Who are you?'

The other girl, looking cross, was now standing at her side.

'I don't know who she is,' said the other girl, who was obviously named Hannah. 'I just found her up here—and in my bed.'

The girl's father came up the stairs in a hurry. 'Who are you, and how did you get into the house?' he demanded.

'I don't know,' said Emma. She felt stupid now. Of course she knew who she was, it was just that she couldn't explain in any way what was going on. 'My name's Emma. It's just—'

Hannah's father looked at her. 'All right, I'll make it simple. When did you come into the house, and where have you been hiding?' he asked heavily.

Emma didn't answer, because there was no sensible answer. She wished that she could just go back into her bedroom, close the door behind her, get into bed and expect it all to come out right again. It could only be some kind of bad dream.

So without saying a word she did just that. She returned to her bedroom, closed the door behind her, leapt into bed, turned out the light and pulled the bedclothes tightly round her chin. Then she closed her eyes. When she opened

them again, it was because the light had been switched on again. Now Hannah and her father were standing at the side of the bed. Hannah's father pulled the bedclothes back.

'Get out of here and get yourself dressed!' he shouted.

Reluctantly, she sat up. Nothing had changed. She was still in the strange room, exactly as it had been before she had returned to it. When she stepped out of the bed and looked round, there were no clothes in there which belonged to her at all.

'Where are my clothes, then?' she asked, bewildered.

A woman now entered the bedroom—Hannah's mother, she supposed.

'What's going on? Who is this girl, Hannah?'

The other girl, Hannah, shrugged. 'I've never seen her in my life,' she said.

'A girl from school, is she?'

'I've told you, I don't know her.'

This would have been ridiculous, had it not been such a nightmare. Nightmare—that was the obvious answer. Emma pinched herself. 'Wake up! Wake up!' she told herself aloud. She had been able to wake herself out of unpleasant dreams before, only this time it didn't seem to be working.

'Now what are you doing?' asked Hannah's father.

'Trying to wake myself up,' replied Emma desperately.

'You're mad,' said Hannah.

'I'm sending for the police,' decided her father. 'She's probably run away from some children's home or something.'

'Let's wait first,' suggested Hannah's mother. 'Perhaps she will tell us in a minute.'

Emma was grateful for that. Only it didn't solve anything. This was impossible. She couldn't have gone to bed as normal then woken up—if that was what she had done—to find herself in what was clearly the same house yet not the same house. Unless, she thought, it was really a similar house to her own and somehow she had been sleep-walking *and* somehow walked into it without knowing what she was doing.

But if that had happened, how had she managed to get inside the house in the first place, and in such a short space of time?

She pinched herself again. It was no use. Hannah and her parents remained staring at her.

'Where do you think you've put your clothes, then?' asked Hannah's mother, almost kindly now.

Emma shook her head. 'They're not here,' she said.

'Then where do you live?' asked Hannah's mother. 'Perhaps we could arrange for you to be taken home, then sort everything out afterwards.'

'Sixteen Oxclose Lane,' replied Emma. At least she was sure of that. At least it was one fact she could keep hold of.

'But this is Sixteen Oxclose Lane,' said Hannah's mother gently.

That was a nasty shock. She looked at herself carefully in the mirror on the wardrobe door. She looked exactly the same as she had done in the few minutes before she had got into bed—less than an hour ago. Then Hannah was reaching forward to touch her, and then grasped her wrist firmly. Emma drew away.

'Just seeing if you were solid,' explained Hannah.

Emma knew what she meant. She was trying to discover if she was real. At any other time that wouldn't have made sense, but just now it did. Emma might have done the same herself, in similar circumstances.

'Don't be silly, Hannah,' said the girl's mother.

'Well, how else did she get here?' asked Hannah. 'What did you say your name was?' she asked Emma.

Emma told her.

'I think first we'd all better go downstairs,' said Hannah's father.

'She can borrow my old dressing gown,' said Hannah.

They went down and into the living room. That, too, was almost as Emma knew it, except that only the walls of the room had not changed . . . and the gas-fire in the fireplace.

The room felt warm, so without thinking Emma went to turn it down, then realized what she was doing. It was only a short time since she had left this room. While she was turning the control knob, she happened to notice the corner of the fire's wooden surround. The little scratch mark was still there, leading towards the back of the fire.

'How did this get scratched?' she asked suddenly.

Hannah's mother looked at her father. 'Why, it's always been there,' she said.

'No, it hasn't,' said Emma in triumph. 'I once lost a hair-grip part-way down the back of the fire and tried to dig it out with a screwdriver. Only it slipped and made that scratch.'

Hannah's parents were now watching her uneasily, and Hannah with much greater interest.

'And how do you explain that little story you're now making up?' asked Hannah's father.

'I'm not explaining it. I'm just telling you, that's how the scratch got there.' Then suddenly she thought of something else. 'There used to be a swing in the garden.'

'Well, there isn't one now,' said Hannah.

'No, there isn't,' Emma agreed. 'When we moved here, the frame of the swing was so old and rickety that my father pulled it down. Only it broke away, and he had to leave the metal bar which held it in the ground because he couldn't get it out. I bet that's still there.'

Hannah's father went out of the room, and returned with a large electric torch. 'You just come into the garden and show me,' he instructed.

'It's too cold for her out there,' protested Hannah's mother.

'No it isn't. Show me,' said Hannah's father again. 'Come on, you show me exactly where you claim that metal bar is.'

He led her into the back garden—although he had no need to. Emma knew exactly where that was. And where the garden shed stood. Hannah and her mother followed them.

'We'll need a spade,' said Emma.

Hannah's father brought one out of the shed. She led them to the end of the path which ran beside the lawn. 'There,' she said, and pointed.

Hannah's father began to dig, while Emma held his torch. First, though, she shone the beam at the house. It was the same house, she was certain of that now. Then she turned it back so that he could see where he was digging.

A rusty metal bar came to light, brown and crumbling. It looked like the base of a garden swing. Hannah's father stopped digging.

'Who are you?' he asked nervously.

'I know who I am,' Emma said, firmly now.

Without a word, Hannah's father returned the spade to the garden shed, and they went back indoors. Emma was feeling calm now that she was absolutely sure that she was in the right house. But she knew she wouldn't be able to stay there, not for ever. Sooner or later somebody would want to take her away, and once out of the house she might never be allowed to return. She mustn't let that happen—not yet.

Hannah herself came to the rescue. 'She might as well stay for the night,' she said. 'After all, she's dressed for bed, and she's got no other clothes, so it's the only thing that makes sense. She can share my bed, just for the night.'

That was true, too, because Hannah had a double bed to herself, just as Emma had—or used to have, Emma thought to herself grimly.

Hannah's father was biting the end of his thumbnail, still nervously. 'I don't know,' he said weakly.

'What's the alternative?' asked Hannah's mother. 'We can sort everything out properly in the morning. It's too late to do anything else about it now. So go on—to bed, both of you.'

The girls went upstairs. Hannah said nothing until the light was out. She was obviously very worried about something—not surprisingly. 'If you really mean you live here,' she said cautiously, 'what does that make us?'

Emma didn't know. She didn't even know what it made herself.

'I think I've seen you somewhere before,' said Hannah, 'but I can't remember where. I think it was a long time ago.'

A sudden thought struck Emma. 'How long have you been living here?' she asked.

'Just about five years. The house caught fire when the previous owners lived here, then—'

'Caught fire? Was anyone killed?'

'I don't think so.'

Emma knew that Hannah was staring at her in the darkness. The same thought had occurred to both of them. What if Emma had died in the fire, but somehow hadn't known?

'I can't be a ghost,' said Emma, but she didn't laugh. It was too frightening for that, now.

'Then when they'd had the house put right,' Hannah was saying, 'that's when they decided to move somewhere else. I don't know why. And that's when my father bought it.'

So where had she been for five years? Emma was thinking to herself. It still made no sense. After a long time, they fell asleep.

When she woke, she could smell something burning. She switched on the light. The room was exactly as it should be. Even her clock was in its right place, on the dressing table. She screwed up her eyes and looked at it. Four o'clock. Hannah had vanished. Everything was now back to normal. Except for the smell of smoke.

Sleepily she climbed out of bed and opened her bedroom door. Out there was normal, too, apart from the smoke coming up the stairs in thick swirls. It just had to have been a nightmare she'd been having. But another nightmare was about to start, a real one this time.

She ran into her parents' room, and shook both of them. 'Fire!' she yelled, then as soon as they were fully awake dashed back into her own room and dressed hurriedly. That was the first essential, she decided, rightly or wrongly.

Her father had made his way downstairs through the thick swirls of rising smoke, and she heard him on the telephone. Then they, with the help of neighbours, all tried throwing buckets of water into the blazing living room, but without success. They were outside the house and in safety by the time the fire-engines arrived. They stood in the small front garden surrounded by what they had managed to salvage of their personal possessions until the last fireman had left.

When the neighbours returned to their own homes, a police car took them to stay at her grandmother's, five miles away, for what was left of the night, and the following morning they returned to survey the damage.

The house was a mess except, surprisingly, most of the living room, which somehow was virtually untouched apart from the smell of smoke which hung in the air.

'If you hadn't woken when you did, we'd all have been suffocated,' said Emma's father.

'Or burned alive,' added her mother.

'So what are we going to do now?' Emma asked.

'It'll all be put right by the insurance,' her father assured her. 'In the meantime, we'll have to stay at your grandmother's.'

'But it'll never be the same,' wailed Emma's mother, 'not after this. All our furniture, and my best things—gone. It won't be the same any more. I don't want to stay here. Let's find ourselves another house and move out as soon as we can.'

So that was what happened. As soon as the damage had been repaired and the house redecorated throughout, the house was put up for sale. It was not long before the first people arrived to look it over and decide if it suited them.

It was a Saturday, so Emma answered the ring on the doorbell. A man, a woman, and a small girl stood there.

'Good afternoon,' said the man. 'Are your parents at home? We'd like to look round.'

Emma started. She recognized them at once. It was Hannah's father and mother. Between them stood a small girl—it was Hannah without a doubt—but looking about five years younger than when Emma had last seen her.

Home

SHIRLEY JACKSON

Ethel Sloane was whistling to herself as she got out of her car and splashed across the sidewalk to the doorway of the hardware store. She was wearing a new raincoat and solid boots, and one day of living in the country had made her weather-wise. 'This rain can't last,' she told the hardware clerk confidently. 'This time of year it never lasts.'

The clerk nodded tactfully. One day in the country had been enough for Ethel Sloane to become acquainted with most of the local people; she had been into the hardware store several times —'so many odd things you never expect you're going to need in an old house'—and into the post office to leave their new address, and into the grocery to make it clear that all the Sloane grocery business was going to come their way, and into the bank and into the gas station and into the little library and even as far as the door of the barbershop ('. . . and you'll be seeing my husband Jim Sloane in a day or so!'). Ethel Sloane liked having bought the old Sanderson place, and she liked walking the single street of the village, and most of all she liked knowing that people knew who she was.

'They make you feel at home right away, as though you were born not half a mile from here,' she explained to her husband, Jim.

Privately she thought that the storekeepers in the village might show a little more alacrity in remembering her name; she had probably brought more business to the little stores in the village than any of them had seen for a year past. They're not outgoing people, she told herself reassuringly. It takes a while for them to get over being suspicious; we've been here in the house for only two days.

'First, I want to get the name of a good plumber,' she said to the clerk in the hardware store. Ethel Sloane was a great believer in getting information directly from the local people; the plumbers listed in the phone book might be competent enough, but the local people always knew who would suit; Ethel Sloane had no intention of antagonizing the villagers by hiring an unpopular plumber. 'And closet hooks,' she said. 'My husband, Jim, turns out to be just as good a handyman as he is a writer.' Always tell them your business, she thought, then they don't have to ask.

'I suppose the best one for plumbing would be Will Watson,' the clerk said. 'He does most of the plumbing around. You drive down the Sanderson road in this rain?'

'Of course.' Ethel Sloane was surprised. 'I had all kinds of things to do in the village.'

'Creek's pretty high. They say that sometimes when the creek is high—'

'The bridge held our moving truck yesterday, so I guess it will hold my car today. That bridge ought to stand for a while yet.' Briefly she wondered whether she might not say 'for a spell' instead of 'for a while', and then decided that sooner or later it would come naturally. 'Anyway, who minds rain? We've got so much to do indoors.' She was pleased with 'indoors'.

'Well,' the clerk said, 'of course, no one can stop you from driving on the old Sanderson road. If you want to. You'll find people around here mostly leave it alone in the rain, though. Myself, I think it's all just gossip, but then, I don't drive out that way much, anyway.'

'It's a little muddy on a day like this,' Ethel Sloane said firmly, 'and maybe a little scary crossing the bridge when the creek is high, but you've got to expect that kind of thing when you live in the country.'

'I wasn't talking about that,' the clerk said. 'Closet hooks? I wonder, do we have any closet hooks.'

In the grocery Ethel Sloane bought mustard and soap and pickles and flour. 'All the things I forgot to get yesterday,' she explained, laughing.

'You took that road on a day like this?' the grocer asked.

'It's not that bad,' she said, surprised again. 'I don't mind the rain.'

'We don't use that road in this weather,' the grocer said. 'You might say there's talk about that road.'

'It certainly seems to have quite a local reputation,' Ethel said, and laughed. 'And it's nowhere near as bad as some of the other roads I've seen around here.'

'Well, I told you,' the grocer said, and shut his mouth.

I've offended him, Ethel thought, I've said I think their roads are bad; these people are so jealous of their countryside.

'I guess our road is pretty muddy,' she said almost apologetically. 'But I'm really a very careful driver.'

'You stay careful,' the grocer said. 'No matter what you see.'

'I'm always careful.' Whistling, Ethel Sloane went out and got into her car and turned in the circle in front of the abandoned railway station. Nice little town, she was thinking, and they are beginning to like us already, all so worried about my safe driving. We're the kind of people, Jim and I, who fit in a place like this; we wouldn't belong in the suburbs or some kind of a colony; we're real people. Jim will write, she thought, and I'll get one of these country women to teach me how to make bread. Watson for plumbing.

She was oddly touched when the clerk from the hardware store and then the grocer stepped to their doorways to watch her drive by. They're worrying about me, she thought; they're afraid a city gal can't manage their bad, wicked roads, and I do bet it's hell in the winter, but I can manage; I'm country now.

Her way led out of the village and then off the highway onto a dirt road that meandered between fields and an occasional farmhouse, then crossed the creek—disturbingly high after all this rain—and turned onto the steep hill that led to the Sanderson house. Ethel Sloane could see the house from the bridge across the creek, although in summer the view would be hidden by trees. It's a lovely house, she thought with a little catch of pride; I'm so lucky; up there it stands, so proud and remote, waiting for me to come home.

On one side of the hill the Sanderson land had long ago been sold off, and the hillside was dotted with small cottages and a

couple of ramshackle farms; the people on that side of the hill
used the other, lower, road, and Ethel Sloane was surprised and
a little uneasy to perceive that the tyre marks on this road and
across the bridge were all her own, coming down; no one else
seemed to use this road at all. Private, anyway, she thought;
maybe they've talked everyone else out of using it. She looked
up to see the house as she crossed the bridge; my very own
house, she thought, and then, well, *our* very own house, she
thought, and then she saw that there were two figures standing
silently in the rain by the side of the road.

Good heavens, she thought, standing there in this rain, and
she stopped the car. 'Can I give you a lift?' she called out, rolling
down the window. Through the rain she could see that they
seemed to be an old woman and a child, and the rain drove
down on them. Staring, Ethel Sloane became aware that the
child was sick with misery, wet and shivering and crying in the
rain, and she said sharply, 'Come and get in the car at once; you
mustn't keep that child out in the rain another minute.'

They stared at her, the old woman frowning, listening.
Perhaps she is deaf, Ethel thought, and in her good raincoat and

solid boots she climbed out of the car and went over to them. Not wanting for any reason in the world to touch either of them, she put her face close to the old woman's and said urgently. 'Come, hurry. Get that child into the car, where it's dry. I'll take you wherever you want to go.' Then, with real horror, she saw that the child was wrapped in a blanket, and under the blanket he was wearing thin pyjamas; with a shiver of fury, Ethel saw that he was barefoot and standing in the mud. 'Get in that car at once,' she said, and hurried to open the back door. 'Get in that car at once, do you hear me?'

Silently the old woman reached her hand down to the child and, his eyes wide and staring past Ethel Sloane, the child moved towards the car, with the old woman following. Ethel looked in disgust at the small bare feet going over the mud and rocks, and she said to the old woman, 'You ought to be ashamed; that child is certainly going to be sick.'

She waited until they had climbed into the backseat of the car, and then slammed the door and got into her seat again. She glanced up at the mirror, but they were sitting in the corner, where she could not see them, and she turned; the child was huddled against the old woman, and the old woman looked straight ahead, her face heavy with weariness.

'Where are you going?' Ethel asked, her voice rising. 'Where shall I take you? That child,' she said to the old woman, 'has to be gotten indoors and into dry clothes as soon as possible. Where are you going? I'll see that you get there in a hurry.'

The old woman opened her mouth, and in a voice of old age beyond consolation said, 'We want to go to the Sanderson place.'

'To the Sanderson place?' To us? Ethel thought. To see us? This pair? Then she realized that the Sanderson place, to the old local people, probably still included the land where the cottages had been built; they probably still call the whole thing the Sanderson place, she thought, and felt oddly feudal with pride. We're the lords of the manor, she thought, and her voice was more gentle when she asked, 'Were you waiting out there for very long in the rain?'

'Yes,' the old woman said, her voice remote and despairing.

Their lives must be desolate, Ethel thought. Imagine being that old and that tired and standing in the rain for someone to come by. 'Well, we'll soon have you home,' she said, and started the car.

The wheels slipped and skidded in the mud, but found a purchase, and slowly Ethel felt the car begin to move up the hill. It was very muddy, and the rain was heavier, and the back of the car dragged as though under an intolerable weight. It's as though I had a load of iron, Ethel thought. Poor old lady, it's the weight of years.

'Is the child all right?' she asked, lifting her head; she could not turn to look at them.

'He wants to go home,' the old woman said.

'I should think so. Tell him it won't be long. I'll take you right to your door.' It's the least I can do, she thought, and maybe go inside with them and see that he's warm enough; those poor bare feet.

Driving up the hill was very difficult, and perhaps the road was a little worse than Ethel had believed; she found that she could not look around or even speak while she was navigating the sharp curves, with the rain driving against the windshield and the wheels slipping in the mud. Once she said, 'Nearly at the top,' and then had to be silent, holding the wheel tight. When the car gave a final lurch and topped the small last rise that led onto the flat driveway before the Sanderson house, Ethel said, 'Made it,' and laughed. 'Now, which way should I go?'

They're frightened, she thought. I'm sure the child is frightened and I don't blame them; I was a little nervous myself. She said loudly, 'We're at the top now, it's all right, we made it. Now where shall I take you?'

When there was still no answer, she turned; the backseat of the car was empty.

'But even if they *could* have gotten out of the car without my noticing,' Ethel Sloane said for the tenth time that evening to her husband, 'they couldn't have gotten out of sight. I looked and looked.' She lifted her hands in an emphatic gesture. 'I went all around the top of the hill in the rain looking in all directions and calling them.'

'But the car seat was dry,' her husband said.

'Well, you're not going to suggest that I imagined it, are you? Because I'm simply not the kind of *person* to dream up an old lady and a sick child. There has to be some *explanation*; I don't imagine things.'

'Well . . .' Jim said, and hesitated.

'Are you sure you didn't see them? They didn't come to the door?'

'Listen . . .' Jim said, and hesitated again. 'Look,' he said.

'I have certainly *never* been the kind of person who goes round imagining that she sees old ladies and children. You know me better than that, Jim, you know I don't go round—'

'Well,' Jim said. 'Look,' he said finally, 'there *could* be something. A story I heard. I never told you because—'

'Because what?'

'Because you . . . well—' Jim said.

'Jim.' Ethel Sloane set her lips. 'I don't like this, Jim. What is there that you haven't told me? Is there really something you know and I don't?'

'It's just a story. I heard it when I came up to look at the house.'

'Do you mean you've known something all this time and you've never told me?'

'It's just a story,' Jim said helplessly. Then, looking away, he said, 'Everyone knows it, but they don't say much. I mean, these things—'

'Jim,' Ethel said, 'tell me at once.'

'It's just that there was a little Sanderson boy stolen or lost or something. They thought a crazy old woman took him. People kept talking about it, but they never knew anything for sure.'

'What?' Ethel Sloane stood up and started for the door. 'You mean there's a child been stolen and no one told me about it?'

'No,' Jim said oddly. 'I mean, it happened sixty years ago.'

Ethel was still talking about it at breakfast the next morning. 'And they've never been found,' she told herself happily. 'All the people around went searching, and they finally decided the two of them had drowned in the creek, because it was raining then just the way it is now.' She glanced with satisfaction at the rain beating against the window of the breakfast room. 'Oh, lovely,' she said, and sighed, and stretched, and smiled. 'Ghosts,' she said. 'I saw two honest-to-goodness ghosts. No wonder,' she said, 'no *wonder* the child looked so awful. Awful! Kidnapped, and then drowned. No *wonder*.'

'Listen,' Jim said, 'if I were you, I'd forget about it. People round here don't like to talk much about it.'

'They wouldn't tell me,' Ethel said, and laughed again. 'Our very own ghosts, and not a soul would tell me. I just won't be satisfied until I get every word of the story.'

'That's why *I* never told you,' Jim said miserably.

'Don't be silly. Yesterday everyone I spoke to mentioned my driving on that road, and I bet every one of them was dying to tell me the story. I can't wait to see their faces when they hear.'

'No.' Jim stared at her. 'You simply *can't* go round ... *boasting* about it.'

'But of course I can! Now we really belong here. I've really seen the local ghosts. And I'm going in this morning and tell everybody, and find out all I can.'

'I wish you wouldn't,' Jim said.

'I know you wish I wouldn't, but I'm going to. If I listened to you, I'd wait and wait for a good time to mention it and maybe even come to believe I'd dreamed it or something, so I'm going into the village right after breakfast.'

'Please, Ethel,' Jim said. 'Please listen to me. People might not take it the way you think.'

'Two ghosts of our very own.' Ethel laughed again. 'My very own,' she said. 'I just can't wait to see their faces in the village.'

Before she got into the car she opened the back door and looked again at the seat, dry and unmarked. Then, smiling to herself, she got into the driver's seat and, suddenly touched with sick cold, turned around to look. 'Why,' she said half whispering, 'you're not *still* here, you can't be! Why,' she said, 'I just looked.'

'They were strangers in the house,' the old woman said.

The skin on the back of Ethel's neck crawled as though some wet thing walked there; the child stared past her, and the old woman's eyes were flat and dead. 'What do you want?' Ethel asked, still whispering.

'We got to go back.'

'I'll take you.' The rain came hard against the windows of the car, and Ethel Sloane, seeing her own hand tremble as she reached for the car key, told herself, don't be afraid, they're not real. 'I'll take you,' she said, gripping the wheel tight and turning the car to face down the hill. 'I'll take you,' she said, almost babbling. 'I'll take you right back, I promise, see if I don't, I promise I'll take you right back where you want to go.'

'He wanted to go home,' the old woman said. Her voice was very far away.

'I'll take you, I'll take you.' The road was even more slippery than before, and Ethel Sloane told herself, drive carefully, don't be afraid, they're not real. 'Right where I found you yesterday, the very spot, I'll take you back.'

'They were strangers in the house.'

Ethel realized that she was driving faster than she should; she felt the disgusting wet cold coming from the back seat pushing her, forcing her to hurry.

'I'll take you back,' she said over and over to the old woman and the child.

'When the strangers are gone, we can go home,' the old woman said.

Coming to the last turn before the bridge, the wheels slipped, and, pulling at the steering wheel and shouting, 'I'll take you back, I'll take you back,' Ethel Sloane could hear only the child's horrible laughter as the car turned and skidded towards the high waters of the creek. One wheel slipped and spun in the air, and then, wrenching at the car with all her strength, she pulled it back on to the road and stopped.

Crying, breathless, Ethel put her head down on the steering wheel, weak and exhausted. I was almost killed, she told herself, they almost took me with them. She did not need to look into the backseat of the car; the cold was gone, and she knew the seat was dry and empty.

The clerk in the hardware store looked up and, seeing Ethel Sloane, smiled politely and then, looking again, frowned. 'You feeling poorly this morning, Mrs Sloane?' he asked. 'Rain bothering you?'

'I almost had an accident on the road,' Ethel Sloane said.

'On the old Sanderson road?' The clerk's hands were very still on the counter. 'An accident?'

Ethel Sloane opened her mouth and then shut it again. 'Yes,' she said at last. 'The car skidded.'

'We don't use that road much,' the clerk said. Ethel started to speak, but stopped herself.

'It's got a bad name locally, that road,' he said. 'What were you needing this morning?'

Ethel thought, and finally said, 'Clothespins, I guess I must need clothespins. About the Sanderson road—'

'Yes?' said the clerk, his back to her.

'Nothing,' Ethel said.

'Clothespins,' the clerk said, putting a box on the counter. 'By the way, will you and the mister be coming to the PTA social tomorrow night?'

'We certainly will,' said Ethel Sloane.

The Extraordinarily Horrible Dummy

GERALD KERSH

An uneasy conviction tells me that this story is true, but I hate to believe it. It was told to me by Ecco, the ventriloquist, who occupied a room next to mine in Busto's apartment-house. I hope he lied. Or perhaps he was mad. The world is so full of liars and lunatics that one never knows what is true and what is false.

All the same, if ever a man had a haunted look, that man was Ecco. He was small and furtive. He had unnerving habits: five minutes of his company would have set your nerves on edge. For example: he would stop in the middle of a sentence, say Ssh! in a compelling whisper, look timorously over his shoulder, and listen to something. The slightest noise made him jump. Like all Busto's tenants, he had come down in the world. There had been a time when he topped bills and drew fifty pounds a week. Now, he lived by performing to theatre-queues.

And yet he was the best ventriloquist I have ever heard. His talent was uncanny. Repartee cracked back and forth without pause, and in two distinct voices. There were even people who swore that his dummy was no dummy, but a dwarf or small boy with painted cheeks, trained in ventriloquial back-chat. But this was not true. No dummy was ever more palpably stuffed with sawdust. Ecco called it Micky; and his act, *Micky and Ecco*.

All ventriloquists' dummies are ugly, but I have yet to see one uglier than Micky. It had a home-made look. There was something disgustingly avid in the stare of its bulging blue eyes, the lids of which clicked as it winked; and an extraordinary horrible ghoulishness in the smacking of its great, grinning, red wooden lips. Ecco carried Micky with him wherever he went, and even slept with it. You would have felt cold at the sight of Ecco, walking upstairs, holding Micky at arm's length. The dummy was large and robust; the man was small and wraith-like; and in a bad light you would have thought *the dummy is leading the man!*

I said he lived in the next room to mine. But in London you may live and die in a room, and the man next door may never know. I should never have spoken to Ecco, but for his habit of practising ventriloquism by night. It was nerve-racking. At the best of times it was hard to find rest under Busto's roof; but Ecco made night hideous, really hideous. You know the shrill, false voice of the ventriloquist's dummy? Micky's voice was not like that. It was shrill, but querulous; thin, but real—not Ecco's voice distorted, but a *different* voice. You would have sworn that there were two people quarrelling. *This man is good*, I thought. Then, *but this man is perfect!* And at last there crept into my mind this sickening idea, *there are two men!*

In the dead of night, voices would break out: 'Come on, try again!'—'I can't!'—'You must.'—'I want to go to sleep.'—'Not yet; try again!'—'I'm tired, I tell you; I can't!'—'And I say try again.' Then there would be peculiar singing noises, and at length Ecco's voice would cry: 'You devil! You devil! Let me alone, in the name of God!'

One night, when this had gone on for three hours, I went to Ecco's door, and knocked. There was no answer. I opened the door. Ecco was sitting there, grey in the face, with Micky on his knees. 'Yes?' he said. He did not look at me, but the great, painted eyes of the dummy stared straight into mine.

I said: 'I don't want to seem unreasonable, but this noise . . .'

Ecco turned to the dummy, and said: 'We're annoying the gentleman. Shall we stop?'

Micky's dead red lips snapped as he replied: 'Yes. Put me to bed.'

Ecco lifted him. The stuffed legs of the dummy flapped lifelessly as the man laid him on the divan, and covered him with a blanket. He pressed a spring. *Snap!*—the eyes closed. Ecco drew a deep breath, and wiped sweat from his forehead.

'Curious bedfellow,' I said.

'Yes,' said Ecco. 'But . . . please—' And he looked at Micky, frowned at me, and laid a finger to his lips. '*Ssh!*' he whispered.

'How about some coffee?' I suggested.

He nodded. 'Yes: my throat is very dry,' he said. I beckoned. That disgusting stuffed dummy seemed to charge the atmosphere with tension. Ecco followed me on tiptoe, and closed his door silently. As I boiled water on my gas-ring, I watched him. From time to time he hunched his shoulders, raised his eyebrows, and listened. Then, after a few minutes of silence he said, suddenly: 'You think I'm mad.'

'No,' I said, 'not at all; only you seem remarkably devoted to that dummy of yours.'

'I hate him,' said Ecco, and listened again.

'Then why don't you burn the thing?'

'For God's sake!' cried Ecco, and clasped a hand over my mouth. I was uneasy—it was the presence of this terribly nervous little man that made me so. We drank our coffee, while I tried to make conversation.

'You must be an extraordinarily fine ventriloquist,' I said.

'Me? No, not very. My father, yes. He was great. You've heard of Professor Vox? Yes, well he was my father.'

'Was he indeed?'

'He taught me all I know; and even now . . . I mean . . . without him, you understand—nothing! He was a genius. Me, I could never control the nerves of my face and throat. So you see, I was a great disappointment to him. He . . . well, you know; he could eat a beefsteak, while Micky, sitting at the same table, sang *Je crois entendre encore*. That was genius. He used to make me practise, day in and day out—*Bee, Eff, Em, En, Pe, Ve, Doubleyou*, without moving the lips. But I was no good. I couldn't do it. I simply couldn't. He used to give me hell. When I was a child, yes, my mother used to protect me a little. But afterwards! Bruises—I was black with them. He was a terrible man. Everybody was afraid of him. You're too young to remember: he looked like—well, look.'

Ecco took a wallet out and extracted a photograph. It was brown and faded, but the features of the face were still vivid. Vox had a bad face; strong but evil—fat, swarthy, bearded, and forbidding. His huge lips were pressed firmly together under a heavy black moustache, which grew right up to the sides of a massive flat nose. He had immense eyebrows, which ran together in the middle; and great, round, glittering eyes.

'You can't get the impression,' said Ecco, 'but when he came on to the stage in a black cloak lined with red silk, he looked just like the devil. He took Micky with him wherever he went— they used to talk in public. But he was a great ventriloquist— the greatest ever. He used to say: "I'll make a ventriloquist of you if it's the last thing I ever do." I had to go with him wherever he went, all over the world; and stand in the wings, and watch him; and go home with him at night and practise again—*Bee, Eff, Em, En, Pe, Ve, Doubleyou*—over and over again, sometimes till dawn. You'll think I'm crazy.'

'Why should I?'

'Well . . . This went on and on, until—*ssh*—did you hear something?'

'No, there was nothing. Go on.'

'One night I . . . I mean, there was an accident. I—he fell down the lift-shaft in the Hotel Dordogne, in Marseilles. Somebody left the gate open. He was killed.' Ecco wiped sweat from his face. 'And that night I slept well, for the first time in my life. I was twenty years old then. I went to sleep, and slept well. And then I had a horrible dream. He was back again, see? Only not he, in the flesh; but only his voice. And he was saying: "Get up, get up, get up and try again, damn you; get up I say— I'll make a ventriloquist of you if it's the last thing I ever do. Wake up!"

'I woke up. You will think I'm mad. I swear I still heard the voice; and it was coming from . . .'

Ecco paused and gulped. I said: 'Micky?' He nodded. There was a pause; then I said: 'Well?'

'That's about all,' he said. 'It was coming from Micky. It has been going on ever since; day and night. He won't let me alone. It isn't I who makes Micky talk. Micky makes me talk. He makes me practise still . . . day and night. I daren't leave him. He might tell the . . . he might . . . oh, God; anyway, I can't leave him . . . I can't.'

I thought, *this poor man is undoubtedly mad. He has got the habit of talking to himself, and he thinks—*

At that moment, I heard a voice; a little, thin, querulous, mocking voice, which seemed to come from Ecco's room. It said: 'Ecco!'

Ecco leapt up, gibbering with fright. 'There!' he said. 'There he is again. I must go. I'm not mad; not really mad. I must—'

He ran out. I heard his door open and close. Then there came again the sound of conversation, and once I thought I heard Ecco's voice, shaking with sobs, saying *'Bee, Eff, Em, En, Pe, Ve, Doubleyou . . .'*

He is crazy, I thought; *yes, the man must be crazy . . . And before he was throwing his voice . . . calling himself . . .*

But it took me two hours to convince myself of that; and I left the light burning all that night, and I swear to you that I have never been more glad to see the dawn.

Hallowe'en

RITA MORRIS

Alan was alone in the graveyard.

He was skulking just inside the gates, behind a wire rubbish bin piled high with withered wreaths. Their brown leaves rustled in the bitter wind. He was waiting for his friend Tommo to join him for their annual Hallowe'en tour of the graveyard, and he had every intention of jumping out from behind the heap to frighten Tommo as he came through the gates. It was traditional. He did it every year.

But minutes passed, and Tommo did not come. Slowly the red sky faded behind the old church. The air was noisy with the twittering of birds settling for the night in the bell tower. Darkness collected on the uneven grass and among the tilted gravestones, while a steady, piercing wind blew dust towards him up the hill and along the tarmac path. Alan wished it wasn't so perishing cold, and that Tommo would turn up soon. He must have been waiting here for *hours*.

In the black tower overhead the heavy bells chimed five: a mournful sound. There was a sinister rattle near his feet as the wind flipped a wreath off the heap and sent it skittering along the path.

'Come *on*, Tommo!'

Alan cursed quietly to himself and jogged up to the church porch, noiseless as a ghost in his sneakers. His toes were numb. He had never been so cold in his life. Whose daft idea had it been to come here every Hallowe'en anyway, his or Tommo's? He couldn't remember. He only knew they'd been daring each other to come here every year since they were seven. Other kids dressed up and traipsed round from house to house, knocking on the doors for sweets; Alan and Tommo braved the church-yard. It was known to be haunted—well, the church was, anyway —and Alan's own granny had told him of the time she'd been woken in the middle of the night by the sound of the church bell, tolling steadily. That was how they rang the bell for deaths. But whose hand had rung it in the hours of darkness, when every living soul was asleep? No, the churchyard was haunted all right, and every kid with a grain of sense steered well clear of it on Hallowe'en. Except Alan and Tommo, of course, who weren't scared of anything.

'Waitin' for someone?'

The sound of that hoarse voice coming so unexpectedly from the deep shadows of the porch made Alan's heart jump into his mouth. He stood poised, ready to run, as a hump-shouldered figure shuffled awkwardly towards him and into the dim light of the overhead lamp.

Alan let out his breath in a sigh of relief. Only old Alice the tramp. Suppose he'd run yelling like a scared little kid from smelly Alice, and Tommo had copped him doing it? Tommo would never have let him live it down.

'Frightened you, did I?' The old woman chuckled richly to herself, fat shoulders heaving under her grubby mac. Beneath the frayed and fluttering headscarf her face was invisible in shadow.

'No.'

Alan spoke loudly but she went on chuckling anyway, coughing to a stop at last. She came stooping across to one of the larger graves, a flat stone the size of a table, and sank down on it, hauling the two plastic carrier bags she trailed everywhere with her up onto the grave beside her. The lamp was now shining on her face. It was a soft, withered old face with tiny sharp eyes, like the face of a fat schoolgirl who had somehow grown old without growing up.

'That's right,' she said. 'Nothing to be afraid of, is there? For all it's a graveyard on Hallowe'en. You're not scared of ghosts, though?'

'Not me,' boasted Alan, shoving his cold hands deep in his jacket pockets. 'I've lived here all my life.'

'In a graveyard?' she cried, eyes widening.

Alan gave her a look; you could do that with Old Alice, you didn't have to be as careful with her as you did with ordinary adults.

'Where?' she asked, persistent. 'Where d'you live now?'

'Up there.' He jerked his head to where a row of orange street lamps showed beyond the graveyard wall. 'Church Road.'

'Ah.' She nodded wisely to herself for a minute, tapping the back of one fat hand with the other. 'Ah.'

You ought to know, thought Alan rudely to himself; you've seen me often enough. And it was true, for Old Alice seemed to have a fondness for the graveyard, and she frequently hung around there—when she wasn't rummaging through the rubbish bins in the supermarket car park down town. It was even rumoured she slept there on fine summer nights. Alan had often seen her as he cut through the churchyard to get to the shops at the bottom of the hill, but she had never spoken to him before. Alice was a crazy woman—not simple, like the children at the special school near the hospital, but *crazy*—and she only ever talked to herself. She was a harmless old soul, said Alan's mum; not that she looked harmless now. A witch she looked, with her dirty face creased in wrinkles and her small, cruel, curious eyes.

'I'm waiting for a mate,' said Alan, and turned his back on her to check the gates again. 'Tommo, come *on*!'

'Well, he won't come looking for you here.'

'He will,' Alan answered with perfect certainty. 'We do it every year. We always meet up for a game on Hallowe'en.'

'He'll be afraid.'

Her mouth fell open and she laughed again, showing one yellow tooth poking up out of a shiny gum. Alan turned away quickly, sickened.

'He won't be scared,' he muttered. 'Not Tommo. Me and him are best mates.'

And it was true, though they were not much alike—Tommo quiet and rather clever, and Alan good at games. But they were always together, closer than brothers, and had been since primary school when they had sat in the same class, Alan Chantler in the front row and Neil Tomlinson right behind. It had been Alan and Tommo ever since.

A great stillness was dropping over the churchyard now as the sky lost its final blue and became black. Despite the nearness of Old Alice, Alan felt with a shiver how lonely it could be up here. The square bulk of the unlit church loomed behind them like a beached ship; clustering trees at the graveyard's edge stood out against the orange gloom of the street beyond. Alan had a sudden weird feeling that every object in the churchyard was playing a Hallowe'en game of its own, a sort of Grandmother's Footsteps with him— that if he turned his back the trees and gravestones might shiver into life of a sort and creep up over the dead ground towards him . . .

He began hopping from one foot to the other, whistling soundlessly through his teeth, banging his fists against his ribs. The stars were coming out, bright and frosty overhead; it would be a bitter night.

'Cold, are you?' said Old Alice comfortably. 'I don't feel the cold any more, me.'

She shifted her large bottom on its stone seat and began tracing the letters cut into the sooty surface of the grave. Nearly all the stones in the churchyard were old, and covered with a kind of furry grime.

'There's eleven of them in here,' she said thoughtfully. 'All one family. Big families in those days.'

Alan ignored her and trotted up the path to the iron gates to peer out anxiously, but Church Road was empty. There was no sign of Tommo.

In the front room of his own house the light came on, and his sister Debbie sat herself down at the table near the window,

homework spread in front of her, chin on hand. Little swot . . .
Of course! thought Alan, *that* would be what was keeping
Tommo! As a friend he had only one fault, which was that he
always did his homework before coming out in the evening.
Alan, on the other hand, never did; he copied his from Tommo
every morning on the bus.

'Makes you wonder how they'll sort themselves out on
Judgement Day, doesn't it?'

'What?' Alan scowled back, irritated. He had almost forgotten Alice was there. He wished she'd shove off.

'On Judgement Day,' she answered patiently, smiling at him
and patting the stone. 'You know—when the dead people rise
from their graves.'

Was she trying to throw a scare into him? Alan would show
her it wouldn't work.

'Yeah, very tricky,' he said. 'Be like trying to resurrect a tin
of sardines.'

And then, to show her how boring her conversation was, he
turned his back again.

'Hear about the accident?' she asked suddenly. Alan slouched
slowly back, unwilling to show he was interested; but he liked
accidents. He had once had the great pleasure of seeing a goods
train derailed.

'Somebody got run over,' Alice said. She leaned towards him
a little, her old face crafty. *I know something you don't know*, it
said. *Ask me*.

'Where?' He made the question a yawn.

'Supermarket. Car park. Young lad, it was.'

She sat back looking pleased with herself, and more cunning than ever; whatever it was she was so proud of knowing, she hadn't told all of it yet.

'Who?' asked Alan, really intrigued now.

She almost giggled.

'Don't know his name. He lived up there, though.' She nodded towards Church Road.

For a second Alan stood bewildered, and then he felt the hair on his scalp prickle and the blood draw slowly out of his cheeks. Tommo lived on Church Road, three doors down from him. They were the only boys on the street.

He whirled and ran towards the gates, and at the very moment he started to run through them he saw with inexpressible relief the bedroom light go on in Tommo's house, and Tommo himself come across to the window and draw the curtains shut. He looked preoccupied, almost sad, but very much alive. A wave of thankfulness swept over Alan; and then he became aware by a chuckle behind him that Old Alice was watching him closely, as if enjoying the effect of her Hallowe'en joke.

For a minute Alan stood without knowing what to say, and then he burst out with appalling and unusual rudeness.

'You toothless old bag! You don't know anything—you just make things up! You're crazy, you are. Everybody knows that. You walk around talking to people who aren't there. And you *stink*!'

For a second she sat facing him, rigid with shock, and then she got to her feet and, without a word, walked away from him down the hill, her two plastic shopping bags slurring and bumping along the ground as she went. Alan stared after her, alarmed by his own rudeness, but secretly comforted to think that being cheeky to Old Alice wasn't as risky as being cheeky to another adult. He could hardly imagine her knocking at his father's door to complain. Anyway—she had no right to go making up that lie about Tommo.

'You're just a smelly old liar!' he shouted after her for good measure. 'Crazy Alice, Crazy Alice!'

'And you're a fool!' she turned her face back over her shoulder, twisting to snarl at him. 'You didn't ask *when* it happened, did you? Two months ago it was!'

Alan laughed aloud.

'You're stupid,' he said. 'You're crazy! I've just seen him!'

Just as he thought she had really gone her voice floated up to him from the shadows at the foot of the hill.

'I shan't speak to you again, young man.'

'Who wants you to?' yelled Alan rudely, and giggled with nerves.

There was a baleful pause.

'You'll be glad of me to talk to, soon enough.'

He heard her slithering footsteps near the far gate and then a moment later saw her slow, bent old figure under the lights of the main road, heading for the town centre, creeping away like a fat old snail.

'Stupid old witch!' called Alan—but not too loudly, in case his father over the road heard him.

It was fully dark now; the last glow had gone from the sky. The birds had fallen quiet. Alan waited shivering under the porch light, wondering what to do. Maybe Tommo wasn't coming; maybe he'd got stuck with his homework. Perhaps they were getting too old for this game, anyway. Maybe it was time to go home.

At the thought of home Alan suddenly felt frozen stiff, lonely and tired. He started up the churchyard path again, towards the lights of his own front room where his sister was turning the page of her exercise book, flattening it down with her thumbnail . . . Coming here on Hallowe'en had been a silly idea. Tommo was right not to bother. He would tell him so in the morning.

The windblown wreath was lying on the path in front of his feet as he came to the gates and he stooped to throw it in the bin with the rest. There was a label attached to the dead flowers, the writing nearly washed away by the rain, but somehow it seemed familiar. Was that Tommo's writing? Alan screwed up his eyes and stared, but it took him a minute to puzzle out what it said.

To Alan, it said, *from Tommo. Best mates.*

The Strange Valley

T. V. OLSEN

The three horsemen came up on the brow of a hill, and the valley was below them. It was a broad cup filled by the brooding thickness of the prairie night. The light shed by a narrow sickle of moon picked out just another Dakota valley, about a mile across as the white men reckoned distance, and surrounded by a rim of treeless hills. The valley floor was covered by an ordinary growth of a few small oaks, a lot of brush, and some sandy flats with a sparse lacing of buffalo grass.

Young Elk said, 'Is this what you wish us to see, Blue Goose?' He made no effort to keep the scepticism from his voice.

'Yes,' said the rider on his left. 'This is the place.'

'Now that we're here, tell us again what you saw the other night.' The third youth, the shaman's son, sounded very intent. 'From where did it come?'

'From there.' Blue Goose leaned forward as he pointed towards the eastern end of the valley. 'As I told you, I'd had a long day of hunting, and I was very tired. I made my camp in the centre of the valley, and fell asleep at once. This was about sunset.

'It was long after dark when I woke. I came awake all at once, and I don't know why. I heard a strange sound, a kind of growl that was very low and steady, and it was a long way off. But it was running very fast in my direction, and I sat in my blanket and waited.'

Young Elk said with a grim smile, 'Because you were too afraid even to run.'

Blue Goose was silent for a moment. 'Yes,' he said honestly. 'I was afraid. I didn't know what the thing was, but I knew it was getting closer. And growling louder all the while, as if in great pain or anger. Then I saw it.

'It was a huge beast, as big as a small hill, black in the night and running very close to the ground, and its two eyes were yellow and glaring. It went past me very close, but so fast I didn't think it saw me. It was bellowing as loud as a hundred bull buffaloes if they all bellowed at once. Suddenly it was gone.'

'What do you mean, it was gone?' Young Elk demanded. 'You said that before.'

'I'm not sure. All I know is that suddenly I saw it no more and heard it no more.'

'I wish you could tell us more about it,' said the shaman's son. 'But I suppose it was very dark.'

'Yes,' Blue Goose agreed. 'Even a little darker than tonight.' He hesitated. 'I thought that the thing might be covered with scales—bright scales like a huge fish—since the moon seemed to glint on it here and there. But I couldn't be sure.'

'You're not very sure of anything,' Young Elk gibed.

Blue Goose sighed. 'I do not know what I saw. As I have said, I left the valley very fast and camped a long way off that night. But I came back in the morning. I looked for the thing's spoor. I looked all over, and there was nothing. Yet I found where I had camped, and my pony's tracks and my own. But the thing left no sign at all.'

'Because there had never been a thing. You should be more careful about what you eat, my friend.' Young Elk spoke very soberly, though he felt like laughing out loud. 'Spoiled meat in one's belly is like *mui waken*, the strong drink. It has a bad effect on the head.'

For a little while the three young Sioux sat their ponies in silence, looking down into the dark stillness of the valley. A silky wind pressed up from the valley floor, a wind warm with the summer night and full of the ripening smells of late summer.

But something in it held a faint chill, and that was strange. Young Elk felt a crawl of gooseflesh on his bare shoulders, and he thought: *The night is turning cold, that is all*. He felt the nervous tremor run through his mount.

He laid his hand on the pony's shoulder and spoke quietly to the animal. He was angry at Blue Goose, his best friend, for telling this foolish story and angry at himself for coming along tonight with the other two because he was deeply curious. And back in their camp only a few miles to the north there was firelight and laughter and a warm-eyed girl named Morning Teal, and Young Elk was a fool to be out here with his friend and with the son of that tired old faker of a medicine man.

Of late, Young Elk thought sourly, there had been more than the usual quota of wild stories of visions and bad spirits running rampant among the people. Early this same summer, on the river of the Greasy Grass that the whites called Little Big Horn, the long-haired General Custer had gone down to defeat and death with his troops. Many warriors of their own band had been among the twelve thousand Sioux, Cheyenne, and Arapaho who had helped in the annihilation of a hated enemy.

In the uneasy weeks since, as the people followed the buffalo, hunting and drying meat in the prospect of being driven back to the reservation by white cavalry, a rash of weird happenings were reported. Men who had died were seen walking the prairie with bloody arrows protruding from them. Voices of the dead were heard in the night wind. It was the shaman's part to encourage this sort of nonsense. A man claimed that a bluecoat soldier he had scalped appeared to him nightly with the blood still fresh on his head. The shaman chanted gibberish and told him to bury the scalp so that the ghost would trouble his nights no more.

Young Elk was disgusted. He had never seen even one of these spirits. Only the fools who believed in such things ever saw them.

The shaman's son broke the long pause, speaking quietly. 'This valley is a strange place. Today I spoke with my father and told him what Blue Goose has told us. He said that he knows of this place, and that his father's fathers knew of it too. Many strange things happened here in the old days. Men known to be long dead would be seen walking—not as spirits, but in the flesh. Still other things were seen, things too strange to be spoken of. Finally all our people of the *Lakotas* came to shun the valley. But that was so long ago that even most of the old ones have forgotten the stories.'

Young Elk made a rude chuckling sound with his tongue and teeth.

'Young Elk does not believe in such things,' the shaman's son observed. 'Why then did he come with us tonight?'

'Because otherwise for the next moon I would hear nothing from you and Blue Goose but mad stories about what you saw tonight. I'd prefer to see it for myself.'

'Oh,' said Blue Goose, 'then there *was* something? I did not make this great story out of the air?'

'Maybe not,' Young Elk said slyly. 'Maybe it was the white man's iron horse that Blue Goose saw.'

'Now you jest with me. Even though I am not all-wise like Young Elk, still I know that the iron horse of the *wasicun* runs on two shining rails, and there are no rails here. And the iron horse does not growl thus, nor does it have two eyes that flame in the dark.'

Another silence stretched among the three youths as they sat their ponies on the crest of the hill and peered down into the dark valley. And Young Elk thought angrily, *What is this?* They had come here to go down in the valley and wait in the night, in hopes that the thing Blue Goose had seen would make another appearance. Yet they all continued to sit here as though a winter of the spirit had descended and frozen them all to the spot.

Young Elk gave a rough laugh. 'Come on!' He kneed his pony forward, down the long grassy dip of hill. The others followed.

Near the bottom, Young Elk's pony turned suddenly skittish, and he had to fight the shying animal to bring him under control. Blue Goose and the shaman's son were having trouble with their mounts too.

'This is a bad omen,' panted the shaman's son. 'Maybe we had better go back.'

'No,' Young Elk said angrily, for his pony's behaviour and the strange feeling of the place were putting an edge on his temper. 'We've come this far, and now we'll see what there is to see, if anything. Where was Blue Goose when he thought he saw the beast?'

Blue Goose said, 'We must go this way,' and forced his horse through a heavy tangle of chokecherry brush. He led the way very quickly, as though afraid that his nerve would not hold much longer.

They came to a rather open stretch of sand flats that caught a pale glimmer of moonglow; it was studded with clumps of thicket and a few scrub oaks. 'Here is the place,' Blue Goose told them.

The three Sioux settled down to wait. Nobody suggested that it would be more comfortable to dismount. Somehow it seemed better to remain on their ponies and accept a cramp or two. It was only, Young Elk told himself, that they should be ready for anything, and they might have a sudden need of the ponies.

Once more it was the shaman's son who ended an interval of silence. 'What time of the night did it happen, Blue Goose?'

'I can't be sure. But close to this time, I think.'

Silence again. The ponies shuffled nervously. The wind hushed through some dead brush, which rattled like dry, hollow bird bones. Idly Young Elk slipped his throwing-axe from his belt and toyed with it. He slid his hand over the familiar shape of the flint head and the fresh thongs of green rawhide that lashed it to the new handle he had put on only this morning. His palm felt moist.

And his head felt slightly dizzy. Now the shapes of rocks, the black masses of brush, seemed to shimmer and swim; the landscape seemed misty and unreal as if seen through a veil of fog, yet there was no fog. *It is a trick of the moon*, Young Elk thought. He gripped the axe tighter; his knuckles began to ache.

'There!' Blue Goose whispered. 'Do you hear it?'

Young Elk snapped, 'I hear the wind,' but even as the words formed on his lips the sound was increasing, unmistakably not the wind. Not even a gale wind roaring through the treetops of a great forest made such a noise. As yet he could see nothing, but he knew that the sound was moving in their direction.

Suddenly the two yellow eyes of which Blue Goose had spoken came boring out of the night. Now he could see the hulking black shape of the monster running towards them at an incredible speed and so low to the ground that its legs could not be seen. All the while the strange humming roar it made was steadily growing.

The ponies were plunging and rearing with fear. The shaman's son gave a cry of pure panic and achieved enough control over his mount to kick it into a run. In a moment Blue Goose bolted after him.

Young Elk fought his terrified pony down and held the trembling animal steady, his own fear swallowed in an eagerness

to have a closer look at the thing. But he was not prepared for the fury of its rush as it bore down toward him. And its round, glaring eyes blinded him—he could see nothing beyond them.

It let out a piercing, horrible shriek as it neared him—it was hardly the length of three ponies away—and it seemed to hesitate. It hissed at him, a long gushing hiss, while the yellow eyes bathed him in their wicked glare.

Young Elk waited no longer. He lunged his pony in an angling run that carried him past the thing's blunt snout, and in that moment brought his arm back and flung the axe with all his strength. He heard it make a strange hollow boom, although he did not see it hit, and then he was racing on through the brush, straining low to his pony's withers, heedless of the tearing branches.

Young Elk did not slow down till he reached the end of the valley; then he looked back without stopping. There was no sign of the beast. The valley was deserted and quiet under the dim moonlight.

Young Elk crossed the rim of hills and caught up with his friends on the prairie beyond. 'Did you see it?' the shaman's son demanded eagerly.

'No. Its eyes blinded me. But I hit it with my axe.' Young Elk paused; his heart was pounding so fiercely in his chest he was afraid they would hear it, so he went quickly on, 'I heard the axe hit the thing. So it was not a ghost.'

'How do you know?' countered the shaman's son. 'Where did it go? Did you see?'

'No,' Young Elk said bitterly. 'It was very fast.'

'Let's go back to camp,' Blue Goose said. 'I don't care what the thing was. I do not want to think about it.'

Joe Kercheval had been dozing in his seat when his partner, Johnny Antelope, hit the brakes of the big truck and gave Joe a bad jolt. And then Joe nearly blew his stack when Johnny told him the reason he had slammed to an abrupt stop on this long, lonely highway in the middle of nowhere.

'I tell you, I saw him,' Johnny insisted as he started up again and drove on. 'A real old-time Sioux buck on a spotted pony. He was sitting on his nag right in the middle of the road, and I almost didn't stop in time. Then he came charging past the cab, and I saw him fling something—I think it was an axe—at the truck. I heard it hit. You were waking up just then—you must have heard it.'

'I heard a rock thrown up by the wheels hit somewheres against the trailer, that's all,' Joe said flatly. 'You been on the road too long, kid. You ought to lay off a few weeks, spend a little time with your relatives on the reservation.'

Johnny Antelope shook his head. 'I saw him, Joe. And then I didn't see him. I mean—I could swear he disappeared—simply vanished into thin air—just as he rode past the cab. Of course it was pretty dark . . .'

'Come off it. For a college-educated Indian, you get some pretty far-out notions. I've made this run a hundred times and I never seen any wild redskins with axes, spooks or for real.'

'You white men don't know it all, Joe. You're Johnny-come-latelies. This has been our country for a long, long time, and I could tell you some things . . .' Johnny paused, squinting through the windshield at the racing ribbon of highway unfolding in the tunnelling brightness of the headlights. 'I was just remembering. This is a stretch of land the Sioux have always shunned. There are all kinds of legends concerning it. I remember one story in particular my old grandaddy used to tell us kids—I guess he told it a hundred times or more . . .'

'Nuts on your grandaddy.'

Johnny Antelope smiled. 'Maybe you're right, at that. Old Blue Goose always did have quite an imagination.'

'So does his grandson.' Joe Kercheval cracked his knuckles. 'There's a turnoff just up ahead, kid. Swing around there.'

'What for, Joe?'

'We're going back to where you seen that wild man on a horse. I'm gonna prove to you all you seen was moonshine.' Joe paused, then added wryly, 'Seems like I got to prove it to myself, too. I say it was just a rock that hit the truck, and I'll be losin' sleep if I don't find out for sure.'

Without another word Johnny swung the big truck round and headed back east on the highway. The two truckers were silent until Johnny slowed and brought the truck to a shrieking stop. The air brakes were still hissing as he leaned from the window, pointing. 'Here's the spot, Joe. I recognize that twisted oak on the right.'

'OK, let's have a close look.' They climbed out of the cab, and Johnny pointed out the exact spot where he had first seen the Indian warrior, and where the warrior had cut off the highway alongside the cab and thrown his axe.

'Look here, kid.' Joe played his flashlight beam over the roadside. 'Soft shoulders. If your boy left the concrete right here, his horse would of tromped some mighty deep prints in the ground. Not a sign, see?'

'Wait a minute,' Johnny Antelope said. 'Flash that torch over here, Joe.' He stooped and picked up something from the sandy shoulder.

The halo of light touched the thing Johnny held in his out-stretched hand. 'Know what this is, Joe?' he asked softly. 'A Sioux throwing-axe.'

Joe swallowed. He started to snort. 'Nuts. So it's an axe . . .' but the words died on his lips.

For under the flashlight beam, even as the two men watched, the wooden handle of the axe was dissolving into rotted punk, and the leather fastenings were turning cracked and brittle, crumbling away. Only the stone blade remained in Johnny's hand, as old and flinty and weathered as if it had lain there by the road for an untold number of years . . .

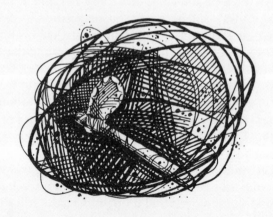

The Haunted Inn

SUSAN PRICE

This story is so true, you'll be told it in a dozen pubs. But I was told it in a pub called The Struggling Man.

A salesman came in one night, I was told, and said, 'Can you put me up?'

Before the landlord could say yes or no, one of the regulars leaned over and said, 'How about giving him the haunted room?'

The salesman, after a hard day's selling, was only in the mood for sleep. He said, 'This isn't another pub with a haunted room, is it?'

'What do you mean?' the landlord asked.

'Every pub I've stayed in had a haunted room,' said the salesman. 'I wish the breweries would think up a new advertising stunt. I'm sick of that one.'

The landlord was hurt. 'I beg your pardon, but my pub really is haunted.'

'What by?' asked the salesman. 'A grey lady? A green lady? A yellow-come-purple-with-orange-spots-lady? It always is a lady of one colour or another.'

'I've never seen it, so I don't know what it is,' said the landlord. 'And I don't want to see it neither, because I do know that whenever anybody's slept in that room, they've been raving screaming mad the next morning. That's why I never let anybody sleep in there.'

'Who told you all that?' the salesman asked.

'Well . . . The man who was landlord here before me.'

'And had *he* ever seen it?'

'Well, I don't know . . .'

''Course he hadn't,' said the salesman.

'You wouldn't catch me sleeping in that room, anyway,' said the regular.

'I would,' said the salesman. 'You want a bet?'

'Don't start that,' said the landlord. 'I've never let anybody sleep in there, and I'm not about to.'

But the regular said to the salesman. 'Will you still be here tomorrow night? I'll buy you a double if you sleep in that room tonight—with the door locked on the outside.'

'If I can search the room before the door's locked, you're on,' said the salesman. 'But I'm not so much green as cabbage-looking. You won't catch me out with tape-recordings of groans hidden in the wardrobe.'

'We won't need to bother with that kind of malarky if you're locked in the haunted room,' said the regular.

'Now I'm sorry to disappoint you gents,' said the landlord, 'but nobody is going to sleep in that room tonight or any other night.'

Everyone disagreed. The regular customers wanted the fun of the bet, and they wanted to see the salesman brought down a peg or two—and the salesman wanted to prove that there was no ghost and bring the locals down a peg or three. All of them badgered the landlord to let the haunted room to the salesman.

The landlord gave way. After all, it was the salesman's business if he wanted to sleep with a ghost, and maybe it was stupid to worry about ghosts in this day and age.

The landlord found the key of the haunted room and led the way upstairs. A lot of customers from the bar followed, as well as the salesman with his luggage. It was quite a crush.

The haunted room was at the back of the pub, at the end of a long and badly-lit corridor that smelt of dust and paint. By the time they reached it, they couldn't hear a sound from the bar, and even the people who'd followed them upstairs had gone quiet. The landlord opened the door and the salesman went in.

'A four-poster bed!' he cried, dropping his suitcase.

'Good, isn't it?' said the landlord. 'It's a hundred years old, you know.' He went over and drew the curtains.

'A four-poster bed in the haunted room!' said the salesman. 'You put it in here on purpose, to make the place look spookier!'

'I bet there's a good many died in that bed,' said the regular. 'Sleep tight!'

Everybody laughed.

'All out into the hall, while I search,' said the salesman, and shooed them out of the room. 'If there's a ghost, watch me find it!'

The regulars and the landlord stood on the landing and watched the salesman make a complete search of every possible hiding-place in the haunted room. He looked in the bed and under it; up the chimney; in the cupboards and the cupboard drawers; behind the curtains at the window, behind the door. He didn't find anything.

'OK, mugs,' he said. 'You can lock me in. I'll see you tomorrow night, and you can have a double whisky waiting for me.'

'Last chance to change your mind,' said the landlord.

The salesman said, 'Get away!' So the landlord locked the door from the outside, and took the key with him. He and his customers all went laughing down the corridor, back to the bar for some after-hours drinking. Once they'd gone, that part of the house was silent.

But the salesman was a man who really didn't believe in ghosts. He undressed and hung his clothes on hangers, brushing them carefully. He peeled off his wig and put it on his bedside table. He put on his pyjamas, put off the light and, in the dark, found his way to the four-poster bed.

A soft curtain brushed his face. The old bed creaked as he knelt on it and, as he rolled back the covers a warm, comfortable smell of clean sheets and blankets rose up. He lay on his side and covered himself, ready for sleep. Then, 'I'm glad we're locked in for the night,' said a voice at his ear.

In the morning, even the salesman's wig had turned white.

I wonder why the pub was called The Struggling Man?

The Fire Escape

ALISON PRINCE

Ever since they had come to this house, Lindsay had been lonely. This evening he stared out of his bedroom window at the bleak view below him. The early winter dusk was falling and the roar of rush-hour traffic drifted up from the streets. A few leaves still clung to the plane tree in the back garden but Lindsay could see between its branches to the landscape of roofs and chimneys which lay beyond the railway track.

Between the railway and the dilapidated fence at the end of the garden was an area of waste land. A fire was burning down there, and people were crouched round it. Not very many, four or five; perhaps. In the fading light, Lindsay could not be sure. He saw the gleam of a bottle as it was passed from one hand to another. The people were always there. Lindsay envied them. At least they had each other.

'Terrific potential,' Lindsay's father had said when they came to the tall, narrow London house. 'Lots of scope for improvement.' Lindsay missed the rambling cottage in Lincolnshire, and missed the friends he had made there. He could not get used to the idea that the house was sandwiched between two others, pressed tightly from either side like someone jammed in a crowded lift. His bedroom was at the top of the house so that, lying in bed, he could only see sky through the sash window. Beside it was a door which led out onto the fire escape.

The fire escape was black and spindly, zigzagging down the outside of the building like a folding foot rule in fancy dress. Lindsay liked it. He had chosen this room because of it. The iron treads were punched with a lattice of diamond-shaped holes and, looking down through them, the earth seemed a long way below. The rickety structure made a tremendous clanging noise if you ran down it quickly, and the whole thing quivered. Bits of rust kept falling off it. The concrete slab underneath it was stained a dark orange because of the rust and the rain.

Lindsay's mother hated the fire escape. 'It's so ugly,' she said. 'And so frightfully high up. I don't like the thought of Lindsay going out onto it from his room. Suppose there was an accident? I think we ought to keep that door locked.'

Lindsay's father had pointed out that emergency exit doors were useless unless they were open. 'Fire regulations,' he said pompously, and his wife did not argue. She never argued, but she sighed and shook her head whenever she saw Lindsay clattering down the iron steps.

A handbell clanged several times from downstairs. That would be tea, Lindsay thought. 'Coming!' he shouted, but without any hope of being heard. There were four floors between him and the basement kitchen which the family found the cosiest room in the house; that was why his mother had instituted the handbell. But the melancholy of the winter evening filled him with depression and he continued to lean his elbows on the window-sill, staring out at the flickering bonfire.

'Go along, Master William.'

The voice was close behind him, chiding and intimate. Lindsay jumped round. The room was empty. 'Who is it?' he whispered.

'Don't keep your mother waiting, there's a good boy.' It was a woman's voice, cosy and slightly lisping. The back of Lindsay's neck felt prickly. He stared round the empty room, telling himself that he was just excited, not really frightened. And anyway, being scared was better than being lonely. He cleared his throat bravely and asked, 'Are you a ghost?'

'Ask no questions and you'll be told no lies,' said the voice smugly. 'Now, run along or Nanny will be cross.'

'But I want to know,' Lindsay insisted. '*Are* you?'

There was silence in the room and the bell clanged again from downstairs. Lindsay waited, half fearing and half hoping to hear the voice of the unseen woman again—but the silence continued. He opened the door to the fire escape and went out.

There was a dull orange glow from the streets and in the gaps between houses he could see the traffic like a moving necklace of headlights. The fire still burned on the waste land and a shower of sparks flew up as someone threw on some more wood. Probably planks from their garden fence, Lindsay thought. His father was always grumbling about it. Lit by the leaping flames, the faces round the fire shone white, like skulls. Lindsay gave a shiver. He glanced over his shoulder at the dark window of his room, and shivered again. Then he ran down the iron steps to the kitchen.

'There's a ghost in my room!' he announced proudly. 'It was talking to me!' He was determined not to be afraid of it.

His mother, turning the crumpets on the grill, looked at him with a troubled frown. 'I know you're a bit lonely here,' she said, 'but you mustn't start imagining things.'

'But there *is*!' Lindsay insisted. His mother pursed her lips as she slid the grill pan back, and he felt his excitement contract inside him, tucking itself away like a small glow of light at the back of his mind. He gave a little sigh. 'I was only joking,' he said. He went to the bench seat beside the scrubbed pine table and sat down with his hands clenched between his knees, waiting for the crumpets to be done.

The next day, Lindsay brought Gary home after school. He was not sure that he liked Gary but his mother worried about him not making friends. Gary sat next to Lindsay in Art, where they shared a dislike of painting 'A Winter Scene', Lindsay because he considered the subject old-fashioned, and Gary because he thought it was soppy.

'You live in Arcot Street? That's where all them old meths drinkers hang out, innit?' said Gary, as he and Lindsay made their way back from the underground station.

'I had a model steam engine once,' said Lindsay, 'and that ran on meths. I didn't know you could drink it, though.'

'You can't,' said Gary. 'Drives you bonkers. The old down-and-outs drink it if they can't afford anything else. Let's go round the back and see if they're about. Always good for a laugh.'

'Mum will get into a tizz if I'm late,' said Lindsay rather feebly. He did not want to go round whatever back Gary had in mind, but he knew he must not appear to be a coward.

'Won't kill her to wait for ten minutes,' said Gary. 'Mine used to make an awful fuss but she got used to it. Come on.' He turned down a concrete alley beside a block of flats and broke into a run. Lindsay had to run as well, to keep up with him. The clatter of their footsteps rang back from the high concrete walls. They came out into a litter-strewn area of muddy grass flanked by the remains of wooden seats, most of whose slats had been torn off, and went through a gap in an old brick wall which looked as if it had once been part of something else. They came out on the waste land beside the railway.

'That's my house,' said Lindsay, pointing across to the un-familiar view of the back of the Georgian terrace. 'The one that hasn't been painted white or pink yet.'

'The one with the falling-down fence?' asked Gary.

'Yes,' said Lindsay. 'Dad says he'll mend it, but he wants to finish stripping the doors first.' He was suddenly rather enviously aware that Gary's parents would never dream of buying a house with terrific potential. He shifted his gaze. 'That's where they have their bonfire,' he said, 'over there beside that—' He stopped short, staring.

'Beside that heap of old rags?' Gary supplied. Then he, too, stared. 'Hang on,' he said, and began to pick his way forward across the rubble and broken bottles. Reluctantly, Lindsay followed. Then they both stopped.

'It isn't a pile of old rags,' Lindsay whispered.

'It's a gonner,' said Gary. 'A corpse. Cor, smashing.' But his voice was a little unsteady and he made no move to look more closely.

'It might be somebody ill,' reasoned Lindsay, trying to still the panic which had swept over him. He went a little closer. There was no movement from the inert figure beside the ashes of the burned-out bonfire. It lay on its side, knees drawn up under the old black overcoat, the arms crossed so that the hands were tucked between the coat and its sleeves for warmth. A man's felt hat, dark and greasy, covered part of the face but Lindsay saw with horror that the skin was puckered and scarred. Most of the nose had at some time been burned away, leaving the nostril as a dark, gaping hole. The scarred chin was beardless and long, grey hair straggled over the hunched shoulders.

'It's a woman,' said Lindsay. In horrified fascination, he bent over the still body. It smelt like the stale reek which came up from the pub cellar when the doors on the pavement were open to let the men lower new barrels into it, but dirty as well, musty and sharp. Then Lindsay gasped. An eye had opened in the puckered, grimy face. Black and malevolent, it glared up at him as the toothless mouth clamped shut then opened again as if it was thirsty. Lindsay jumped back.

'What is it?' asked Gary, who had been watching from a safe distance.

'She's alive!' said Lindsay, and they both ran as if the old woman was a bomb which might go off at any moment.

'This way!' gasped Lindsay, veering aside to make for the fence at the bottom of his garden. They ducked through the gaps left by the missing planks, pelted across the over-grown grass and down the short flight of stone steps under the fire escape, and burst into the kitchen.

'Goodness!' said Lindsay's mother, looking up from her ironing board. 'What on earth's the matter?'

'Nothing,' panted Lindsay, trying to look casual.

'Just had a race,' said Gary. He grinned at Lindsay sheepishly and Lindsay grinned back, knowing that Gary, too, was wondering why they had taken to their heels in such panic. The woman was only an old down-and-out. She couldn't hurt them. And yet, in that moment when Lindsay had found himself looked at by the beady black eye, so horribly alive in the ugly face, he had been terrified.

'Why don't you two go and play upstairs?' suggested Lindsay's mother. 'Just while I finish the ironing. I was getting quite worried about you, being so late back, but it's nice you've found a friend. Can you stay for tea . . . er . . . er . . . I don't know your name, do I?'

'Gary,' said Gary. 'Yes, please. Smashing.'

Lindsay took Gary up the fire escape to his room, despite a pained glance from his mother. He could tell by the way Gary stamped up the iron treads that he liked it.

'Here we are,' said Lindsay. He opened the door to his room and switched on the light.

'Great,' said Gary. He glanced round at the faded wallpaper and the iron fire surround with a gas fire behind a brass fender. 'Bit old-fashioned, innit?' he asked.

'My parents like old-fashioned things,' said Lindsay defensively.

Gary grinned. 'I seen a play on telly where there was a room like this. About a kid who had a nanny what hit him with a slipper. Right old bat she was. Skinny. Wore a black dress with buttons down the front.'

'Oh, yes,' agreed Lindsay. 'There's one of those here.'

'Whatcher mean?' asked Gary.

Lindsay blushed. It had been a silly thing to say. 'I mean, I expect there was,' he said quickly. 'You could imagine there was.'

'Yeah,' said Gary. He grinned again. 'What about the old bird out there, then? Gave you a turn, didn't she?'

'I like that!' protested Lindsay. 'You didn't even come close enough to look!'

'Them old dossers can get quite nasty,' said Gary with dignity. 'If you got any sense, you don't get near enough so's they can grab you.' He embarked on a long series of tales about dossers and their habits and Lindsay listened, fascinated. Like a small pain, the thought of the woman in a black dress nagged at him. She was not skinny, as Gary had said. He had seen her last night when he was in bed, just dozing off to sleep, and she was quite fat. She had thick wrists. But then, Gary had only seen some silly television programme; he couldn't be expected to know. Lindsay toyed briefly with the idea of telling Gary about it, and decided not to. Gary would laugh.

Lindsay's father moved the blowlamp flame slowly down a cream-painted door panel. 'Time you were in bed,' he said without looking round.

Lindsay didn't answer. He had been thinking hard since tea. 'Yes, run along, dear,' said his mother.

'Actually,' Lindsay ventured, 'I was going to ask if I could swap my bedroom.'

'Not *now*?' enquired his mother, pained.

'Some time,' said Lindsay. 'If I could just—swap.'

The scraper gave a long, shrill squeal as Lindsay's father shaved off the newly-blistered paint. 'You made your choice,' he said. 'Now stick to it.' He applied the blowlamp to the next area of paint.

'But—' began Lindsay.

'You heard what your father said,' his mother reproved him. 'Now, off you go. And not up the fire escape.'

Lindsay reluctantly did as he was told. There was a kind of mounting dread about going up the lino-clad stairs. The brass edgings with their worn criss-cross grooves were somehow sinister, and so was the dark wallpaper, although its pattern of brown leaves was interrupted by stark white streaks where the new wiring had been chanelled into the walls. He wished he had not brought Gary home. The casual reference to a woman in a black dress had brought the strange presence in Lindsay's bedroom a big step further forward. It was as though, without realizing it, Gary too had known that the woman was there. Until now, Lindsay had been able to persuade himself that it had just been a dream last night. But it had seemed so real. The owner of the cosy voice was a solid, bulky woman; and yet there had been something different about her. Underlying the cosiness was something impatient and angry. Something frightening.

Lindsay sat on his bed and glared round at the mauve-striped wallpaper with its knots of roses. 'You just stay away,' he said fiercely. 'Do you hear?' And in the same instant he tingled with shame, as if he had been slapped for his cheekiness.

He got up defiantly and went to the window. He was aware that the unseen presence was watching him but he tried to look casual. Down on the waste land, the fire burned. Lindsay thought of the woman who looked like a pile of rags and remembered the toothless mouth in the scarred face, and the black, accusing eye. He shuddered. And behind him, close enough to make the hair on his scalp crawl, there was a dry, unpleasant chuckle. He would not let himself turn round. If she was there, he did not want to see her. But at last the feeling that he was not alone overwhelmed him and he spun round with a gasp of terror. The mauve-striped wallpaper mocked him with its emptiness.

Lindsay tried to stay awake that night. He stared with prickling, wide-open eyes at the ceiling, where a faint shifting of the light reminded him that the bonfire still burned. It's all right, he thought determinedly. I'm still awake. She can't come. She only comes when I'm dropping off to sleep. But the comfort of that thought brought with it a warm, fatal relaxation and the hands were there before him, clasped in front of the black, silky fabric, smug and white and threatening. The voice was as quiet as a confidential whisper. 'Master William,' it said, 'you were a wicked boy today. You disturbed me.'

Lindsay wanted to protest that he was not William, that it was all wrong. But he could make no sound. He stared at the hands and at the thick wrists tightly buttoned into the black sleeves. The line of small black buttons led up the bodice to the high collar, the roll of fat under the chin, the mouth clamped into a sagging line. And the black eyes stared down at him with the same hatred which had sent him running across the waste land that very afternoon.

'See what has become of me,' whispered the woman. 'I lost my position, Master William. All because of you.'

No, shouted Lindsay, you've got it wrong. But he made no sound.

'A little bit of comfort,' the lisping voice went on. 'That's all I wanted. But you had to interfere, Master William. You had to spoil it all.'

Lindsay shrank down in his bed and covered his face with his hands. The sleeves of his pyjamas felt tight on his wrists and he fingered a cuff cautiously, unable to understand what had happened. His curiosity overcame his fear and he opened his eyes. He found that he was wearing a white nightshirt, the full sleeves gathered into tight cuffs. This must be a dream, he told himself. But it did not feel like a dream.

Stealthily, he pulled the sheet down a little so that he could see out. The table beside his bed, usually bare except for his books and his alarm clock, was covered by a dark green chenille cloth with a fringe of bobbles round the edge. On it stood a brass oil lamp, burning with a steady yellow flame. Across the room, the woman in a black dress sat by the coal fire in a rocking chair which creaked rhythmically as she rocked to and fro, humming to herself. She held a small glass in her hand and a bottle stood in the fireplace, its neck just visible above the brass fender. She drained the contents of the glass and reached forward for the bottle, glancing across at the bed as she did so. She frowned when she saw the boy watching her.

Instinctively, Lindsay flinched at the scrutiny of the black eyes, remembering with someone else's mind that he had been savagely punished on previous occasions for seeing what he was not supposed to see. Once again, he covered his face with his hands.

'We going to have another look at the old dossers, then?' asked Gary after school the next day.

'No, we're not,' said Lindsay promptly. 'And you can't come home to tea today because Mum says I've got to go with her to get some new shoes.'

'OK,' said Gary easily. 'Didn't ask, did I? Might as well go home your way, though.' He whistled loudly after a girl in high heels, and Lindsay blushed.

There was a shop on the corner of Arcot Street with milk crates stacked on the pavement outside it, and a litter bin overflowing with empty cans. Gary casually picked a Coke can out of the bin and tossed it ahead of him to kick noisily along the pavement. Lindsay ran to get a kick in as well and they made their way cheerfully down Arcot Street, pushing and barging at each other to get a turn in at kicking the can.

'Hey!' said Gary suddenly. 'Look!'

Ahead of them, a shapeless figure in a dirty black overcoat shuffled along the pavement. Grey hair straggled from under the battered hat and the bare, mauve-blotched legs ended in a gaping pair of army boots with no laces.

Lindsay stopped. 'It's her,' he said.

Gary grabbed the can, took a couple of quick steps and drop-kicked it at the shuffling figure. It hit the woman a glancing blow on the shoulder. She turned with surprising speed and let loose a stream of invective. Lindsay did not understand most of the words she used but their intention was unmistakable. The old woman shook her fist in a passion of hatred and her face, contorted with loathing, was the face of Lindsay's waking dream.

Gary indicated Lindsay with a cheerful jerk of his thumb and shouted, 'He was the one what done it!'

'It wasn't!' protested Lindsay. He started to tell Gary what he thought of this calumny but the old woman stopped swearing and took a couple of purposeful steps towards them. Her black eyes blazed with fury.

'Come on!' said Gary, and took to his heels. It seemed an age to Lindsay before he could tear his gaze away from the black eyes. His feet felt leaden as he tried to run and each step was a painful jolt which clanged in his brain like the echo from high walls.

Lindsay left his light on that night, but his father came in and switched it off. 'No need to have the place lit up like the Blackpool illuminations,' he said. 'Costing me enough as it is, what with gas for the blowlamp . . .' He went grumbling out.

In the dark, Lindsay lay with his fists clenched and his eyes wide open. The nameless threat seethed all round him as the light from the bonfire flickered faintly on the ceiling. I didn't do it, he said silently. I didn't throw the can. Honest. But he knew it was no good.

He stayed awake for a long time, lying as rigidly as a soldier at attention. He heard his parents go to bed in their room below his, and after a while he heard the click of their light being turned out. He ached from lying so stiffly on his back, and turned on his side to be more comfortable. It was much better like that. Warm . . .

'So, Master William,' whispered the voice, very close to him. 'The wicked must be punished, must they not?' One plump finger tapped implacably on the back of the other hand.

'Please,' Lindsay begged. 'I didn't do it. I didn't.'

The plump fingers reached out and gripped him by the ear, twisting it mercilessly until he cried out with pain. Somewhere, a part of his mind was angry that he could make no sound. And then he was awake again, staring at the light on the ceiling. His ear was throbbing. I shouldn't have let myself go to sleep, he thought.

The light on the ceiling was concentrated in a circle, he noticed, a warm, yellow glow, much closer than the dim flicker

of the bonfire. It was the light of an oil lamp. Oh, no. Horror flushed through his veins like cold water. He was awake; he was sure he was awake. But he was in the room of his dreams. Somebody was singing; a tuneless, moody song accompanied by the regular creak of the rocking chair.

Furtively, Lindsay looked out. The woman clasped the bottle to the tight black silk of her bosom as she rocked by the fire. Her head turned restlessly from side to side against the back of the chair; her hair was escaping from its pins and dangled in grey-streaked locks across her shoulder. Her unfocused gaze met Lindsay's and the black eyes were suddenly sharp. She stopped singing. She got up from the chair, lurched a little then recovered herself and advanced towards the bed, the bottle dangling by its neck from one hand.

'I told you before,' she said thickly, 'little boys who pry come to a bad end. My bit of comfort—nothing to do with you. You hear?' With her free hand, she shook Lindsay by the shoulder, digging her nails into his skin.

'Don't,' he begged. 'You're hurting.' And as he spoke, he knew he was awake, for he could hear his own words.

'You must be punished,' she said. 'Nobody will hear if you scream. Your parents are out. I am in charge of you.'

'They're not out,' said Lindsay bravely. 'They're in bed. I heard them put their light out.' He sat up and pushed the bed-clothes back.

'We are not going to be silly, are we, Master William?' said the woman through tight lips. She stared at Lindsay until he subsided back on to the pillows, then, still looking at him, raised the bottle to her lips. She tilted her head back to drink, closing her eyes.

Lindsay seized his opportunity. He jumped out of bed and ran to the door. It would not open. He grappled desperately with the handle and heard the swish of silk as the woman came up behind him. Her fingers gripped him just above the elbow in a knowing pressure which made him scream out with the pain of it. But the scream was loud and real, and it was music in his ears. Despite the nightshirt he was wearing, despite the frowsty immediacy of the room and the coal fire burning in the grate, despite the awful presence of the woman, he was Lindsay and his real life was not this one. He wriggled round in the woman's grasp and kicked her hard on the shins.

'Ow!' she shrieked. 'You little devil!'

'Mummy!' yelled Lindsay. 'Daddy! Come up here, quickly! *Mummy!*'

The woman swung the bottle at him viciously but Lindsay ducked away, grabbing the bottle and twisting it out of her grasp. She swore at him and seized a handful of his hair. Lindsay's eyes watered with pain. He hurled the bottle into the fireplace so as to have both hands free to fend the woman off.

The bottle hit the edge of the grate and splintered into pieces. The woman gave a shriek of fury, released Lindsay and rushed to the fireplace just as flame broke out from the spilt spirit, licking across the fender. The woman swung round to scream abuse at Lindsay and the skirt of her black dress swirled out across the path of the flame. The silk flared up with terrifying speed.

Somebody was rattling at the door handle. The woman's dress was engulfed in flame. She beat at it with her hands, uselessly. Lindsay saw that the hearth rug was smouldering. The whole place was going to catch fire. And the door was locked. She probably had the key. Lindsay ran to the fire escape door and flung it open. The woman was close behind him, a human bonfire determined to engulf him in her flames. She grabbed him by the back of his nightshirt. He turned and pushed her away with all his strength. The black, burning, reeking weight of her body was impossibly heavy. 'No, Master William!' she shouted. 'You are coming with me!'

Lindsay found the outside wall of the house at his back, rough and cold and real. He leaned hard against it, thrusting the awful bulk of the woman away with a foot as well as both hands. There was a creaking, rending sound—and suddenly the weight fell away from him, down into the night air.

Lindsay stood on the iron platform at the top of the fire escape in his pyjamas, panting. And somebody panted beside him.

In cold terror, Lindsay turned his head. But it was somebody his own size who stood beside him, and it was a boy's voice which said, 'Thank you very much!' Brown eyes smiled into his, and dark hair curled over the high collar of the nightshirt. 'I've been stuck with that old horror for years,' the boy went on. 'And you've let me escape. *Thank* you.'

'You're William!' said Lindsay in astonishment.

''Sright!' said William. They grinned at each other. The rail in front of them gaped away into space, grotesquely twisted outwards. Then Lindsay heard footsteps running up towards him, and felt the iron platform quiver under his feet. Was it the woman? He shrank back into his room. William had gone. It was dark. There was no fire, no oil lamp. He switched on the light and clenched his fists, waiting.

'Good God!' said the voice outside. 'Look at that rail!' It was Lindsay's father.

Lindsay sat down on his bed and began to shiver. His father came into the room, his face almost comic in its consternation. 'Why on earth did you lock the door?' he demanded. Lindsay's mother pushed past her husband. 'Oh, darling, are you all right?' she asked, running across to kneel beside Lindsay. 'Whatever happened?'

Lindsay felt terribly cold. 'Did you see her?' he asked. His parents glanced at each other. 'The woman in a black dress,' Lindsay persisted. 'She caught fire.'

'Nothing to do with fire, old chap,' said his father gently. 'The rail gave way on the fire escape and she fell through. She's—she's down there.'

'Is she dead?' asked Lindsay. Again, his parents looked at each other uneasily. '*Is* she?' demanded Lindsay.

'Yes, darling,' said his mother. 'I'm afraid she is.'

Lindsay nodded. 'That's what I thought,' he said. He fished under his bed for his slippers and put them on, then went across to the door to take his dressing-gown off the hook. A thought occurred to him and he tried the handle. The door opened. 'It wasn't locked,' he said calmly as he put on his dressing-gown.

'It jolly well was!' said his father hotly. His wife put out a restraining hand. 'Lindsay, what are you going to do?' she asked as her son tied his dressing-gown cord firmly and pushed his hands into his pockets.

'I'm going to look,' said Lindsay, and made determinedly for the fire escape. His mother gave a shriek of dismay. 'The rail! Oh, do come away!'

'It's all right,' Lindsay assured her as he started down the iron steps. He smiled to himself as he made his way down in the cold night air. A little thing like a broken rail was nothing to be afraid of. Beside him, William smiled as well.

The body huddled on the concrete slab looked at first glance like a pile of rags. The light from the basement kitchen shone across the putty-coloured face and the out-flung hands. The toothless mouth gaped and the grey hair straggled into a still-spreading pool of blood. Lindsay stooped and gazed steadily into the open black eye. It stared at nothing and its spark of hatred was gone.

William gave a little sigh of relief and Lindsay felt a surge of happiness. Then, quite unexpectedly, there came a kind of anguish for the crumpled body which had been a person and, more, for whatever nameless thing had made that person so terrible. He found that he was crying. William crouched beside him, his face anxious. 'It's all right,' he said. 'It isn't your fault, you see. You're just the person who had to do it.'

Lindsay's mother swept him into the kitchen, wrapped him in a blanket and sat him by the Aga while her husband phoned the police.

They had to bring the body through the terraced house to reach the ambulance standing at the front door. Lindsay glanced at the shapeless heap under the red blanket as the men carried the stretcher through. William waved goodbye to it and Lindsay smiled into his cocoa. His mother looked at him curiously. 'I . . . I was just thinking what Gary will say,' he invented rather wildly.

'Yes, quite a story to tell him,' said his mother. 'I'm so glad you're making friends.'

Lindsay nodded dutifully and smiled again. His friend was not Gary.

The policeman who had been talking to Lindsay's father closed his notebook and stood up. 'That's all we need for now,' he said. 'Thank you very much for your co-operation. And for the cocoa.'

'Who was she?' asked Lindsay's mother. 'Have you any idea?'

The policeman smiled briefly as he buttoned his notebook into his tunic pocket. 'The ambulance chaps know her of old,' he said. 'Been brought in drunk countless times. Sarah Hodden. Old Sal, they called her. She used to work in this house, you know—donkey's years ago. She was a nanny. But the parents came home one night to find the place in flames. The little chap she looked after was screaming blue murder. He blurted out some story about there being a struggle, but he was very badly burned. He died a few days later.'

'How awful!' said Lindsay's mother. William made a face at Lindsay and shrugged cheerfully.

'Pity it wasn't the old woman who died,' said Lindsay's father. 'It would have saved everyone a lot of trouble.'

'I don't think she ever worked again,' said the policeman. 'The fire left her face in a mess—enough to give any kid nightmares. She just became a down-and-out.'

'Certainly not the sort of person you'd employ as a nanny,' Lindsay's father agreed. He glanced at his wife but she was frowning inattentively.

'I can't think why she came back,' she said.

'Trying to burgle the place, I expect,' said Lindsay's father. 'But thanks to Lindsay scaring her off, she didn't get away with it. Not that I'd wish such a ghastly accident on anyone,' he added hastily.

'I think it's rather sad,' said Lindsay's mother. 'Poor old thing—perhaps she was wandering in her mind and thought the little boy was still here. She might have seen Lindsay and confused him with the boy she used to look after. I wonder what his name was.'

'William,' said Lindsay.

Everyone looked at him and William said: 'You are a twit, Lindsay.'

'I mean,' Lindsay amended quickly, 'it *might* have been William.' He yawned in an off-hand sort of way.

'Back to bed,' said his mother firmly. She turned to her husband and added, 'We *can* let him change his bedroom tomorrow, can't we? After what happened tonight—'

'Of course we can,' said Lindsay's father benevolently. 'That's the great thing about a house like this, there's plenty of room. Stacks of potential.'

Lindsay shook his head. 'Oh, no,' he said. 'It's quite all right now. I like that room, really I do.'

William nodded. 'So do I,' he said.

Lindsay smiled as they all stared at him dubiously. They were so funny, looking through William as if he wasn't there. 'I'll go to bed now,' he told them, and opened the door to the hall. He wouldn't suggest going up the fire escape. Not tonight. They would only be upset.

He smiled again at their puzzled faces and closed the door gently behind him. Then he started up the lino-covered stairs, whistling. His shadow zigzagged across the brown leaves on the wallpaper. William, whistling beside him noisily, cast no shadow, but he grinned at Lindsay as they reached the first floor and started up the next flight of stairs. 'Race you!' he said, and they pelted side by side up through the narrow house to the empty, welcoming bedroom.

With
Vacant Possession

ROBERT SCOTT

She pushed open the gate and crunched up the drive between massed hydrangeas. The house was smaller than she had expected, old certainly, and—withdrawn. She felt that it had regarded her first appearance with mild interest, weighed her up as she approached, then dismissed her, indifferent, unconcerned.

The door opened as she walked up to it but did not, she thought, welcome her presence. She looked round the large hall—solid old furniture lovingly polished, fine pictures, brassware, silver—and turned to the first door she saw. As she reached for the knob (flowered porcelain with a delicate finger-plate above) she was suddenly overwhelmed by fear, by the sense, the certainty, that someone—some thing—stood behind her silently watching, threatening. She turned, panicking, and—woke up.

That was her first visit. Over the months that followed the dream returned, each time more distressing, more stifling. Sometimes it came on successive nights, sometimes after an interval of several weeks, but it always started in the same way: the wrought-iron gates with the initials—*her* initials—worked into them, the drive, the opening door. Always it ended with the conviction that if, turning, she were to see what stood so threateningly close behind her she would be lost, imprisoned forever in her nightmare. Yet each time, as she turned, she woke: shivering, gasping, terrified, but free still. What it was that so nearly claimed her each time she could not decide.

Not everything was the same. Time passed. The hydrangeas faded; the sycamores shed their leaves; rain soaked the lawns, though not her; frost, then snow, covered the drive. And she explored the house: sitting room, drawing room, library, kitchen, the wide oak staircase, bedrooms, attics. Each time a little more and each time with greater longing, a longing to be welcomed, to possess the house even though it barely tolerated her. What would happen, she wondered, when she had been everywhere, seen everything? The time couldn't be far away. Would the house then dismiss her and the dreams stop? Would she turn and finally see that cold, hard presence standing always just behind her? And what then?

It was a year or so after the dreams started that she saw the house itself. On a frustrating drive through unfamiliar lanes to visit friends who had just moved to the country, she caught a glimpse of the gates and braked hard, dangerously. The car skidded on to the verge as she tried desperately to meet the next bend, swung round, rolled, and ended in the ditch horn and alarm blaring. The windscreen crazed before her eyes.

When she recovered her senses she found that she was already half out of the car, held only by her seat belt. She struggled free and pulled herself back up to the road. Headache—a violent headache—blood from somewhere, clothes torn and stained but nothing else, nothing worse. As the horn and alarm continued to clamour for attention, she made her way back along the road to the gates. Help, she thought, they must help. And behind this urgency another, quieter, voice was insisting that now at last she would find out about the house. Now, at last, she would know.

The notice attached to the pillar by the gate was certainly not part of her dream. The house was for *sale*. But, as she pushed open the wrought-iron gates—gates with her initials worked into them!—and crunched up the drive between massed hydrangeas, she had the odd, discordant feeling that everything was quite, quite unreal. Soon it would all disappear and she would, indeed, wake up.

There was the wail of an approaching siren as she hesitated, looking at the house. It seemed larger than she remembered, old certainly, and—inviting. She felt that it had regarded her first appearance with some interest, weighed her up as she stood before it, then recognized and welcomed her. The lane beyond the gates was suddenly silent.

The door opened invitingly as she walked up to it. She looked round the large hall, expecting the familiar furniture, pictures, brassware, silver—but it was empty. She turned to the first door, hand outstretched already, and saw him there, tall, gaunt, and cold, watching her grimly.

'Well?' he said. 'Are you satisfied?'

What was he talking about? She let go the breath she had been holding without realizing and began to relax. Forbidding he might be, but at least he was human. Her dreams had led her to imagine some ghastly monster who would claw her to pieces, but now . . .

The accident. She needed help. She opened her mouth to ask him to—but he cut in:

'You can give someone else the pleasure of your company now. If there's anyone foolish enough to buy the place—which I doubt—you can haunt *them*.'

He crossed to the door and nodded curtly at her. Before he closed it, closed it and locked it, locked her in, she caught a glimpse of the ambulance passing the gate, its siren wailing.

Love Letters

LAURENCE STAIG

G reg Slope smiled, or as near as he could get to a smile; not quite a sneer—but close. Angie hugged her books more tightly, whilst glancing from side to side. She bit her lip so hard it almost bled.

'So come on then,' she said after a moment, 'are we meeting later or not?'

His grin collapsed and a hardness entered his eyes. She backed off as he looked her up and down, tapping his fingers on the wall.

'Probably not. I thought I might surf a little on the Net, see if anyone has left me any e-mail. Just chill out—play a computer game. I mean, is that *all right with you*?'

His eyes met hers as he almost spat out the end of his sentence. He pushed his face towards her and her pulse quickened in response. Angie looked at the floor.

'Sure, I only asked so that I could sort out my evening, that was all. I have a life, you know. No big deal, really.'

'No, you're right there, it is *no big deal*.'

Greg turned on his heels, pulled his Red Sox baseball cap further down onto his forehead and made his way to the new block.

'It's just that . . .' she called after him, realizing it was a mistake to continue, even as the words left her mouth. He glanced over his shoulder, keeping his back towards her.

'Just *what*?' His back stiffened—if he were a cat it would have arched. Any moment now and fur might fly.

She weakened. 'It's just that all you seem to do these days is mess about with those machines. Surf! I thought you wanted to go out with me—I'm flesh and blood. I have feelings, you know. Perhaps you'd rather go out with a box of micro-chips!'

'I find the machine . . . shall we just say—more interesting. We speak the same language. The machine—as you call it—is more fun.'

He laughed, and continued on his way. She was lucky; he had kept his temper. Angie watched him dance his way along the path. He was very much aware that everyone else must be watching him. From across the green, Jane Garrat and her friends gave him a wave. He lifted his cap and tossed his fringe away from his eyes as though he were a catwalk model. Their faces shone with delight, Jane almost collapsing into a girlish giggle. After all, 'Mr Lurve' himself had responded. Angie sighed.

'I don't know why you bother,' said a voice.

There was a moment of silence.

Angie didn't turn, she knew very well who it was. Myra always badgered her about him.

'I know,' she said quietly.

'You're worth more,' the voice continued. 'He's a big-headed bully, a braggart. You've got brains and savvy, come on! He thinks he's *so* cool, he wouldn't know how to ask a polar bear out and you know it. In fact, let's face it, he wouldn't know a relationship if it bit him on the backside!'

Angie laughed. Myra looked up at her with her big eyes, but she didn't smile.

'I *know*,' she said again, in a 'faraway' voice. 'But he's still a dreamboat, you've got to hand it to him.'

'Dreamboat! More like the *Titanic*! He's got a nasty temper . . . which reminds me—how's your eye?' Myra's face remained serious. 'He used to go out with Jenny Gee. Stories go around that . . .'

'Gossip,' said Angie sharply. 'And my eye's fine, thank you.'

'Yeah—walked into a door, didn't you. I bet he's sniffing around in Reilly's Computer Club, I bet that's why he spends all his time there. I bet he's looking for someone new to mess up!'

'No,' said Angie thoughtfully. 'I overhead Mr Reilly talking to another teacher. He thinks Greg is good at this computer stuff and that's why he goes.'

Myra sighed and linked her arm through her friend's. It infuriated her that Angie always gave him the benefit of the doubt. They watched 'Mr Lurve' turn the corner of the Science Block.

Greg stopped as he approached the bright brick-red of the new buildings. He heard the cries of the black crows above him. They swooped like hooded assassins and landed on the green with an ungainly stance. A nearby pair turned and squawked at him, their beaks huge and seemingly hungry.

'Go away,' he called. 'Ugly things—get out of here!'

It suddenly occurred to him that there was nobody else around. The birds had begun to visit recently for no apparent reason, ever since the new block had been completed. The students had been told that it was because of the building work, and the new landscaping of the grounds. New fresh worms and other goodies were easy picking and they would go away eventually. He still didn't like them, and he was certain they watched him. Dark hooded things.

Ahead of Greg were the swing doors that led through to the computer laboratory. The round windows looked like dead soulless eyes. As usual he felt uncomfortable and that fact annoyed him because he didn't know why. It was something about the place. He couldn't put his finger on it, and he had certainly never spoken to other kids about his feelings. After all, he had his image to consider. Despite an early summer breeze, he felt a chill. He'd better hurry. There would be company in Reilly's Computer Club, even if a high percentage were trainspotting techno-headed nerds. It was the most popular Twilight Class of them all, and Reilly thought Greg was the best in the group.

'That new girl,' he whispered to himself suddenly. *She* might be there. She was interested in computers and had even written her own programs.

'Yeah,' he smiled to himself. 'Go for it. Stuff Angie Walters. Give me a cyber-chick any day.'

He braced himself and walked through the swing doors. The silence closed behind him like the sudden pull of a shade.

The new science block had quickly gained a reputation as a strange place even before the computer laboratory was completed. During the construction it was somehow a place to avoid. Builders had complained about feeling uneasy there, and according to one story a groundworks team had refused to continue unless their wages were increased. There was even a rumour that the police had visited the Principal about something to do with the place. But nobody knew what, although the visit had fuelled weird stories. One builder had found part of an old font, and someone said that a chapel had stood there once. But it was a long time ago.

Greg listened to his footfalls as they echoed on the shiny red tiles. He was late, that was why he was alone. The dark tunnel of grey which connected the buildings seemed longer than usual. The white conduit piping that ran along the ceiling reminded him again of milky veins, of something which pumped life rather than simply electrical lines and computer network cables. They had installed the best, the very latest in fibre optics, and the special in-line ran beneath the ground. Neat and tidy. For a moment he glanced away: no, not veins—bleached bone. He caught his breath, wondering why the idea had suddenly entered his head. *Bloody bones.* His eyes flickered from side to side.

Slowly, he proceeded to the end of the corridor. Through the glass window of the door he could see the other students at their computer stations. Reilly, the computer teacher, eccentrically bounced from one computer to the other, busily advising students through his enormous grey moustache.

'Nutter,' said Greg, catching Reilly's eye. He could hear his own breathing. The silence was going to press in on him. He opened the door.

The room had been filled with the hum of electricity, the whirring of cooling fans and disk drives, the click-clack of busy fingers on keyboards; only a few voices echoed across the room along with the jovial encouragement of Mr Reilly. Greg Slope's appearance at the door removed the human input at a stroke. There were a couple of dozen students this evening, some familiar faces and several he didn't know. Mr Reilly stared at him, frozen mid-crouch beside a computer bench. Then he spoke up.

'Why, Greg! Come on in. I wondered where you had got to.'

Greg Slope moved forward and looked towards the corner of the room where he usually worked. A short, plump girl whom he had never seen before sat at his computer, *in his place*. For a moment he glared at her.

'Oh, don't you worry now,' said Reilly suddenly, noticing Greg's stare. 'We've another machine just as good. That's young Mary in your usual spot, just for now.'

Mr Reilly was quick to move across the room to defuse the situation. With the grace of a waiter showing a customer to a 'better' table, he ushered Greg to another machine by the door.

'We're networked here, my boy,' said Mr Reilly. 'Doesn't really matter where you sit, now does it.'

For a moment the room went quiet once again. But Greg smiled a shark smile as Mr Reilly eased him into the chair.

Greg sat down without a word and powered up the computer. For a moment he felt uncomfortable. This machine was in an open space and he felt vulnerable. At his usual machine— *his place* for goodness' sake—he could work within shadows. He could surf with some privacy, seeking out secret corners of the Net, giving good verbo to anyone who took his fancy anywhere in the world, frightening the life out of those who had crossed him, stroking and encouraging those he liked the sound of.

No sooner had he settled down, when a bright light flashed to his right. He glanced upwards. From the corner of the room, from his usual computer station, came a cry. The corner was lit for several seconds, the short plump girl pushed her chair away from the computer screen and stood up. She buried her face in her hands.

'Whatever is it?' said Mr Reilly. 'Nothing serious, I hope?'

The girl looked over at him anxiously, 'I don't know exactly, it was a sudden burst of light, it happened earlier, just after the screen froze. It . . . it was as if the machine spat at me!'

'Spat at you?' said Mr Reilly, wrinkling his face into a semi-grin. He peered into the screen. Suddenly, the screen saver dropped into place. A message innocently floated across the monitor screen: *Hello there!*

The girl looked down in embarrassment. 'Perhaps . . . perhaps I imagined it.'

'No,' said a voice from a nearby bench. 'I saw it too, a flash of light.'

Greg looked for the source of the voice, it had melody and intrigue. It was the new girl who sat quietly at her computer. Her blonde hair was arranged into bunches, set behind her ears. She had put on a little make-up, nothing too garish, it was perfect. Her blue eyes sparkled. For a moment she seemed to notice him, *really* notice him.

'It's been acting up, ever since I switched the thing on,' continued the plump girl.

'Then swap with me,' said Greg softly, still looking at the new girl.

'Would you?' said the girl with a beaming smile of gratitude.

Mr Reilly watched in silence, grateful for the apparent change in Greg Slope's manner. Could he be trying to impress? It didn't matter, he wanted peace at any price.

'That'll be fine,' said Greg. 'It's the machine I usually use anyhow. The keyboard knows my fingers. I have the touch see.' The shark grin returned.

'I don't think there's any danger with it,' said Mr Reilly. 'But keep an eye on it, Greg, something obviously startled her.' He led the girl over to where Greg had been sitting.

Greg Slope sat at the machine and glanced again at the new girl, who still looked in his direction.

His fingers ran across the keyboard like a master's, making sure she could see his skill in action. Had he any e-mail he wondered? Sometimes he was left little messages. Some were abusive (usually from boys, jealous of his charisma) and some were cute messages from those he had chatted up on the Net. A recent 'correspondent' had especially intrigued him.

He moved the mouse across his mouse pad.

Suddenly, the screen saver cut in again. The message floated across the screen: *Hello there, Greg!* He tapped the space bar again. At first it hadn't registered with him. Then after a second he realized.

'My name,' he said. 'It used *my* name, didn't it?'

He waited to see whether anything else was going to happen. Behind him the hum of the classroom melted into a drone. He moved his mouse and clicked on the mailbox icon. The little picture of a mailbox with a flag upturned exploded into a window. There were several files listed which he clicked with the mouse pointer. A message flashed up: *Corrupted files—unable to access.*

'Damn,' he said. 'Someone's interfering with my mail!'

Mr Reilly's face appeared over Greg's shoulder. 'Problems?'

'Just can't open my e-mail,' Greg said. He turned to face Reilly. He could feel Reilly's breath, warm and stale. 'Nothing, no nothing at all. I can manage—OK!'

Mr Reilly stood up. He knew better than to stay with Greg Slope when he wanted to be on his own.

Greg noticed a file in the corner of the window which he hadn't opened. He clicked on it and a message window burst on to the screen: '*Greg, did you get my message? You don't want to read all those others, all those other admirers. I am waiting for you.*'

Greg moved away from the screen. He felt uncomfortable. A sudden thrill—a prickle of cold—was creeping through his bones. He looked at the message again. There was no return address. He found himself twisting nervously in his chair. The new girl was looking at him from across the room. Did she wink just then? He caught his breath as a sudden thought occurred to him. Was it *her*? She seemed to know what he was reading. The girl toyed with a strand of her hair with an index finger and gave him a smile. Greg found himself staring back, then he twisted round to face the monitor again. His fingers trembled as he moved the mouse and closed the message window. For a moment his hand rested on the mouse. It felt different somehow this evening, it had a warmth to it. The plump girl must have been grasping it in her sweaty hand. The screen saver dropped in again, right in the middle of working: *See you again soon, my love!*

Greg swallowed. A small cry caught in the back of his throat.

'What's up, matey?'

The nasal voice startled him. Bottle-bottom Barry was at his shoulder now. His goldfish eyes stared through his spectacles. Greg relaxed.

'Bog off, Bottle,' he sneered.

'Come on, matey, you're as jittery as a bug, what's up? I've been watching you.'

'Oh, have you?' said Greg. 'You haven't been leaving stupid messages for me by any chance?' Greg's lip curled like the corner of burnt paper.

'More than me life's worth, matey,' chirped Bottle-bottom, who many agreed was too stupid to know fear.

'I'm just getting some strange things here.' Greg clicked on the mailbox again, but it was empty.

'Well?' said Bottle-bottom.

'I don't understand it, it was here a moment ago.'

Bottle-bottom snorted and stood up straight. 'Imagining things, matey. Perhaps the place is having an effect on you. Word's out that the Principal is making some statement or other about the building.'

'Statement?' said Greg.

'Barry Bresslaw, back to your place, please!' snapped Mr Reilly.

The new girl giggled and made a deep blink in Greg's direction. Bottle-bottom moved away. Greg returned to the screen. The screen saver had drifted in again: '*I've a loving eye for you. Look for my messages.*'

Greg swallowed hard. The screen went dark with a sizzle and a crackle. Suddenly, almost immediately afterwards, the lights went out. For just a moment Greg felt stifled, the darkness like tar, and he smelt something strange. It pressed against him like cold earth.

It was peculiar. Greg wondered whether she was doing it on purpose, almost avoiding him. In the daily round of things he saw only *glimpses* of the new girl. Often she was in crowds, or was passing through to some place or other. Changing classes. But she *was* interested in him, he was certain of that, because she caught his eye at every opportunity. He pondered over why attempts to make contact in person failed.

It was lunch time, and he knew that Reilly would let him into the computer lab.

'OK—but you're on your honour. Nobody else.' Mr Reilly paused by the door. Greg was quieter than usual and Mr Reilly wasn't certain what to make of it.

'I just want to do some e-mail, that's all.'

'Touch nothing else,' said Mr Reilly, suspiciously. 'We still don't know what it was exactly that caused the power failure. If that nice new girl in your year drops by, tell her I've left her disks at the front office. She was in here earlier, doing the same as you, I think. She's a bright lassie.'

Greg listened with interest. So she was here. He was itching to access his mail. Perhaps she had been leaving messages for him—for his eyes only. Reilly closed the door behind him.

He powered up the computer and waited. The disk drive made a sound like the crunching of gristle and sinew against bone. There might have been a dog inside the machine, gnawing away. Greg frowned. Was it going to crash? And surely it didn't usually take this long to boot?

The e-mail box icon flashed onto the screen. The flag was upright—he had mail. Usually the icons for the files were square boxes, but these were in the shape of a heart. A dark red colour made them look as though they were burning into the screen. An emblem—a sign. He moved the mouse pointer to the first of the three files. A double click and a message window opened: '*You have nice hands, and I like the way you look at me. You're a saucy one.*' That was it.

A grin spread across his face wider than a crocodile's. 'Boy, she's keen. *Saucy* though? What a goofy expression! She's a weird chick.'

Behind him the door opened and Angie looked in.

'Greg, I thought you might be here and I wondered whether we could talk. I know that . . .'

He twisted round in his chair, the rage on his face taking her by surprise. 'Can't you see I'm busy? Get out of here, leave me alone or else! You're nothing, do you hear me? A waste of space. Go and play with your dumb little friend!'

Angie held back the tears.

'I'm arranging a new date, with someone who knows where the future is! Saucy, eh, perhaps I like that. Wild!'

She quietly closed the door.

'There's got to be more, I know there has.' He closed the message box and clicked on the second heart: *'I'd like to meet you alone, my love is strong and it's been so long.'*

He closed the message box and spun round in his chair. 'Yes!' Just then he saw her. The new girl was outside on the green about to join a queue boarding a school coach. She stopped by the window and looked in at him. He waved and she approached and placed her face next to the glass. Greg pointed at the computer and made a thumbs up sign. She laughed and gave a thumbs up sign in return.

'So it is you, *saucy!*' He could hardly remember when he last felt like this. His heartbeat thundered like an engine as he reached forward and grabbed the mouse. He clicked on the third heart: *'Tonight, at 9.30. I'll be waiting, the moon is full. I'm sure you'll find a way.'*

'9.30?' he said. 'But the place will be locked, why not just give me a number and . . . She's testing me. *Me!*'

For a moment he remembered her thumbs up sign in return to his. He switched off the computer, without going through the shutting down process properly. For a moment the whir of the disk drive seemed louder, almost angry, and the screen went blank with a crackle and a spit. Greg thought for a moment and before leaving the computer lab he crossed to the fire door. It was an old trick he knew well. The earlier power shut down had caused a temporary fault with the burglar alarm, he'd heard Reilly telling the caretaker. He wedged a ten pence piece in the mechanism of the emergency exit bar. Reilly would never notice.

Getting in was a cinch. The caretaker had even left the rear gate open from the earlier evening classes. The place was as silent as the grave, a perfect setting for a meeting. 'Mr Lurve' could be romantic, couldn't he? He had already pulled the blinds and now all he had to do was just wait. Greg laughed and sat in his usual seat in front of his machine. At first it had been easy to see in the dark, but now as the seconds ticked past, the shadows seemed to be deepening and becoming denser.

'Something's wrong,' he said to himself after a moment. He couldn't quite figure out what it was. Just a feeling. What was it that her message said? *I'll be waiting. I'm sure you'll find a way.* 'But she isn't here,' he said. 'I mean how could she have got in? I had to do it . . .'

For a moment as he wrestled with the logic, his thoughts became scrambled. From his left came the unmistakable click and whir of the start-up of the computer. He caught his breath and faced the screen. Instead of the usual boot-up routine the screen showed a pinprick of light in its centre.

'What's going on?' he said.

The darkness around him became blacker—somehow it was more intense than he had ever experienced before. The thud of his heartbeat was now inside his head, and seemed to be all he could hear. There was that smell again—was it drains? His hand dropped to the keyboard. Usually his fingers met plastic buttons which yielded as he typed. But this time he did not feel plastic. The surface felt smooth, warm, and slightly pliable, not unlike . . . (he swallowed) *flesh*.

He reached out his right hand to hold the mouse. Something thin, which moved slowly, cautiously, met his touch. He shuddered. Cold fingers caressed his own. It was a hand, and now it held his. First a light touch, then suddenly it grasped him with an iron grip.

'No!' he cried out.

The pinpoint of light opened wide like the huge iris of an eye. He found himself gawping into a tunnel of red light. The sides seemed to be fibrous like tissue and in the distance he could hear a gentle rustling. Something was coming, scraping and scratching, struggling and pushing its way upwards. He looked down at the mouse. Instead of a round plastic device, he could now see the hand more clearly. It was feminine with long nails. The nails pressed into his flesh but the hand was somehow transparent—a ghostly, filmy grey. He groaned as he saw that instead of the usual cable a bare arm joined the hand. It came from somewhere at the back of the computer.

The screen flashed into the screen saver. A new message floated by: '*I'm so glad you came, now we can be together. Be faithful and kind. Always.*'

Greg Slope screamed as he involuntarily pushed his face into the screen. A far off girl's voice sang softly, but the voice had an older tone. He knew immediately that the voice was not that of the new girl. The truth hit him like a lightning bolt: the messages had not been hers. *They had come from somewhere else.*

Beneath him, a crack split the tiled floor. He looked down. It was as if he could see deep into the earth, deeper than he had ever wanted to see. He noticed for the first time that cables at the back of the machine descended into the crack. They thrashed like angry eels, twisting and whipping. Another hand appeared within the screen, from deep within the blood red tunnel. But this hand, which was of bleached bone, extended a greeting. Greg glimpsed a cracked grey forehead, adorned with a wisp of white hair, as it appeared at the end of the tunnel. The kiss that was coming was of bare teeth. The eyes—dark holes. Something dead was coming.

Greg Slope's new girlfriend had arrived.

Now we can be together.

An awful, terrible smile yawned open and with a sudden yank, he felt himself pulled into the screen, sucked down and drawn into a dark embrace. The last words he heard were, 'Saucy boy. *Saucy.*'

Greg missed the local news item that evening on TV. He was otherwise engaged with a new date. The Principal had made a short statement concerning rumours of 'a find' during the recent building work at the computer wing of the new science block. He had been advised to keep the matter quiet until now.

The 'find' was thought to be the remains of a girl and they had been there for a very long time indeed. A local historian revealed that the science block had been on the site of a small local graveyard attached to a chapel, well over a hundred years ago. It was uncertain who the girl might be, but an old story maintained that a village girl had been found dead after being rejected and mistreated by a 'gadabout' local boy with whom she had been deeply in love.

The Principal admitted that new optical communications cables of the latest technology had been run beneath the ground. He regretted that they had indeed passed through a grave. They would be re-routed as soon as possible.

The Sinister Schoolmaster

ROSEMARY TIMPERLEY

Peter wanted to go to the comprehensive school because most of his friends in the area were going there. His mother, however, wanted him to go to a small, private school, where he'd get 'individual attention'. His father kept quiet and left mother and son to fight it out.

'I don't want "individual attention",' Peter said. 'I'd rather be one of the mob. I don't mind a bit of roughness, if that's what you're afraid of. If I'm bashed, I can bash back.'

'That,' said his mother, 'is the very attitude I want you to discard. You tend to turn life into a battlefield. This nice little school should make you more gentlemanly.'

Peter gave a voiced imitation of someone being sick.

'Don't be disgusting!' she snapped. 'It's time you were taught some manners.'

'They say on the telly that it's parents that's responsible for their children's manners,' said Peter, 'so if I'm awful it's because of the way I've been upbrung.'

'Brought up,' she corrected him automatically.

'Why?' said Peter. 'You cling, you clung; you ring, you rung; you bring, you brung—'

'You ring, you rang, or you have rung,' she corrected him.

'You ding, you dung,' he muttered.

'*What* did you say?'

'Nothing.'

'I should think so. You start at St Edmund's tomorrow, Peter, and nothing you can say will make me change my mind.'

'*Saint* Edmund's,' he moaned. 'I expect the Head has long white hair with a halo balanced on top.' But he knew that the battle was lost. His mother was only a woman, but she was tough as old rope when she set her mind on anything, and she wanted her son to be a 'gentleman'. It made you mad. He thought longingly of the state school, where his mates were going, and where some of the teachers even looked like human beings. He was full of gloom when he set out next morning for the first day of term.

He got on the bus, wearing his prissy uniform and carrying a small case with pencils, pens, rubber, compasses and similar daft things. The bus ride took about fifteen minutes, then, 'Church Road,' the conductor said, and Peter knew that was where he must get off. He alighted, and the friendly old bus trundled away, leaving him alone on the edge of a new world . . .

It was then that the fog descended. It came down suddenly, cold and grey and blanketing, sending a shiver through him. He had been told which way to walk and now began to plod along a road with tall trees on either side. They were menacing, like sentinels. They watched and whispered. Peter was usually quick enough to be brave and defiant when there was something to defy, but in this blind-making fog all he could do was put one foot in front of the other and grow more and more uneasy.

He suddenly felt *afraid* of this new school.

All the same, he was grateful to see a light at last, though it must be a light from the hated school. Yes, there was a driveway, and a building crouching further on, with one single golden eye glaring at him. It struck him as odd that there was only one light on in the building. He knew it was a small school, but surely there should be more than one lighted classroom. For the window was that of a classroom, and class had started, so he realized with dismay that he must be late. He could say he was 'delayed by the fog', of course, although he hadn't got lost or anything—had he?

He went closer to the window and looked in.

About a dozen boys sat there, in similar uniforms to his own. That meant he'd found the right school, anyway. The boys sat very attentively. They were pale of face and their eyes were scared. The teacher was at the desk in front of them. He was a short, bull-shouldered man with a red face and white hair, which was long at the sides but left a pink 'halo' of baldness top-back of his head. He was gesticulating with his right hand and carried something tucked under his left arm, ready for use.

It was a cane.

He asked a boy a question. The boy answered. Peter couldn't hear what was said, but the teacher gave a wolfish smile and beckoned to the boy, who came out to the front and bent over.

The schoolmaster seized the cane in his right hand, raised it, and brought it down crackingly hard on the boy's bottom. He hit him again, and again, and again, and his expression was joyful.

'Stop that!' shouted Peter.

The class froze. The teacher turned towards the window. Pale grey eyes peered into dark grey fog. Then the man marched across and flung open the window. 'Who is that? You—boy—out there—what did you say?'

'I said "Stop that",' Peter answered.

Thick arms, like a couple of little tree trunks, shot out of the window and grabbed him by the shoulders. He dropped his case on the grass. He struggled. Useless. He was lugged inside. The window was closed again. Peter was dumped on the classroom floor, the man with the cane looming over him.

A terrible stillness seemed to have descended. The boys were quiet and motionless, seeming hardly to breathe. The man stood like a statue of wrath. Peter had to admit to himself that he was very frightened indeed.

Then the silence was broken. 'And who,' asked the sinister schoolmaster, 'are you?'

'Peter Lorrimer.'

'And what are you doing here?'

'I'm a pupil here. It's my first day.'

'Your first day—what?'

'My first day being here.'

'Your first day being here—what?'

'My first day being here at this school.'

'Your first day being here at this school—what?'

'This school called St Edmund's,' said Peter.

'This school called St Edmund's—what?'

'A rotten dump!' said Peter, exasperated.

'Stand up!' Peter stood. 'Bend over.' Peter bent. Crack! The cane came down on his bottom.

'Did you enjoy that, Peter Lorrimer?'

'No.'

'No—what?'

'No, I didn't enjoy it!'

Crack came the cane.

'No, you didn't enjoy it—WHAT?' screamed this maniac.

A whisper from the class: 'Ssssay "ssssir".'

Silence for a moment. The fog thickened outside. The oppressiveness of fear thickened too. Peter felt half-paralysed in this nightmare. He was full of pain, yet it was a dead sort of pain, felt yet not felt. Weird.

Now the teacher spoke. 'There is no pupil called Peter Lorrimer in this school. You are an impostor. Why are you wearing our school uniform?'

'I am a pupil—my mother sent me—'

'Your mother sent you—WHAT?'

'SIR!'

Another swish from the cane.

'That's not fair,' said Peter. 'I said "sir".'

'That was for being a liar.'

Swish . . .

'And that was for arguing about it. Now go and sit at that desk.' Peter obeyed. 'Let's see how much you know, you impostor in the uniform of St Edmund's, of which I am proud to be Headmaster. I go—I went. I come—' He stopped and waited.

He really is stark raving bonkers, thought Peter. But lunatics must be humoured, so he said hopefully, 'You come, *sir*.'

'The boy is a half-wit. A dunderhead. I come—' Again he waited.

'Thank you for coming,' said Peter, adding a hasty, 'sir.'

'Heaven grant me patience. Listen. I go—I went. I come—'

Light dawned. The silly clot wanted the past tense of 'come'.

'I came,' said Peter.

'I bring.'

'I brung.'

'You WHAT?'

'I brung, SIR!'

'Brung, brung, brung? Anyone heard the word "brung"?'

A titter of sycophantish laughter from the class.

Peter's conversation with his mother came blessedly back to him. 'I brought,' he said.

'I ring.'

'I rung. No—take that back—I rang, or I have rung. Like you'd say "I rang up" or "I have rung up".'

'I wonder what strange country this boy comes from,' mocked the teacher, 'and what strange language they speak there. Rang up, rung up—what does it mean?'

'It means what it says, sir. Like when you ring someone up, on the telephone.'

'The what?'

'The telephone. *Tele*. As in television, telegram, tele-communications—' His voice faded as the teacher's face turned a deeper shade of crimson.

'Thank you,' said the man. 'Thank you, Peter Lorrimer, for breaking into my class, disturbing my lesson, dressing up in our school uniform, pretending to be a pupil and then talking a lot of gibberish. If there are any words to be invented here, *I* will do the inventing.'

'I'm not inventing anything!'

'You are not inventing anything—WHAT?'

'SIR!'

'Stand up! Bend over!' *Swish, swish, swish* went the cane. In Peter's ears, it seemed to turn into the sound of a raging wind, or a thundering waterfall. His ears would burst!

And it seemed suddenly as if they did. There was a sort of explosion in his head. Light blazed. He found himself lying on the pavement, and people were gathering round him. He supposed that the teacher had beaten him unconscious, then carried him here, bleeding and bruised, for he saw the tall trees which lined the road to the school. The fog had gone.

'He's coming round,' a woman said. 'It's all right, lovey. You're all right now.' She helped him to his feet.

'What happened, old son?' a man asked.

'He was trying to beat me to death,' said Peter. 'He's mad.'

'Kid's been dreaming,' said another voice. 'No signs of damage on him, are there?'

'No. Just a little faint, that's all it was,' said the woman, brushing the pavement dust from his blazer. 'Where do you live?'

Peter told her. One of the men offered to drive him home. He hardly spoke in the car. He felt exhausted. The driver dropped him at his own gate. 'Shall I come in with you?' he offered. 'Will anyone be there?'

'Yes, thank you. My mother's there. Thanks for the lift.'

'You go in and have a good rest,' said the man, and drove off.

Peter let himself into the house. His mother heard him and came into the hall, frowning. 'Oh, Peter, how could you be so naughty?' she said. 'The Headmaster has been on the phone to me—'

'I don't care what he said about me,' Peter said. 'He was horrible and cruel and mad. I'm never going back there. He tried to murder me!' And he poured out the whole story.

His mother listened. His tone was so convincing that she half-believed him. Then she said, 'If you had such a beating, let's see how sore you are.'

'I should think I'll be scarred for life,' said Peter, pulling down his trousers and wondering, as he did so, why his bottom didn't hurt. His mother looked.

'There isn't a mark on you,' she declared. 'Not even the smallest bruise. You've been telling me lies—dangerous lies, too. If you were older, you could be had up for slander for making accusations like that against the Headmaster. And I know for a fact that you did *not* turn up at school at all this morning, because the Head rang up to ask why you hadn't arrived. Oh, Peter, what am I going to do with you when you behave like this? I know you didn't want to go there, but to tell these wicked lies—'

'I wasn't telling lies!' cried Peter. 'It happened! And all in that dreadful fog—'

'There has been no fog—none at all—except in your perverse mind,' she said.

He went very cold. All the indignation died out of him. He whispered: 'If it didn't happen—yet it did—*what* happened? Who was that man with the white hair and the red face, and thick arms and shoulders, and a beastly smile—and a voice which seemed to cut through you, just as the cane did? Who was he?'

'An invented character in your story,' said his mother. 'The Headmaster of St Edmund's is tall, dark, rather thin and has a very nice smile. I went to see him before I decided to send you there.'

Peter felt dazed and ill. It had all been too much. You could go on fighting against circumstance for just so long, and then— he broke into tears.

As he melted, so did his mother. She took him in her arms. 'Oh, darling, what is all this about?' she said. 'Why did you make up that story? Did you really think I'd believe it?'

'It happened,' wept Peter.

'Where have you really been all morning?'

'Where I said. Then I found myself lying in the street and a man drove me home.'

'What man?'

'I don't know—a nice man—they were all very nice—the passers-by who stopped to pick me up—they were kind—people should always be kind—not like *him*! That . . . that sinister schoolmaster!'

Even if his home was sometimes a battlefield, his mother now proved a gentle victor. She was so unaccustomed to seeing him cry that she realized something must be badly wrong. She took him up to bed, tucked him in with a hot-water bottle, kissed him on the forehead and told him to go to sleep. He did sleep, too. Deeply, dreamlessly. It was evening when he woke, blinking contentedly in the safety of his own little room. Then his father came in.

'Your mother's been telling me—'

'It all happened, Dad. Honest!'

His father sat on the end of the bed. 'We know now that you went to the school, Peter, although no one saw you there. Your case was found outside one of the classroom windows.'

'That's right,' said Peter. 'I dropped it when that dreadful Headmaster dragged me inside.'

'No one dragged you inside,' said his father. 'Your mother did wonder if there could be something in your story, as you were so upset, so she went to the school this afternoon. She thought maybe one of the teachers was like the man you'd described. No one there is even remotely like him. No one there *now*, that is.'

'No one there *now*?' Peter echoed.

'The Head, Mr Rennick, has come to see you. He wants to talk to you about it.' He went to fetch the other man, and Peter waited. If that villain with the cane walked in—

A tall, dark, anxious-faced man came in and closed the door behind him. He had a book under his arm, not a cane. 'Hello, Peter. I'm Mr Rennick, the Headmaster of St Edmund's.'

'Then who was the man with white hair?' Peter asked.

'Ever heard of John Bashman, nicknamed "Old Basher"?' Mr Rennick asked him. Peter shook his head. 'Here's a picture of him.' Mr Rennick opened the book, called *History of St Edmund's School*, and displayed a full-page illustration. It was a reproduction of the portrait of a man, in colour. A white-haired, red-faced thick-bodied man. It was labelled: 'John Bashman, the First Headmaster'.

'That's him,' said Peter. 'That's the man who beat me.'

'That man has been dead for a hundred years. He wasn't nicknamed "Old Basher" for nothing. He caned the pupils for the smallest misdemeanour. He was a sadistic bully, to my mind, but in those days beatings in school were more common than they are now. It was an age of violence. Now your story is that you looked through the classroom window and saw him there; that he dragged you inside, and so on—'

'He did! In that awful fog!'

'There was no fog. It was a bright morning. The teacher who spent all morning in that classroom was taking physics. It's a lab, rather than an ordinary classroom. You realize now, don't you? You had some sort of dream-awake. A hallucination of some kind.'

'You mean I saw ghosts of the past,' Peter said calmly. 'That would be why he'd never heard of the telephone or television. He said I was talking gibberish and that if anyone was going to invent words, he would do it.'

'It was all a dream, Peter. You never wanted to come to my school. You were resentful about it. Your mother says you dashed out without any breakfast, so you were empty. You got to the school, couldn't face going in, dumped your case, fled back to the road—and then you fainted. Overwrought nerves. While unconscious, you had this dream. Does that make sense to you?'

'I suppose so. But it must have been more than an ordinary dream, as Old Basher really did exist.'

'Yes. And I expect you'd read about him somewhere and forgotten. What the conscious mind forgets, the unconscious retains. That's my explanation. It makes more sense than "ghosts". There are no such things.' He spoke confidently, almost arrogantly.

He wouldn't be so cocky about it if *he'd* had Old Basher standing over him with that cane, Peter thought—and, suddenly, behind the Headmaster's shoulder, he saw a shadow forming . . .

The shadow gained colour and solidity. It seemed to have sprung in some curious way from the illustration in the open book, which Mr Rennick had placed on a shelf behind him. There was the white hair, the red face, the thick body—the raised arm with the cane in it—the curling smile—the pale eyes, glaring at the back of the Headmaster's head. 'Imposter!' spat the lips— or that could have been the sound of rain falling on the leaves in the garden. The arm with the cane was raised higher—

'Look out!' screamed Peter. 'Old Basher is just behind you! He's going to wallop you!'

As the cane descended, Mr Rennick gave a cry, and the light went out. Peter went right down under the bedclothes, in case Old Basher started on him next.

A few moments later, the bedclothes were pulled away from him. His mother was bending over him. The room was dimly lit by light from the passage. His father was outlined in the doorway. Mr Rennick was rubbing his head.

'It's all right, Peter,' his mother was saying. 'The electric bulb fell out of its socket and hit poor Mr Rennick on the head. That's why the light went out.' She turned to the Headmaster. 'My fault, that. I couldn't have fixed it properly when I put it in the other day.'

'I've always told you to leave that sort of job to me,' Peter's father said irritably. 'Sorry about this, Mr Rennick. Come downstairs and have a drink.'

The two men departed, but before he left the room, Mr Rennick gave Peter a long, suspicious look.

Now his mother fussed over him a little and he lay down to sleep. Strangely, he no longer felt afraid of Old Basher, who had so obviously had it in for Mr Rennick rather than himself. Resented anyone else taking over the school, even a hundred years afterwards. That would be it. Peter did, however, feel a little afraid of the look Mr Rennick had given him. When he went to St Edmund's there wouldn't be any beating or cruelty, but he wouldn't be popular. The Head definitely didn't like or trust him. Oh, life could be hell sometimes. It really could. He slept.

In the morning, his mother brought him breakfast in bed.

'You're going to stay at home today,' she said, 'then your father and I will arrange for you to go to the comprehensive.'

'Wow!' He nearly hit the ceiling with relieved delight.

'Peter, be careful, you'll spill your tea.'

'What made you change your mind?' he asked her.

'I didn't,' she said, rather grimly. 'Mr Rennick changed his. He said he didn't want you at the school. He said some neurotic children cause outbreaks of poltergeist activity, and he didn't want the pleasant atmosphere of St Edmund's disturbed. He struck me as pretty neurotic himself,' she added. 'What a fuss to make over a falling light-bulb! As if *you* could possibly have been responsible for that.'

It was Old Basher, thought Peter. Clever old ghost!

Then his father descended upon him. 'Enjoying your breakfast and the "good news"?' he said sardonically. 'You cunning little devil! You were determined to get your own way, weren't you? Tell me—how did you wangle that poltergeist effect?'

'I didn't,' Peter began. 'It was Old—' Then he stopped. It would be no use telling his father the truth. He had a sceptical nature, limited, lacking in imagination. Still, he wasn't a bad sort. Peter smiled. His father winked and departed.

In fact Peter felt friendly towards everyone this morning. Even Old Basher. Especially Old Basher! But for him, Peter would have had to go to St Edmund's . . .

'Thank you,' he said, impulsively and aloud—and an echo in the air—or maybe it was only the gurgling of a water-pipe—said: 'Thank you—WHAT?' and Peter bellowed back: 'SIR!'

The
Honeysuckle Trap

BARBARA KER WILSON

The Carringtons 'collect islands'. That's the way they describe it. For several years now they have chosen to spend holidays on various islands—the Hebrides, the Isles of Scilly, and, farther across the sea, Majorca, Corsica, and Sicily. One year they went as far as Rhodes. From all these expeditions they bring home to London amusing tales of their experiences, gossip about the people they've met, colour slides of land- and sea-scapes, as well as objects, things—Mary Carrington would never refer to them as mementoes, still less as souvenirs—to remind them of the places they've seen. A silver brooch from Skye which Mary often wears; a painted plate from Majorca which they use at their wine-and-cheese parties; terracotta pots from Greece that Peter has hung on the walls of their courtyard garden, trailing decorative ivy. They're a pleasant couple: young, good company, both practical by nature. Each a little unimaginative, perhaps—at least, that's what I used to think. Now, I'm not so sure.

When they returned home last month from their latest holiday, they asked me to visit them. I expected the usual post-holiday gathering of their friends, the wine and cheese, the colour slides slotting into position one after another, with Peter's lighthearted commentary and additional remarks thrown in by Mary from time to time. You know the sort of thing. I was to be surprised.

I decided to walk to their house. They live in Chelsea, not far from my flat. It was a fine evening in late summer, and part of my way lay beside the river. I enjoy walking beside the Thames at dusk; that night the sunset seemed to reproduce a Turner painting. St Paul's was silhouetted against the bloodshot sky— a similar effect, I thought, to the way it must have looked during the Blitz. But, as always, I firmly turned away my thoughts from the wartime years. I do not care to dwell on them.

Possibly it is hindsight to say now that I felt some premonition that the evening was to bring the strangest experience of my life—I don't think *that* is an exaggeration. Maybe it was only the dusk, the river, and the sunset: a powerful enough combination, surely.

When I got to the Carringtons' house, I wondered if I had mistaken the time, or the day. There were no cars parked outside. Clearly, however, I was expected. Mary greeted me warmly.

'We've not asked anyone else,' she said. 'We decided we'd like to have you all to ourselves, Edward.'

Did I discern a slightly—defensive—note in her voice?

'That sounds rather as though you intend to serve me up as an entrée,' I remarked, smiling. It was the sort of facetious remark I often found myself making in the Carringtons' company. Yet their company was always pleasant.

Strangely, there seemed to be a time-lag in Mary's responsive smile. Why, I wondered? It wasn't a very good joke, but then Mary's code of polite behaviour did not grade her response to jokes—they were automatically accorded a smile or a laugh.

Peter had just opened a bottle of whisky. He seemed the same as ever. 'The usual duty-free loot,' he said with a grin as he handed me my drink.

That was a Carrington post-holiday cliché. Don't, by the way, misunderstand me. I don't mean to jibe at the Carringtons, or sneer at them. Not at all. It is good to have some friends of reliable temperament. I relax and bask in the warmth of their clichés, their predictable social behaviour. Which fact only made my experience that evening the more unusual.

As we sat down to eat—and it was really most pleasant to be given a delicious casserole for a change, instead of nibbling on Camembert or coping with an adhesive *fondue*; moreover, Peter's loot also comprised an extremely acceptable bottle of Burgundy—I could sense that Mary was longing to tell me something; it was almost as though I were sitting next to a child who had a confession to make. But I could sense, too, that she did not know how to begin her telling, her confession, which-ever it was. Perhaps it was both.

'And how was the holiday?' I asked. Helpfully, I hoped. 'Interesting? Good weather? Food tolerable?'

'Oh yes. The sun shone. Beautifully quiet and relaxing, just what we needed. Good swimming. We enjoyed the inn. One or two amusing people.' Mary's somewhat stacatto reply was, in effect, the sort of message she'd scrawled on innumerable scenic postcards which I had received from various islands over a handful of summertimes. It sounded dismissive of my enquiry, as though such things as those I'd listed were not of real importance.

'You've added another island to your collection,' I remarked. The odd thing was—I realized that while I was speaking their language, as it were (the habit I fell into, chameleon-like, when-ever I crossed their threshold), this evening they, I felt sure, were trying, even with some measure of desperation, to make contact with me on a different level than our usual one. The immediate problem was, how were we to meet one another?

'Another island—yes,' Peter said, in what for him was a remarkably serious tone of voice.

The choice, I recalled, had been Peter's that year. Some months ago, they'd sought information from me about the island, wanting to know something of its history. I had bored them a little, I fear; when you are used to teaching history all day long, it is difficult not to relapse into a classroom attitude.

No, there is more to it than that. Much more. I must relate the whole experience properly. I had bored them deliberately; not from any unfriendly feeling, but to compensate— instinctively, I suppose—for the sudden surge of adrenalin through my veins when, here in this same room, those few months ago, Peter had said quite out of the blue: 'Tell us about Sark, Edward.'

Sark: The word, and his seeming—but, as I quickly realized quite unintentional—implication that something was known of a connection between the island and myself in past years, had the effect of a pistol pointed at my head. *A Luger automatic, held by a man in field-grey uniform* . . .

My meticulous wartime training had taken charge, im- mediately, even after all the years that had gone by. Hooding my eyes, I had expounded—pompous word—on the history of the Channel Islands, my boring monologue serving to mask the shock I had received. I remember likening the Channel Islands to stepping-stones lying between the coasts of France and England, England and France.

I positively lectured the Carringtons, telling them how as stepping-stones the Islands had been used by French refugees escaping from religious persecution, so that many Huguenot family trees, transplanted, had flourished there; and, during the Second World War, by Germany, who invaded the Islands in 1940 and occupied them until the end of the war—as the first stage, so it was thought, of Hitler's invasion of Britain. This is disputed as fact, yet, at the same time as the ports of north-west France were filled with German invasion troops ready to embark for England, sixty-one barges lay in the seas between Guernsey, Herm, and Sark, ready to transport troops and equipment to England, while Guernsey's airfield was filled with planes ready to escort the invaders. *I saw these things.*

'Tell us about Sark, Edward': it had, after all, only been Peter's way of revealing their latest choice of island for the annual holiday. They'd stayed at the inn on Little Sark, which is connected by a narrow causeway to the rest of the island.

'A picturesque old place—the inn, I mean,' Mary said now, turning the stem of her wine-glass between her fingers as we sat at the table. 'Lots of tales about smugglers—you know the sort of thing: laces for a lady, letters for a spy . . .'

And watch the wall, my darling, while the gentlemen go by.
But I didn't finish the quotation aloud. I am squeamish about
finishing off other people's quotations; it seems too much
like jumping down their throats. Nor, this time, did I deduce
any unfounded implications from Mary's particular choice of
line. 'Tell us about Sark, Edward': what an extraordinarily
unfortuitous stringing together of five simple words that had
been.

Well, the next moment, and on my part quite inadvertently,
I returned shock for shock. 'Any ghosts?' I asked.

The effect of my lighthearted query was, almost literally,
shattering. Mary dropped her wine-glass; although it did not
actually shatter, Burgundy ran over the polished table top like
uncongealing blood.

'How did you *know*?' she gasped.

Peter, too, was staring at me. 'We haven't told anyone else
about it; you must be riding a thoughtwave, Edward.'

I was astonished by their reaction; inevitably, too, my former
training raised in me a faintly critical attitude in the face of such
undisguised revelation of feeling. But at least, at last, we'd found
our stepping-stone, our causeway for communication. I up-
righted Mary's glass and then dispensed what wine remained in
the bottle between the three of us. It seemed only natural at
that point to assume Peter's role of host.

I sat back, cupping my wine-glass in both hands, 'Tell me,' I
said.

Mary mopped at the spilled wine with her table napkin.
Conversely, this action seemed to help her words to flow. 'It
was—oh, so strange, Edward. Yet all rather vague, really. You
see, we decided to go for a walk one afternoon—'

'One does, in Sark,' Peter broke in. He had collected his
thoughts, momentarily scattered as the wine was spilled. 'No
vehicles have ever been allowed on the island, as you probably
know. Only the farm tractors—otherwise it's horse-and-buggy,
and bicycle.'

I could, if I'd wished, have corrected him on a technical point
there. During the Nazi occupation, the ban on cars, lorries, and
motor-cycles had been broken for the first and only time. *How
strange it had been to hear the revving of engines; how the
vehicles had stirred the dusty roads.*

Mary resumed the story. 'We set off after lunch. It was a lovely day, sunny with a slight breeze—just right for walking. We crossed the causeway and set off right across the island, heading for Dixcart Bay.'

Involuntarily my senses became alert as I heard that name, but I am sure they noticed nothing.

'Everything seemed airy and clean—the sea sparkled and the seagulls looked extra white, like television ads for some detergent.' Mary laughed softly. 'We took great gulps of sea air and felt madly healthy and energetic. It took us—oh, a couple of hours to reach the far end of the island, and then we thought we'd look for a place to have some afternoon tea. We couldn't find anywhere in the village, so we wandered on quite a way past the pub—it was shut, of course—and then we suddenly found ourselves walking in a narrow lane, completely over-grown with honeysuckle and dog-roses.'

Here I closed my eyes for a second. This was unbelievable. I could have spoken Mary's next words for her.

'It was like walking through a warm, sweet-smelling tunnel. The scent of honeysuckle was overpowering. I felt almost—choked—by it.'

Peter smiled uneasily. 'That lane really scared Mary. And do you know, Edward, it was quite silent. That was—eerie, I must admit. It was just as though all sound had been abruptly cut off. There were none of the usual hedgerow noises—you know, birdsong, bees humming, that sort of thing. It was—stifling.'

Choking. Stifling. They chose the right adjectives, these Carringtons. But silent? No. In my memory the lane was hideous with noise. I eased my collar with one finger. What else?

Mary's eyes were wide as she went up that lane again in her imagination. 'At the end of the tunnel—the lane—we came upon the entrance to a big, old house. There were huge ornamental gates, rather in need of a lick of paint. They stood wide open, and there was a name on one of the posts: *Vieux Clos.*—There are lots of houses with French names there, you know.'

I nodded. Yes, I knew. *The gates were freshly painted when I saw them. A military notice in German, French, and English was attached to the iron scrollwork.*

Peter took up their tale. Clearly, the memory of that afternoon was just as vivid in his mind as Mary's. 'The driveway—it was very neglected and overgrown—went between tall trees into the distance. You could just glimpse the house through the trees. I thought, we both thought, it might be a place where summer visitors stayed, and we might get our cup of tea there.'

'It was still awfully quiet,' Mary said. 'Only our feet scuffling through long-fallen leaves and crunching over weedy gravel.'

Leaves had been swept up, gravel weeded and raked, the day I went to Vieux Clos. Slave-labourers imported from France were employed there as gardeners.

'We reached the house and wandered in,' Peter went on. 'The place was furnished, but everything was shabby and dusty; there was no one else around. We found a large room with lots of cane chairs and rattan tables, and sat down, but there was simply no sign of life at all.'

'Our visions of lovely thirst-quenching tea and hot scones oozing butter and jam and cream completely evaporated into thin air.' Mary attempted her more usual style of conversation. 'Yet it was funny—we felt that there *were* people about, that at any moment not just one person, but lots of people might come rushing into the room. We didn't feel as though we were alone.'

'Then,' Peter said, 'we realized that the room opened out, through glass doors at its far end, on to a long, covered veranda. And the strangest thing was—we both at the same time said exactly the same thing—'

And here Mary joined Peter in the exclamation they had made at that point: 'Oh, *there* they are!'

'You see,' Peter reiterated, 'we had been expecting to see some people—we *knew* we were not alone.'

'And—who were *they*?' I asked, hoping my voice did not sound unduly agitated.

'We had no idea, then,' Peter said flatly. 'We think we know now, because of what happened later. But all we knew at that moment was that we saw a number of young men dressed vaguely in the same way, grey trousers, open-necked shirts, playing ping-pong at tables set out along the veranda.'

Ping-pong! That, surely, must be the last word one would expect to hear in a ghost story. The sound of that aptly alliterative yet basically frivolous word eased, for me, the tension that had been building up. I gave a short, involuntary laugh, as much from relief as for any other reason. 'Ping-pong!' I repeated.

'Table-tennis, then, if you prefer it,' Mary said almost crossly. 'It really wasn't funny, Edward—it's the most extraordinary thing we ever—'

'I could hardly fail to realize what a deep impression the whole business has made on both of you,' I said hastily. 'Please go on.'

'They were playing fast and furiously—aggressively, you might say,' Peter said deliberately, 'and we were only a few yards away from them, with shabby glass doors that surely could not be soundproof between us. Yet we heard nothing. They were obviously calling out to each other as they played, but we heard no voices. Their feet made no noise on the wooden floor. There was silence, absolute silence, as they hit the ball and it bounced and ricochetted across the table. It was like watching a silent film. And they—were completely oblivious of our presence. It was just as though we did not exist.'

'We felt—like ghosts ourselves,' Mary said, oddly.

I looked at her curiously. 'Well, why not?' I said. 'I suppose ghosts may belong to the future as well as to the past, for all we know.'

'It was like that,' Peter said. 'Like being out of time. It wasn't frightening or creepy—at least, not at that moment. Just—strange.'

'We decided to go,' Mary said. 'It wasn't until we'd nearly reached the gates at the beginning of the driveway that I remembered about the lane. Suddenly I felt—quite terrified. I just knew that something—that someone—was waiting in the lane.'

Be calm, I told myself.

'I felt,' Mary said, 'as though to walk into that lane was to walk into a trap.'

A trap. The honeysuckle trap. To lure two people into itself, as though it were some monstrous insectivorous plant grown vast beyond all imagining. I could not believe the strangeness of what these two young people were describing to me. Its full impact had not really hit me until that moment. What eerie coincidence had led them to relive an experience that belonged to my past? I recalled a remark Peter had made earlier in the evening: 'riding a thoughtwave'. Could it be, perhaps, that my strong initial reaction to his first mention of Sark, those few months ago, had triggered off some supernatural association between our three minds? Or my suppression of that reaction, perhaps, in a poltergeistic manner? That might be more likely. I recalled that the frenzied actions of a poltergeist, the hurling of furniture, crockery, or lumps of coal, are often said to arise from a frustrated spirit trapped, perhaps, within a crippled body. I would never consciously reveal to anyone what happened to me one summer's day in Sark in 1941—yet perhaps my story had escaped from me in spite of myself, in some subconscious way I would never understand.

'We had to return along the lane,' Peter said. 'There was actually a wider road leading away from the house, but that would have taken us miles out of our way. I practically had to drag Mary into the lane! Oh, I wasn't indifferent to the atmosphere, either. I just wanted to get through it—to get away from the whole place as quickly as possible. To get the hell out of it.'

'*Get the hell out of it!*'—*Robson's voice, screaming down the lane, choked with blood, after the pistol shot. Blood streaming over stems of honeysuckle vines, over the creamy, waxen flowers. The sickening stench of blood.*

Mary's voice sounded almost breathless now that she had reached the climax of the story. 'We walked more and more quickly and then we ran. There was that stifling feeling again, the feeling we'd had the first time—'

At that moment, for all three of us, I think the well-remembered, sickly, cloying scent of honeysuckle actually seemed to pervade the air around us, above the dining-table where a few beads of red wine still lay on the polished surface. Almost, I could tell, Mary got up to open the window wider. Almost I myself rose to do that.

'Then we were out—it was all over!' Mary said. 'We came out into the open air and breathed freely and smelled the sea air. We were safe!'

'By this time the pub was open—we needed a drink,' Peter went on. 'And while we were drinking we got into conversation with the barman. We didn't say much, just told him we'd been up the road and into the big old house at the end of the lane. I think we'd even forgotten its name, for the moment. Then Mary asked him what it was being used for. We still weren't quite sure, you see—'

'He did a double-take,' Mary said. 'You could only call it that. "*Vieux Clos*?" he said. "Been empty ever since the occupation, has that place. Been empty for years and years." Then he told us that during the occupation it had in fact been the headquarters of the Gestapo. Young SS officers were billeted there, as well as their Commandant. One day there was a British Commando raid on Sark from England—apparently there were several such raids on the Channel Islands during the war, with the British seizing Nazi prisoners and information, and sabotaging communications.'

I said nothing, but held her gaze as she continued.

'Anyway, on one raid, two Commandos apparently went up to *Vieux Clos* and took all the records they could find. Somehow the Commandant found out they were there. He went up to the house by the back way and waited for them to come out—he waited halfway down that lane, under the honeysuckle, and he shot one of the men as they were escaping, running down the lane just as we ran . . .'

'But the other man killed the Commandant,' Peter said. 'He . . . strangled him.'

They stopped talking then. I replaced my wine-glass on the table, flexing my fingers. Did they expect me to comment on their story? I could find no words for that. But they had given me more than enough to think about, if I chose. I thought of the ultimate cliché: food for thought.

'Edward, I'm so glad we've told someone. Of all our friends, you seemed the only one we could possibly tell. You're such . . . such a safe person, you see. And we knew you'd listen quietly, and not think it all too stupid for words.'

'No,' I said, 'I don't think it stupid. Not at all.'

Then Mary stretched out one hand to me—an unusual gesture. She is not a demonstrative person.

I took hold of her hand gently, cupping it between my two hands. Hands that could . . . soothe.

'It's time you made coffee,' I said.

The Ghost in the Summer Kitchen

MARY FRANCES ZAMBRENO

When the little girl first visited the summer kitchen, I didn't realize that she was a ghost. It was Sunday, and I was baking pasties for my father to take with him to work during the week. Making pasties is hot work, so I'm always glad when I can use the summer kitchen. The little log building out in back has an iron woodstove and screened-in windows on all four sides. It would get uncomfortably hot with cooking as the day wore on, but not unbearably so, and at least the house would stay cool.

I was rolling out the stiff dough for the crust, as my mother had taught me, when there was a shadow from the doorway.

'Hello,' said a strange girl, outlined against the morning sun. 'What are you doing?'

I froze, staring at her with more than a little rudeness. She was a few years younger than I was, about my little sister Sara's age, and she was wearing a thin white dress that looked like a nightgown. Her fair hair hung loose down her back, and her feet were bare.

'Who are you?' I asked sharply. I'm not used to being surprised by strangers when I'm cooking. And after all, our nearest neighbour lives half a mile down the paved road from us. 'Where did you come from?'

The girl drew back from the door, her eyes widening slightly.

'I didn't mean to bother you,' she said. She sounded frightened, and I was sorry for it; I hadn't meant to scare the child. 'I'm Annie Pennick. I'm visiting my grandmother because she's sick. I just wanted to see what this funny little building was, and then —I'm sorry. I'd better go.'

Moving more quickly than I could speak, she slipped away and down the hill. I would have called after her then, and apologized for having spoken so sharply, but there wasn't time. In a moment I was glad that I'd kept my mouth shut.

It was as I was watching her out of sight down the hill that it happened. First the white nightgown started to shimmer, as if a fog had passed over the sun. But the day was bright and warm, with achingly blue sky behind the deep green of the pines, and never a cloud in sight. Then her long golden hair started to shiver with light, and fade from gold to silver to white to—

Nothing. She was gone. I blinked and rubbed my eyes, but there was no fair-haired little girl running down the hill. She had vanished as if she had never been.

Well, I may be only fourteen years old and not as sharp as I think I am (or so Aunt Grace is always telling me), but I know a ghost when I see one. Mother had often spoken of the summer kitchen as haunted. Before she died, she'd said that she saw spirits over this way whenever she was wakeful at night, and that that was how she'd know when her time was coming. I hadn't exactly believed her then, she'd been so weak and even feverish much of the time, but now . . . I felt a shiver trickle down my spine.

Perhaps I should have gone for help right then. But what could I have said? There was no proof that anyone had been in the summer kitchen with me, not even a bare footprint in the dusty earth outside the door. And anyway, who would I have told? Aunt Grace? She would never believe me. Aunt Grace wouldn't believe me if I said that the sky was blue and winter was cold. Father was at work, and the children were no help— Elizabeth and Sara had taken little Ben to the Makis' farm, to see the animals. They'd play with the Maki girls and help with chores, too, and probably finish by bringing home fresh eggs. That was more important than my fears.

And the ghost hadn't *seemed* threatening. She was no taller than my sister Sara, and with Sara's big blue eyes and golden hair, too. Surely she couldn't mean any harm? So long as she didn't frighten the children . . . but then, would they be afraid of another child? I doubted it. More likely they'd see her as another playmate and would frighten *her* away, as I had done. And father had enough to worry about. The mines had been on strike for part of the spring and were only just back to full production. We'd small enough savings to get by, without him thinking that it wasn't safe for me to be alone most of the days, and spending good wages on a housekeeper. He fretted enough about that as it was.

I really don't mind being alone during the day. It's mostly only when the children are at school, and not so bad during the summer. At mother's funeral Aunt Grace asked me if I wouldn't rather come to live with her in town—she said that father could easily hire a woman to tend the little ones—but I told her firmly to mind her own business. Why should I do Aunt Grace's washing and ironing and cooking and cleaning, instead of doing it all for my own family? That was what she had in mind, of course; she knew how well mother had taught me, much better than she'd taught her own lazy daughters.

Besides, it isn't as though Ironvil were a big city. We're just a little mining town on the shores of Lake Superior—there isn't much to do except dig for iron and chop down pine trees for timber. Living in town is much like living just outside of it, only outside we have room for a proper garden. Even Aunt Grace had to admit that my garden was something special. This year I would have swedes and beans and lettuce and tomatoes and carrots and sweet basil and red and yellow cabbages, and of course potatoes and onions enough to share with all the neighbours. I had meant to try squash, but hadn't got the seeds into the ground in time. That was my only failure, though. Even the old raspberry bushes looked as if they would be heavy with fruit by mid-July.

So in the end I held my peace about the ghost. In a way, I was sorry that she'd left so quickly. Mrs Jenks, the minister's wife, says that ghosts walk because they are unquiet spirits and need to finish something that they should have done in life. Reverend Jenks says it's foolishness and not to listen—he even scolded her at the church picnic for talking like that—but I wasn't so sure that I agreed with him. I would regret frightening the poor little girl ghost away from finishing some task that she needed to accomplish before she could rest.

It must be a terrible thing, to be an unquiet spirit, I thought, and one so young at that. Privately, I wondered how she had died, and if she was unhappy. I would have liked to help her, if I could. I wondered if she'd come again, though I'd of course no way of knowing. If I'd had a clue as to why she'd come in the first place, I might have guessed—but I didn't, and that was that.

Until she *did* come back, about two days later. I was boiling the jars to get ready for raspberry preserving season—it really looked like being a bumper crop of berries, though the bushes were older than I was—when I saw her shadow in the doorway again. She was wearing the nightgown again, and the sun shining behind her made her look as if she were glowing in the morning light. Perhaps she was.

I managed not to look up from my work, though it was an effort to keep my hands moving.

'Hello,' I said and was proud that my voice was steady. I could feel the pulse beating in my throat, and I had to work to breathe evenly, but I didn't want to scare her off this time. Not until I'd found out a few things. 'I was wondering if you'd come back. Would you like to sit down and stay a while?'

'I don't . . . know if I can,' she said, sounding puzzled. She moved in from the door, as lightly as a leaf on a spring breeze. 'Am I dreaming? I feel as if I'm dreaming, sort of.'

'I'm sure *I* don't know,' I said—sensibly, I thought. Do ghosts dream? I'd have to ask Mrs Jenks, the next time I saw her. I glanced up at the ghost. 'Why don't you sit down and see?'

'I don't . . . want to bother you,' she said, looking me full in the face for the first time.

'You won't bother me,' I started to say, and then our eyes met, and the words went cold in my throat. An electric spark flashed from the ghost to me, burning me as it passed. A thin, invisible cord hung in the air, connecting us, making me feel as if she was a part of me as much as my sisters and brother were. I couldn't help it. My hands trembled, and the jar I was holding slipped between them to shatter on the floor. The sound broke the spell, if spell it was, and I jumped.

'Oh!' the girl said, and she was gone. Just like that—no fading into mist this time, just disappeared between one breath and another.

I stood for a long while, staring at the space where she had been, before I realized that I'd been holding my breath and let it out slowly. The question was, who was she? Annie Pennick, she'd said. Pennick was a Cornish name, not uncommon in these parts. 'Seek ye by Tre, by Pol and Pen, for thus shall ye know the Cornishmen,' says the old rhyme. And Anne, or Anna, is not an uncommon name. My mother's name was Anna, in fact, and it's my own middle name, though I've always been called Rose. Father used to call me his Wild Rose of the North Country, because I loved to go hunting and fishing with him so much—though I'd no time for such amusements any more . . .

But the ghost. Who could she be? Someone who had lived in this house before us? That was possible. It's an old house, though sturdy, and we just rented the land that it stood on, from the mines. Possibly it had even been moved from one of the rows of company houses, over on the other side of town; the structure was similar, and people often moved houses. Why, there was a wealthy woman in Marquette who'd had her great mansion taken apart and shipped, stone by stone, all the way to the east coast—just because she was angry with her neighbours. People who survive on the shores of Lake Superior tend not to let a little thing like picking up a house and moving it down the road stop them from living where they want to live. Any number of families could have called this house 'home' before us.

And probably had, since miners' families tended to move even more often than miners' houses. If this little Annie had been a miner's daughter, her father might have died in a cave-in. I didn't recall the name from any of the lists of the lost, but it might have been when I was too young to remember. Or no, wait, she'd said she was visiting because her grandmother was dying. Did I know of any ailing old ladies in town? Perhaps. There were always a few widows about, with or without grandchildren. It's a difficult life for a woman, being married to a miner, but the ones who survive the early years and childbirth usually live to a great age. We have to be tough, we northern mining folk. If mother hadn't had Benjamin, she might—no. That was no way to think. Mother lived long enough to see to it that I knew how to take care of the family, to teach me to cook from grandmother's recipe book, and to sew and clean by her own exacting standards. I would teach Sara and Elizabeth, and my own daughter someday, who would teach hers in turn . . . The family was what mattered.

Or perhaps the 'grandmother' whom the ghost referred to was long dead, and she was simply confused. It was difficult to guess without more information. This time, however, I didn't wonder whether or not she would come back. I knew that she would. And sooner or later one of the children would see her and perhaps be frightened, and father would be upset.

That wasn't good. I had to find out why little Annie Pennick couldn't rest, and then see to it that she could. If I could. I still hadn't figured out what she wanted from me, but I was beginning to have an idea. Why else would she come to the summer kitchen, and only when I was cooking there? This would bear thinking on—unless next time she came someplace else.

She didn't. It was on a Saturday, baking day, when father had taken the children out to the woods with him to keep them out of my way. Baking day is always a tricky business, even in the summer kitchen, and I was late. I often overslept on Saturdays, because father was around to see to the early morning chores. Mother wouldn't have approved, but she would have understood how tired I was. Anyway, that was why I was still kneading the first batch of bread, before setting it out to rise, when I suddenly realized that I wasn't alone.

I looked up. The ghost was standing in the doorway, as usual, but this time she was a few steps inside. She smiled uncertainly.

I swallowed. 'Come in,' I said, as warmly welcoming as I could be. I'd had several days to think of what to say, and I knew that this was important. Knew *what* was important, too—first things first. 'Please. Don't leave—if you mean no harm, I mean no harm.'

She hesitated. 'I don't mean any harm to anyone, I don't think . . . but who are you?'

'Rose Palmer,' I told her gravely. She started a little at that, and I wondered if she'd known the name of the person she was visiting. Perhaps not, if it was only that she'd lived in our house once upon a time. 'I live here.'

She looked around the summer kitchen. 'In here?'

'No, of course not.' I chuckled. It was going just as I'd planned. 'This is just the summer kitchen. I cook out here, when the weather gets too hot. The big house is behind us, up the hill.'

'I see.' She seated herself on the bench near the wall, carefully, as if sudden movements—even her own—might frighten her. I hadn't imagined a shy ghost before, but why not? Careful, now, I told myself. Don't rush things. Let her make the first move. 'What are you doing?' she asked.

I waved at the bread dough. 'I've been kneading bread. Then I'll cover it and set it to rise, and pretty soon I'll be able to punch it and shape it.'

'You're baking bread?' Her brow wrinkled. 'Do you like to bake?'

I shrugged. 'It's all right. Better than some chores—canning, for instance. I hate canning.'

'Then why do you do it?' she asked, sounding confused. 'I mean, if you don't like it . . .'

'Well, *someone* has to do it,' I said. What a strange question, even for a ghost. 'Or else we wouldn't have food in the pantry next winter.'

She was quiet for a few minutes, watching me work. That suited me; I did need to pay attention to my bread, and I also needed time to think what next to say. I had a chance now, but I wasn't sure . . .

When the dough was covered and set to rise, I was ready.

'How is your grandmother?' I asked casually. 'You said she was ill.'

For a moment I didn't think she was going to answer. Then she said: 'The doctor says she's as well as can be expected. She doesn't really know anyone any more—just sleeps all the time. I never even got to say goodbye.'

'That's sad,' I said, wiping my hands on my apron. 'But surely you said goodbye the last time you saw her.'

Annie shook her head. 'I was really little. She let me bake cookies with her, and said the next time I came to visit we'd do some more, but then we moved to Chicago and I never saw her again. She used to send presents for my birthday and Christmas, and mother kept saying we'd visit, but we never did.'

'Why not? Chicago isn't far.' This was it, I realized—my best chance, the one I'd been hoping for. If she'd never gotten a chance to say goodbye to her grandmother, then that was why she was unquiet. But how could she say goodbye now? She was trapped. I thought I saw a way out, but it would be tricky. It all depended on whether I was right about her coming to the kitchen. 'You could have come up on the train.'

'I think it was the divorce,' Annie said, looking away. 'Mother visited sometimes, but after she and Dad got divorced, I had to stay with him in California over the summer, and—I couldn't come during the school year.'

I thought about that for a while. Divorce was a terrible thing, I'd heard—Reverend Jenks could get quite upset on the subject —and California was a terrible long distance, but it seemed hard to deny a child visits with her grandmother because of it. Still, I had my opening.

'You said you used to bake cookies with your grandmother,' I said. 'Well, I'm baking today. Would you like to help me? Sara sometimes does—she's almost old enough to be a real help, and you look about her age.'

She looked at me strangely. 'Is Sara your sister?'

'Yes, my eldest little sister,' I told her. 'She's nine, five years younger than I am. Elizabeth is a year younger than she is, and Ben—my brother—is three years younger than that. There were two other babies in between Ben and Elizabeth, but they died. Sometimes it happens that way.'

Annie took a deep breath. 'I'm eleven now. So I guess I'm old enough to learn to bake for real.'

Well, of course she was. Eleven! I couldn't believe that her mother hadn't started teaching her already. I found her a spare apron from the hook on the wall—one of mother's old ones, but we pinned it up so it didn't drag on the floor. She seemed much more solid now, made of flesh and blood instead of mist and sunlight. Perhaps it was that she was doing something that would help her. I hoped so. Or perhaps it was just that we were baking bread. There is something about bread that makes everything more real.

We baked together most of the morning, until the last batch was in the oven and the first was already cool enough to eat. Annie didn't know anything; I had to teach her how to measure salt in her hand, how to punch and shape the loaves—everything. She worked hard, without saying much, but I could see that she was enjoying herself.

I found myself oddly glad of the company, too, even the company of a restless spirit. Perhaps Sara was old enough to start learning to cook, as I had learned. She wasn't much younger than I had been when Ben was born and mother became ill. It would be nice to have company for the baking, at least . . . I had sprinkled sliced apples and raisins on one loaf, as a treat for the children, and when the last batch was baking, I cut it, and Annie and I shared it, with fresh butter from the dairy. I was interested to see that being a ghost did not prevent her from dripping melted butter on herself as she ate.

She stopped with her mouth full of bread and put her head to one side. 'Do you hear something?' she asked when she could speak.

We listened. I didn't hear anything, and said so, but Annie slipped off the bench anyway. She took off her apron and laid it across the table. 'I'd better go. My mother might be worried —she wasn't sure I should come here any more.'

'Come tomorrow,' I offered. 'Or no, tomorrow's Sunday. But Monday's washing day, which is no fun. Well, come tomorrow, then, and I'll teach you how to make pasties. That's what I was doing the first time you visited. I've a special recipe I use that mother got from a Cornish woman. It's very good. Pasties were invented in Cornwall, you know.'

'No, I didn't,' she said. I'd thought she might like hearing about pasties, being Cornish herself, but she only smiled a little. 'Goodbye, Rose.'

She didn't say yes or no to making pasties with me. Perhaps she was afraid that she wouldn't be able, poor little ghost. I'd no idea what sort of restrictions were placed on her wandering,

and I couldn't ask. But I didn't watch her out of sight, this time—just in case it made a difference.

Sunday was grey and cold. The children would stay indoors on a day like this, reading and playing games, and father, too, would be resting up for his work week. I didn't really need to cook in the summer kitchen in that weather—the house could have used some heating—but somehow I found myself out there anyway, rolling out the stiff dough for the pasty crust as mother had taught me. Pasties need a sturdy crust, if they are to stay together in a miner's lunch. I planned to slice a baby carrot or two into the potatoes and onions and swedes for the filling; father would like that, and it would add a bit of colour. The beef was fat enough that I didn't really need pork, but I put some in anyway, for flavour.

The air all around me was heavy and dark, filled with the tension that meant a storm was near; I kept one ear open for thunder as I worked.

Annie came as I finished crimping the crust on the first pasty and cutting it with a knife three times, so that the filling could breathe properly. Again, she was just there in the doorway. She wasn't wearing her nightgown any more—she had on a blue jumper with a white blouse, and her hair was combed neatly back from her face and braided. And she didn't step inside.

'Annie!' I said, looking up. 'You came, in spite of the storm. I'm so glad. Come in, then, before it starts to rain. Don't stand there, you'll get wet.' If ghosts could get wet. She was dressed up so—perhaps because it was Sunday, for church? But it had been a Sunday the first time she'd come, too.

She looked back over her shoulder, briefly, but didn't move. 'I have to go now. I just came to say goodbye. My grandmother died this morning.'

'Goodbye?' A little flicker of something touched my heart. Fear? Surely not. 'But we aren't finished—I haven't taught you how to make pasties yet.'

'No, you haven't,' she agreed. Her hands clenched against the door frame until I thought she'd give herself splinters. 'I guess I'll just have to learn on my own. Because you have to leave now. Don't you?'

'Me? But—father, the children—oh, don't be silly. I can't go anywhere.'

'You can go wherever you want to go,' she said, looking at me steadily. 'Your family's all grown and gone—and we even had a chance to say goodbye. Didn't we, grandmother? I'm only sorry I couldn't come sooner. Mother is sorry, too, and even Dad. I talked to him on the phone last night, and he said he never meant—never mind. We just didn't think, any of us—but now it's done.'

We stared at each other for a long, long moment. I could see the mist swirling behind her. As it parted, I caught a glimpse of a tall red-headed woman in a blue dress, looking worriedly towards the summer kitchen. Annie's mother. She seemed familiar. Like someone I had seen once, in a dream . . .

Then I heard something else. Faintly, a voice was calling that I had never thought to hear again. I took a deep breath, understanding at last, and sorry for the burden that I had placed on this child. Or perhaps it hadn't been a burden, but a choice? I hoped so.

'Done, and past done,' I said finally, feeling as if I wanted to cry. Strange to realize—we have so little time in this life. So little, and so much. 'And if you didn't think, then neither did I. Thank you, child, for helping me to see—to finish. I'm glad we got to cook together, as I promised we would. And as you remembered. Tell your mother that you're to have my recipe book, if you want it. It's on the shelf in the kitchen, next to the clock. You'll find the pasty recipe in there. Be careful—if you use too much stiffening in the crust, it will be as tough as old shoes.'

She nodded, her eyes bright with tears, and she looked so much like Sara that I wanted to run to her and comfort her, but I couldn't. She was too far away. Then, as she had that first time, she melted slowly into the sunshine and mist of another daylight, somewhere I could not go any more. As she left, for a moment I saw the summer kitchen through her eyes: an old, broken down log shed with a dusty space where the great iron stove had once stood, screens long since torn and gone, roof broken open to the sky. Through one of the half-boarded windows, I caught a glimpse of fresh green, like a garden. Then that faded, too.

In the distance I heard my mother call. 'Rose! Rose Anna, my dear!'

There were others standing with her. It was time for me to go.

Acknowledgements

Marian Abbey: 'Watching Over You', copyright © Marian Abbey 1999, first published in this collection by permission of the author. **Francis Beckett:** 'A Separate Peace', copyright © Francis Beckett 1999, first published in this collection by permission of the author. **Ruskin Bond:** 'Topaz' from Ruskin Bond (ed.): *The Penguin Book of Indian Ghost Stories* (Penguin Books India, 1993), reprinted by permission of the author. **Tanya David:** 'Dogends', copyright © Tanya David 1999, first published in this collection by permission of Celia Catchpole Ltd. **Louise Francke:** 'Alicia', copyright © Louise E Francke 1974, first published in Mary Danby (ed.): *The Sixth Armada Ghost Book* (Collins, 1974), reprinted by permission of the author. **Shamus Frazer:** 'Florinda', first published in *London Mystery Magazine 29*, June 1956, copyright © the Estate of Shamus Frazer, reprinted by permission of Mrs Joan N Frazer. **Adèle Geras:** 'Rowena Ballantyne', copyright © Adèle Geras 1999, first published in this collection by permission of Laura Cecil Literary Agency on behalf of the author. **John Gordon:** 'If She Bends, She Breaks', copyright © John Gordon 1982, from *Catch Your Death and Other Ghost Stories* (Patrick Hardy Books 1984), reprinted by permission of A P Watt Ltd on behalf of the author. **Catherine Graham:** 'Snookered', copyright © Catherine Graham 1999, first published in this collection by permission of the author. **Dennis Hamley:** 'Incident on the Atlantic Coast Express', copyright © Dennis Hamley 1999, first published in this collection by permission of the author. **Kenneth Ireland:** 'Who is Emma?', copyright © Kenneth Ireland 1992, from *A Ghostly Gathering* (Knight, 1992), reprinted by permission of Jennifer Luithlen Agency. **Shirley Jackson:** 'Home', from *Just an Ordinary Day: The Uncollected Stories* (Bantam Books, 1997) copyright © 1997 by the Estate of Shirley Jackson, reprinted by permission of Bantam Books, a division of Random House, Inc. **Gerald Kersh:** 'The Extraordinarily Horrible Dummy', from *The Horrible Dummy and Other Stories* (Heinemann, 1944). **Rita Morris:** 'Hallowe'en', copyright © Rita Morris 1983, first published in Mary Danby (ed.): *The Fifteenth Armada Ghost Book* (Fontana, 1983), reprinted by permission of the author. **T V Olsen:** 'The Strange Valley', copyright © 1968 by T V Olsen, first published in Betty Baker (ed.): *Great Ghost Stories of the Old West* (Four Winds, 1968), reprinted by permission of Golden West Literary Agency. All rights reserved. **Susan Price:** 'The Haunted Inn', copyright © Susan Price 1987, from *Here Lies Price* (Faber, 1987), reprinted by permission of Faber & Faber Ltd and A M Heath and Co Ltd on behalf of the author. **Alison Prince:** 'The Fire Escape', copyright © Alison Prince 1984, from *The Ghost Within* (Methuen, 1984), reprinted by permission of Jennifer Luithlen Agency. **Robert Scott:** 'With Vacant Possession' and 'The Opening Match', both copyright © Robert Scott 1999, first published in this collection by permission of the author. **Laurence Staig:** 'Love Letters', copyright © Laurence Staig 1999, first published in this collection by permission of the author. **Rosemary Timperley:** 'The Sinister Schoolmaster', copyright © Rosemary Timperley 1978, reprinted by permission of The Agency (London) Ltd. All rights reserved and enquiries to The Agency. **Barbara Ker Wilson:** 'The Honeysuckle Trap', copyright © Barbara Ker Wilson 1976, from Barbara Ker Wilson (ed.): *A Handful of Ghosts* (Hodder Australia 1976). **Mary Frances Zambreno:** 'The Ghost in the Summer Kitchen', copyright © Mary Frances Zambreno 1994, first published in Bruce Colville (ed.): *Bruce Colville's Book of Ghosts* (Lions, 1994).

Despite every effort to trace and locate copyright holders before publication this has not been possible in all cases. If notified, the publisher undertakes to rectify any errors or omissions at the earliest opportunity.

The illustrations are by:
Jason Cockcroft: 17, 37,44, 46, 65, 78, 139, 142, 179, 183, 189;
Paul Fisher Johnson: 79, 84, 114, 119;
Ian Miller: viii, 20, 24, 126, 130, 143, 146, 163, 165;
Brian Pedley: vi, 1, 6, 10, 47, 52, 56, 60, 105, 147, 157, 190, 196, 201, 210, 212;
Tim Stevens: iii, 25, 31, 98, 101, 121, 125, 166, 177.

The Opening Match

ROBERT SCOTT

When David returned to his flat he wasn't too surprised to find Peter stretched out in his armchair. Perhaps he should have been. Peter had died nine months before, hit on the head by a cricket ball in the last match of the season.

But they had an understanding. If either should die he would try to return to the other with the answer to that all-important question: was there cricket in Heaven?

He told Peter how upset he had been . . . such a fine fast bowler . . . such a promising career . . . tragic that it should have happened like that . . . and so on. And then:

'Well?' he demanded.

Peter had no doubt what David wanted to know, but he hesitated.

'Do you want the good news first, or the bad news?' he asked.

'Let's try the good news.'

'We were right. Heaven without cricket would be unthinkable.'
David grinned widely.

'In fact,' Peter added, 'I've been picked for the opening match of the season this Saturday. Traditional fixture. Against . . . er . . . the Other Place.'

David was shocked. 'You mean, they play cricket in Hell too? That really is bad news.'

'Oh, *that's* not the bad news. The bad news is that you're down to bat for them.'